MURDER
ON
ICE

A Joe Ezell Mystery

Book Three

———◆———

P.J. Conn

Book and cover design by eBook Prep
www.ebookprep.com

October, 2017
ISBN: 978-1-947833-07-4

ePublishing Works!
www.epublishingworks.com

CHAPTER 1

Los Angeles, California, 1947

Joe Ezell yanked on his trousers and hurried to answer the furious pounding on his apartment door. It was 8 o'clock in the morning, the first Wednesday in September, and as far as he knew the police weren't looking for him. His fiancée, the delightful Mary Margaret McBride, would use only a genteel tap to announce her presence, so the only person he cared to see hadn't come calling.

"Hold on, I'm coming," he yelled, and jammed his feet into his slippers. When he swung open the door, he found the apartment manager, Leon Helms, a jovial man in his sixties who loved wearing Hawaiian shirts. Today's had brightly colored tropical fish swimming in a vivid turquoise ocean.

"What's wrong, Leon? Is the building on fire?" Joe took a deep breath, but didn't smell smoke.

Leon Helms leaned against the doorjamb and struggled to catch his breath. "You've got to come with me, Joe. Something awful has happened in apartment three."

"Where the new couple moved in?"

"They've disappeared. Come look at what they left behind."

Joe grabbed his keys, closed his door, and buttoned his

shirt as he followed Helms down the outdoor stairs into a central patio. There were six units in the building. Joe's was number six on the west corner of the second floor overlooking the street. Number three was in the back on the ground floor. He'd only seen the new tenants a few times, coming and going to work. Now that he was in his thirties, the couple had looked impossibly young, but they had to at least be in their twenties.

The door to number three stood ajar, and Helms pushed it open. "I watered the plants on the patio this morning, and noticed their door wasn't latched. Something struck me as wrong, maybe they were ill, but they've gone, and taken everything they moved in with. The bed was stripped, there are no towels in the bathroom, and the medicine cabinet is empty."

"Do they owe you rent?"

"No, they're paid up until the end of the month. Go take a look at the refrigerator."

Expecting to find it empty, Joe walked into the kitchen to oblige. The refrigerator racks had been removed and placed on the counter. That would leave the Frigidaire as empty as a new freezer. A very bad feeling snaked up his spine. Gathering his courage, he yanked open the door.

"Good God!" he gasped.

"That's exactly what I said," Helms responded. "If my hair weren't already gray, it would be now."

A nude young woman had been folded in half; her chin rested on her knees and her arms were looped around her ankles. Her skin had a bluish cast, and a deep purple handprint showed clearly on her upper arm.

"How long do you suppose she's been dead?" Helms asked in a fearful whisper.

"A while."

Sun-streaked highlights brightened the thick waves of her long brown hair. Joe gently tucked a strand behind her ear to see her face, and her skin felt as cold as ice. She'd been a very pretty girl, but even without knowing her name, he recognized her as big trouble.

"I don't know her. Do you?" Joe asked.

"There's something familiar about her, but no, I can't place her. I wanted you to see her before the police arrived. Just to have a witness, you understand."

"I do. I don't have any early appointments, so I'll wait with you." Joe couldn't bring himself to close the refrigerator door, but he walked into the living room to wait. He had a fairly good idea who'd answer Leon Helm's call, and he wasn't disappointed.

Detective Jacob Lynch took one look at Joe Ezell and swore under his breath. "Has it even been a week since I last saw you?"

"One week and a day," Joe replied, equally uneager to see Lynch.

"I'm Leon Helms, the manager here. Actually, I'm the owner, but I call myself the manager to simplify things." He told the detective how he'd come across the body. "Scared me to death," he explained. "I asked Joe to come take a look, just to prove I wasn't crazy."

Lynch turned to Joe. "I can't help but wonder why you were here."

"I wasn't merely lurking in the neighborhood. My apartment is number six upstairs."

"That's right," Leon Helms assured the detective. "He's one of my best tenants and never causes a hint of trouble."

"Wonderful. Now where is the body?"

Leon led the way into the small kitchen. "The couple renting the place moved out without giving notice. The refrigerator was on, you can hear it humming, and I opened it to see if they'd left any food I'd need to toss out."

Lynch crouched beside the body to better study the deceased. "Do you recognize her?"

"No. I haven't asked the other tenants though. Should I try and catch them before they leave for work?" Leon answered.

"We'll handle it." The detective stood and smoothed his jacket. His suit was a light-weight whiskey plaid wool, perfect for autumn in Southern California. His brown silk tie had threads of muted gold, along with his matching handkerchief. His brown wing-tipped oxfords were highly polished.

Joe wondered how early Lynch rose to be so well-dressed before nine o'clock in the morning. He bought most of his own clothing in thrift stores so he'd easily fit into the crowd when he followed someone or conducted a surveillance. No matter what he intended to do, he couldn't afford Lynch's elegant wardrobe, but he'd heard the man had a wealthy wife. He wondered if she laid out his clothes in the morning so he wouldn't embarrass her when he left the house. He turned away to hide a totally inappropriate grin.

Detective Lynch led them into the living room. "I'll need the renters' names, along with their apartment application, and references. Is your office here in the building?"

"No, I live just down the street. It will take me only a minute to fetch it all."

"Go," Lynch directed with a hasty wave. He turned to Joe. "You've served your purpose as a witness, and you needn't stay."

"Leon has had such an awful shock, I'd rather hang around and offer support," Joe replied.

"Snoop, you mean." Lynch took a quick tour of the apartment and found it as empty as Leon had discovered. "Did you know the couple renting the place?"

"Just on sight to say hello. I didn't know their names."

The detective pulled out his notebook. "Can you describe them?"

"Early twenties, maybe younger, tall young man with a slim build, and black hair clipped short. The girl had long brown hair, and had a cute figure. They were usually laughing when I saw them, teasing each other, and she had a high-pitched giggle."

"They behaved like newlyweds?" Lynch asked.

"I suppose. They were nice looking, and could have been college kids."

"Did you notice their car?"

"Yeah, they drove a 1939 Buick sedan. Too big a car for a young couple, but someone in the family might have owned it first."

"Save the speculation." He stepped out to speak with the uniformed officer who had come with him.

Joe wished he'd had time for a cup of coffee before Leon Helms had come to his door. A piece of sourdough toast with strawberry jelly would have been welcome too. He felt a brief surge of guilt for missing his breakfast with a dead girl crammed in the refrigerator. He wondered how she had died. There were no obvious wounds, and no blood he could see.

Leon came sailing through the door, puffing as though he'd run all the way home and back. "Here's the file I had on them. Their names were Vince and Peggy Thornton."

"Do you have a previous address?" Lynch asked.

Leon shuffled through the few papers in his file. "They said they had graduated from college in June, gotten married, and had been on their honeymoon before coming to Los Angeles to live."

"That's a no, I take it?" the detective asked.

"Yes, that's a no. They seemed like such swell kids, and I didn't ask for their parents' addresses."

"You remember the name of the college where they studied?" Lynch asked.

Leon looked flustered, and Joe spoke, "They had a decal from the University of Colorado on the Buick's rear window."

"Yes, that's it," Leon added. "They were from Colorado." He smiled as though he'd correctly answered a radio quiz show's sweepstakes question.

"Fine. How about work addresses?"

Leon ran his finger down the rental agreement. "He's with the Walt Disney Studios, not in the art side of it, but business. He emphasized that and joked he couldn't draw as well as a two-year-old."

"And the wife, Peggy?"

"She's a teacher at one of the Los Angeles elementary

schools." He paused a moment. "This might look like I keep sloppy records, but they were such wholesome kids, I was happy to rent to them."

"Which you now regret?" the detective asked.

"Not really, they were very good tenants, but now I do wish there was more information on the rental agreement."

The crime scene photographer arrived carrying his 4 x 5 Speed Graphic camera and kit of flashbulbs. Joe had met him when he'd found a dead body outside his office one morning in July. He followed him to the kitchen door.

The photographer knelt to photograph the girl, and rose suddenly. "Do you have her name?" he called to Lynch.

"No, do you recognize her?"

"If I'm not mistaken, this is Cookie Crumble, one of the strippers from Sherry's."

Lynch and Leon edged through the doorway to get another look at the girl. "I told you she looked familiar," Leon offered. "I'm seldom in Sherry's, but I remember her now. She wore her hair in pigtails and had a cute act, more playful than risqué."

"Thank you for the review," Lynch replied. "Did your disappearing tenants leave their keys?"

Perplexed, Leon's eyebrows knit together. "They had two, and I haven't seen them. Let me look around a minute. Help me, Joe?"

"Sure." Joe went through the drawers in the kitchen while Leon checked the bedroom and bath. The keys weren't in the drawers of the end tables in the living room either.

"We didn't find them. Could Cookie be holding them?" Leon asked.

Lynch joined them in the living room. "We're not touching her body until the man from the coroner's office arrives. Why do you suppose your tenants left a dead girl in the refrigerator and didn't lock the door? It seems like the obvious tactic to employ."

"How should I know?" Leon asked. He sat down in the living room, leaned forward, and held his head in his hands.

"This is the worst thing that's ever happened here."

"Never had a death among tenants?" Lynch asked.

Leon looked up. "One years ago. A sweet little old lady didn't wake up from her afternoon nap, and a friend coming for tea found her. That was different from this tragedy by a long shot. With an elderly woman, we were prepared for her natural death. This is a horrifying murder."

"I'm continually horrified," the detective muttered under his breath.

Joe took the comment as sarcastic rather than sincere. "Maybe the tenants had nothing to do with Cookie's death," he mused aloud. "Someone else might have noticed the apartment was empty before you did, Leon."

"I'm trying to recall the last time I spoke with them," he replied. "When did you see them last, Joe?"

Joe had had an exciting week, including being attacked by a razor-wielding murderer. His arm itched where he'd been slashed, reminding him he ought to have Mary Margaret remove the stitches.

"I saw them last week, Thursday maybe. I was going out as they arrived home, and we passed each other by the mailboxes. Someone else living here might have seen them after that."

"Who are the other tenants besides Mr. Ezell," Lynch asked, pencil poised above his notebook.

Leon leaned back in his chair. "Brett Wayne lives in number one. He writes screenplays for Western movies. I don't know if any of them have ever actually been filmed, but he calls himself a screenwriter."

"How long has he lived here?"

"Five or six years. Miss Abby Hicks has number two. She's a checker at the market on the corner. Sweet girl, she's been here three years, and never causes any trouble."

"All right, that's Mr. Wayne, Miss Hicks, and Mr. Ezell who are model tenants, as were the couple who disappeared. Tell me about who lives in four and five."

Leon raised his brows and glanced toward Joe. "Joy and Morris Kemble have number four, and they've been known to get into a loud argument or two, but no one has ever called the police on them. He's a restaurant critic, and she's an office manager at some firm downtown. They're long-time tenants.

"Melissa and John Todd have number five. They moved in last year right before Christmas."

"I'll bet they're a real sweet couple," the detective observed.

"I'd describe them as standoffish," Joe responded.

"Yes, indeed," Leon agreed. "They keep to themselves. Both work at the central library and seem to prefer books to people."

"How fortunate they found each other."

Lynch was full of snide comments today, but Joe let it pass. From any angle, he regarded the detective as an arrogant ass, so today was no worse than any other with him. One of the coroner's men came to the door, clipboard in his hand, and the conversation took a sharp turn.

"Where's the body?" he asked. His name, Roberts, was embroidered over the left breast pocket on his blue jacket. Coroner was stenciled in white letters across the back.

Lynch showed him into the kitchen, where the photographer was packing up. "Can you tell me when she died?" the detective asked.

"It's getting crowded in here," the photographer announced. "I always leave before the science gets too deep." He slipped around them, nodded to Joe and Leon, and let himself out the door.

Roberts took hold of Cookie's hand, and her arm fell away from the body. "She's been in a refrigerator, and the cold may have skewed the timing. Rigor mortis usually sets in the first twelve or so hours, and passes in forty-eight to sixty hours. She may have been dead two days, or three. "

He knelt down to get a better look at her. "Hey, is this Cookie Crumble?"

"We believe it is," Lynch replied. "You saw her act at Sherry's?"

"Many times, she was really cute, dressed in schoolgirl

uniforms and wore her hair in braids. This is a real shame. I need to get another man and the stretcher." Lynch let him go.

"Mr. Helms, do you have a key to lock the apartment when we leave? We'll mark it as a crime scene, and you won't be able to come back in until we clear it, but the door should be locked."

"I have the key on my ring." He stood to tug it from his pocket, and sorted through the keys once, and then again. "I would have sworn I had a key for number three. I have all the others."

"Who has access to your keys?" the detective asked. "Does your wife borrow them, or someone else in your family?"

Leon again searched through the keys. "No, my wife has no reason to touch my keys, and my son, Stuart, why would he want them?"

Lynch caught Joe's eye. "Perhaps he needed a good place to hide a body."

CHAPTER 2

Leon gasped and paled, and Joe grabbed his arm to guide him back into his chair before he fainted. "My son is a good boy, and he'd never be involved in a murder," he insisted. "I hang my keys on a hook by the back door, and didn't notice number three had fallen off my key ring. I often walk back and forth between my home and here, and could easily have lost it."

"Perhaps," Lynch responded. "Do you have another extra key, or do you need to call a locksmith?"

"Whenever a tenant moves out, I have the locks changed. I always ask for plenty of extra keys because they are so often mislaid or lost. Do you mind if I call my wife and ask her to bring a key for number three? I don't think I can walk home and back again just yet."

"Did you tell her about the murder on your last visit home?" Lynch asked.

"No, she was in the bathtub, and I didn't want to disturb her. This will be an awful shock to her as well."

There was a telephone on the end-table beside his chair. He fumbled with the dial and needed three tries to reach his wife. "Doreen, we've had an emergency here. I need you to look in the top drawer of my desk for the canvas bag of keys. Will you please bring me a key for apartment three? No, it's not a plumbing problem. I'll explain when you get here. Yes, of course, drive if you'd rather not walk." He ended the call. "She'll be here in a minute."

"Where is your son at this time of day, Mr. Helms?"

"He's probably having breakfast at the Kappa Sigma fraternity house at USC. He's an excellent student, and has never been in any trouble."

"Like most of the people you know," Lynch observed. "Call him and have him meet us here, but don't provide the details of why he's needed."

Leon stood to remove his wallet from his back pocket, and pulled out a small card with the number. He rolled back into his chair before he reached for the telephone. "He may already have left for class."

"If so, leave a message asking him to contact you as soon as he can," the detective instructed.

The phone was answered by a new fraternity pledge, and it took several minutes for Stuart Helms to be located and summoned to the phone. "Good morning, son, I don't mean to interrupt your classes, but we have an emergency at the apartment building. I need you to meet me here at apartment three as quickly as you can. No, nothing has happened to your mom or me."

"I'll write him an excuse for any missed classes if he needs one," Lynch offered, but his sly smirk made him look more menacing than helpful.

Leon hung up the telephone. "He's on his way."

Joe had met Stuart and remembered him as a skinny kid who wore glasses and looked like he'd be more interested in books than girls. He was surprised Stuart had joined a fraternity, but maybe they were all studious lads rather than loud cutups.

Doreen Helms stepped into the apartment, and her husband rose to meet her. She was petite, and her curly dark hair framed sparkling brown eyes. She preferred dresses in subdued patterns and colors and provided a quiet balance to her husband's far more flamboyant wardrobe.

"I brought the whole bag of keys, honey. Hello, Joe." She appraised the police detective with a puzzled glance.

"Mrs. Helms, I'm Detective Lynch, and I've come to investigate a homicide."

"Homicide? Who's dead?" she whispered, as though unwilling to disturb them.

"A young woman who goes by the name Cookie Crumble."

"The stripper?" Completely confused, she reached for her husband's hand. "What has she got to do with apartment three, Leon?"

Leon shrugged slightly. "Her body is in the refrigerator."

"What! How did she get in there?" She moved closer to her husband, and he hugged her shoulders.

"That's what we're attempting to discover," Lynch responded. "How well did you know the couple who rented this apartment?"

"I met the Thorntons on the day they moved in," she responded. "I introduced myself and welcomed them so if there were ever a problem and Leon wasn't available, they'd know me. I haven't seen them since. They were such a charming couple, not a pair I'd suspect of murder."

"Appearances are often deceiving," Lynch answered.

The coroner's man returned with his partner and a stretcher. "Pardon us, we need to get by. Maybe you'd all like to wait outside." Leon led his wife out the door and Joe and Lynch followed.

Brett Wayne had been out to the mailbox to check his mail, and seeing them standing in the patio ambled over. "Good morning, everyone. Looks like another beautiful day."

"That all depends on your point of view." Lynch introduced himself, got Brett Wayne's name and handed him his card. "Have you seen the couple who rented apartment three in the last few days?"

Brett studied the detective's card. "I saw them sometime last week. No, wait a minute, I just saw him out by the trashcans empting his trash when I was there doing the same. I don't recall when I last saw her."

Joe knew Brett better than his other neighbors, but they

weren't buddies by a long shot. He could understand curiosity had prompted Brett to join them, but the man didn't appear to be surprised to meet a homicide detective. Perhaps he wrote so many shoot-outs in his Westerns, he was jaded to death in real life.

Lynch glanced toward Joe. "What are the odds he knows Cookie Crumble?"

Before Joe could reply, Brett did. "The stripper? I've seen her a time or two. Sorry, Mrs. Helms, we shouldn't be discussing that type of woman in front of you."

Doreen pursed her lips as though she agreed and looked up at her husband.

Stuart jogged up to meet them, saw his father and mother appeared to be fine, and relaxed visibly. "What's happened, Dad?"

Stuart had inherited his mother's dark eyes and hair. He'd grown a couple of inches and filled out since Joe had last seen him. With a slight curl in his dark hair and black-framed glasses, he reminded Joe of Clark Kent. He wondered if Stuart could shift personas as quickly as Superman. Maybe there was a lot more to the young man than what he'd remembered.

Detective Lynch introduced himself. "Your father called the LAPD this morning. The tenants have moved out, and left us with some puzzling questions. How well do you know Cookie Crumble?"

An incriminating blush filled Stuart's cheeks. "The stripper? I don't know her at all."

"Yet you knew she stripped for a living," Lynch continued.

"Well, everyone knows that. With a name like Cookie Crumble, what else would she be?"

"Just answer my question, Mr. Helms, don't editorialize."

The young man straightened up. "No, sir, I've never met the woman. Why do you ask?"

Lynch nodded toward the apartment. "Her body is in the refrigerator."

"Her body? My God, she's dead?" Stuart asked in a

startled croak. He looked to his parents, but they simply shrugged.

"Cold as ice," Lynch replied. "What do you know about it?"

"Nothing at all. Why aren't you asking the couple who lives here?"

Leon stepped forward. "That's exactly what the police need to do rather than hassle you. Does my son have your permission to return to USC and attend to his classes?"

"For the time being," Lynch answered. "We'll keep in touch."

They all moved back as the coroner's men carried a sheet-wrapped Cookie Crumble out on their stretcher. Joe half-expected to see a slender arm dangle over the side the way dead dames were always posed on the covers of the paperback mysteries he loved to read. He regretted never having seen Cookie Crumble perform, but he did know a girl who worked at Sherry's, and this afternoon might be the perfect time to stop by for a chat.

Located on the Sunset Strip, Sherry's was a popular hangout for the mobsters who called Los Angeles home. The food was delicious and the strippers gorgeous, even if much of the clientele were on the shady side. Joe had met Mae, one of the bartenders, three weeks ago while pursuing a case. He hoped she'd be working the lunch crowd that day, and she was.

Mae was a pretty brunette, a co-ed at UCLA who used her wages toward her college education. Joe doubted she'd remember him, but she did.

"Hey there. Whatever we've got on tap, right?"

"Right." He'd worn sunglasses on his previous visit to hide a black eye. He took them off now and smiled. "A friend told me I should come by some night to see Cookie Crumble. Why is she a standout?"

Mae was awfully cute herself in black satin shorts and a close fitting white blouse. She leaned against the bar and whispered, "She does a naughty school girl act that lots of men like, but she hasn't shown up since Saturday night, so you may have missed your chance to see her."

"Aren't strippers unreliable by nature?" Joe asked, as though he'd given the subject a great deal of thought.

"Not if they want to work here," Mae answered. She moved down the bar to refill a Scotch and soda for a man seated alone and came back to talk. "I liked her, but she had awful taste in men."

"How so?" Joe sipped his beer. He'd found appearing to have a casual interest in a subject made people far more talkative than a practiced set of direct questions did.

"She bounced from college kids, who would never take her home to meet their folks, to men who were Mickey Cohen's muscle."

Cohen was a well-known mobster, and Joe didn't care to meet him or any of his stooges. "That's quite a swing," he mused.

"I'll say. You should come in more often."

She smiled as though she really wished he would. He'd met her boyfriend, a mathematics major at UCLA. Rather than believe she was sincere, he took it as practiced encouragement to keep him drinking at Sherry's bar, something the management would insist upon.

"Sure, I'll make a point of it," Joe responded, and he left her a generous tip. He had a natural interest in a murder in his own apartment building, and he might have to come by several times to learn what more there was to know about the late Cookie Crumble.

The telephone rang as Joe entered his office. Unsure how many times it had already rung, he hurried to answer. "Discreet Investigations."

"Joe, this is Leon Helms. I didn't want to speak with you this morning when there were others listening, but I'd like to hire you to work on Cookie Crumble's murder. Detective Lynch didn't impress me, how did he strike you?"

"We've met, and I also have reservations about him. I've

already stopped by Sherry's where Cookie worked." He thought better of mentioning his source had revealed Cookie dated college boys. That was a direction he'd investigate, but he'd not worry Leon needlessly over it this afternoon.

"Would you give me Stuart's telephone number? He might remember more than he did this morning." He waited while Leon again fumbled through his wallet and made a note of the number. "Do you have a contact number for Vince Thornton?"

"No, just Walt Disney Studios. I sure hope you find him there, but I suppose if he killed Cookie, he and his wife would have promptly left town."

"There is definitely something strange about the way they disappeared. Don't worry, I'll check every possible angle. The school district should know where Peggy Thornton is working, if she is a teacher."

"This is an awful mess, isn't it?"

"Leave everything to me, Leon. I'll talk to you soon." Joe hung up grateful he had a more challenging case than usual, but also disappointed it was right in his own back yard.

Mary Margaret prepared chicken and dumplings for dinner and Joe summoned all his will power to stop at two servings. "If I eat this well after we're married, I'll hit two hundred pounds before Valentine's Day."

She laughed. "I'll serve smaller portions so there's no danger of that. I'd still love you if you were pudgy, but I'd much prefer to keep you lean. Are you sure you won't have another dumpling?"

He raised his hand. "Absolutely not. Say, today I received a post card in the mail for a free dinner for two at the Jumpin' Plate. Let's go Saturday before we go to the movies."

"Sounds like an excellent idea." She blotted her mouth with her napkin.

"Are you going to be such an agreeable wife?" he asked.

"As long as you prove to be an agreeable husband. Did

you take on any new cases today?"

They'd finished eating so a mention of murder wouldn't spoil their meal. "You could say one dropped into my lap." He recounted the morning's story while she stared at him big-eyed, but he didn't mention how closely Stuart Helms might be involved.

"Let's go to Sherry's Saturday night," she suggested. "I've never been to a strip joint, and it's a classy place, isn't it?"

"Some might say so, but I doubt many men take their girlfriends there." He was appalled by the idea, but she was such a good-natured sweetheart, he didn't want to refuse her suggestion out of hand.

"We'll be working your case," she insisted. "Scouting the place where Cookie worked, and you might learn something to help you solve the case before Detective Lynch even gets around to looking into it. Please?"

She left her chair to cuddle in his lap, and he hugged her tight. "I don't suppose there's anything wrong with stopping by Sherry's, but if you're shocked, or insulted, we'll leave right away."

"Agreed."

His arm began to itch, reminding him of his stitches. "I don't see any reason to go back to the hospital just to have my stitches removed when you could do it here, couldn't you?"

"After you've been so nice about taking me to Sherry's, I don't see how I can refuse." She gave him a quick kiss and hopped off his lap to fetch her scissors and tweezers. Not only was his beloved a wonderful cook, she was a great kisser, and he considered himself one lucky man. Now all he had to do was solve a stripper's murder and collect his fee to pay for their honeymoon.

Thursday morning, Joe searched the *Los Angeles Times* for a mention of Cookie Crumble's murder. The article, titled "Popular Entertainer Found Dead", was buried inside the first section and gave few details. Her name had been

Alice Reyes, AKA Cookie Crumble. She'd been strangled, and her body had been found in a vacant apartment. There was a headshot that could have come from her agent, identified as Archibald Sutton, rather than a suggestive photo to advertise her routine at Sherry's. Sutton described her as a beautiful girl who'd been on the verge of stardom.

Joe wanted to talk with him, but he'd not call ahead and give Sutton a chance to refuse an interview. Instead, he looked up the agency address in the telephone book, and arrived at 11:00 o'clock.

The secretary, her desk nameplate read Charlotte Stafford, greeted him warmly. "You're exactly the type Mr. Sutton wants to represent." She checked a list on her desk. "Do we already have your name?"

"I doubt it. I'm Joe Ezell. What type would you say I am?"

The secretary wore her blonde hair in a riot of curls and blew one out of her eyes before she replied. "You've got rugged good looks and could play a variety of roles and be believed. Do you have any acting experience?"

As he saw it, he frequently disguised his identity to get information on a case, and this was such an example. He prided himself on being convincing and played along. "Mainly live theater," he responded.

"Great. I'll ask Mr. Sutton if he can see you now." She left her desk to approach the agent's door. She had a shimmy in her walk, as though she were the one auditioning.

Joe caught only part of their brief whispered exchange, but it worked and Sutton welcomed him into his office. The agent stood to shake Joe's hand and looked him up and down. "I like your looks. We see too many pretty boys who work as models, and it's good to see a real man. Did you bring photos?"

"I'm picking up some new ones this afternoon." The agent's plaid suit was too loud for Joe's tastes, but it probably went unnoticed in the entertainment industry. Archibald looked to be in his late forties, with brown hair and eyes, and the intense gaze of a scientist observing a critical experiment. However, Joe had never trusted a man with a thin mustache. Archibald's was so perfect, he might have pasted it on that morning.

"Good. You have to stay current. I can get roles for you in half a dozen films preparing to shoot. War movies need men who look like they actually served."

"I did, in the Coast Guard."

"You ought to have photos taken in your uniform, and you'll have more work than you can do. Before I send you out on an audition, I'll need you to sign our agency contract." He opened a side drawer on his desk and withdrew the document.

Joe took it. "What's your cut?"

"The standard ten percent, and you'll work often with me representing you. How did you get my name?"

"From Alice Reyes, Cookie Crumble, mentioned you, but I never expected her to turn up dead before we met."

"Awful shame. She had it all, face, body, and talent. The one thing she lacked was good judgment about men, present company excepted, of course."

"You think a boyfriend killed her?"

"I'm sure of it. She dated more than one of Mickey Cohen's goons, and they aren't known for their manners."

"What do you suppose happened?" Joe asked as he flipped through the contract.

Sutton shrugged. "She probably broke up with a creep who didn't take it well. More than one man has killed a woman he'd sworn he couldn't live without."

"He must have had a terrible temper," Joe observed.

"I'll say."

The secretary peeked in the door. "You have a luncheon engagement at Ciro's."

Joe stood. "I want my attorney to review this, and I'll come to see you next week."

"Don't wait too long," Sutton advised. "Guys who can play weary war veterans are in high demand, next month it might be cowboys."

"I can ride a horse," Joe promised, and he meant it.

* * *

Marty Streech, a reporter with the *Los Angeles Examiner,* came down Joe's office stairs just as he started up. "I'm glad I caught you." He turned to go back up the stairs and waited for Joe to unlock his door. As usual, Marty's clothes were rumpled, and his shoes could use some polish.

"I've got a theory about the dead stripper, Cookie Crumble. The papers didn't say so, but a reliable source told me they found her naked in a Frigidaire."

Joe took his chair behind his desk. He preferred to listen rather than share his own inside information. "What's your theory, Marty?"

The reporter leaned back in his chair, stretched out his legs, crossed his ankles, and consulted his notes. "Clearly she knew a man capable of incredible violence."

"You're thinking of the Black Dahlia's killer?"

"I am. Elizabeth Short loved to party, and she may have gone to Sherry's multiple times. She could have been a friend of Cookie's. Maybe the murderer feared Cookie could identify him."

Joe could think of no reason to dispute Marty's supposition. "It's possible."

"It is. The police don't often find dead women in refrigerators. That's way past peculiar, so the man must have a sinister bent."

"You plan to link the murders in a story?" Joe asked.

"I do. You proved Georgia Dixon's murder was unrelated to the Black Dahlia's, but that doesn't mean Cookie wasn't killed by the same evil bastard."

"Go ahead and pursue it," Joe encouraged. "Do you know anything about Archibald Sutton, Cookie's agent?"

"He represents what I'd describe as the second tier of stars. I've never heard anything bad said about him. Do you think he might have had something to do with her murder?"

"No, I just wondered about him." The telephone rang, and Marty got up to leave as Joe reached to answer. "See you." *Not too often,* Joe hoped.

CHAPTER 3

Stephen Bennett, a CPA, had an office in Joe's building. Joe walked down the hallway to ask him to take a look at the contract Archibald Sutton had given him. "I know you're not an attorney, but how does the math look to you?"

The accountant frowned as he gave the document a swift review. "Ten percent is standard, but he's asking you for a three-year commitment. Are you actually taking up acting in your spare time?"

"No, I just let him think so."

"Then you don't want to sign anything, Joe, or it might come back to bite you later."

"I can see how it could. Thanks, Stephen." Joe went back to his office to think it over. He glanced at his watch, and reached for the telephone book for the number of the Disney Studios in Burbank. He asked to speak with Vince Thornton in the business department. The Disney operator promptly connected him to John Marks, and Joe used an imaginative story that always worked.

"My name is Joe Ezell, and I'm attempting to locate a man who has come into a large inheritance. The family has mislaid his contact information, but they believe he's working at Disney. His name is Vince Thornton. Do you know him?"

"Vince Thornton? Never heard of him." Marks's gruff

voice fit his curt manner perfectly.

"He's a graduate of the University of Colorado, and would probably have been hired in June. Does that sound familiar?"

"No. This is a small department, and we haven't taken on anyone new since last March."

"Is there another department where he might work, budgeting or accounting perhaps?"

"No, again. We're all in one office. Lots of people want to work for Disney, but that doesn't mean they actually do."

Joe gave him his telephone number. "Thanks for talking with me, Mr. Marks. Give me a call if Mr. Thornton appears, but don't tell him the good news. Let me surprise him. He'll thank you and maybe even give you a reward."

"Yeah, sure he will."

Disney was known for their beautifully animated characters, and Joe pictured John Marks as a grumpy bullfrog whose lily pad was rapidly sinking beneath him.

The main offices of the Los Angeles Unified School District were downtown, and rather than make a trip and get caught in the late afternoon traffic, Joe gave them a call as well. Unfortunately, his inheritance story failed to work on the secretary who answered the telephone in personnel.

"We never give out names of teachers, or where they're assigned. You may be a well-meaning person, Mr. Bell,—"

"It's Ezell," Joe emphasized.

"Whatever, sir, as I said, you may be a lovely man, but others are not. If a teacher wishes you to know her school, she'll contact you herself."

"That's an excellent policy for security," Joe complimented. "Would you take a message and see that it gets to Mrs. Thornton? Unless she has my number and knows I'm calling about a substantial inheritance, she won't know to call me."

"If you insist, but I'll make no promises."

Joe gave her his number and said good-bye. The police would find her school, if she really worked for the LAUSD, but they had the authority to ask, while he only represented Discreet Investigations.

That night, Joe told Mary Margaret how easy it had been to fool the agent into believing he was an aspiring actor who could handle a part in a war movie.

She clapped her hands. "You should do it, Joe. Even if you aren't given any important lines, playing a soldier might be fun. And you'd get paid."

Being paid was what appealed most to him. He needed money for a honeymoon, and at present, he could only afford a day trip to Santa Catalina Island. "I suppose I could go on a few auditions. It might lead to more information about Miss Crumble."

"Yes, do it, Joe. Humphrey Bogart isn't nearly as handsome as you, and he works all the time."

"You're forgetting he's a fine actor, while I'm a private eye. Although I can usually convince people to talk to me."

"Exactly, Joe, now all you have to do is convince a camera."

Saturday morning, Joe met Hal Marten and Gilbert Werner, both former clients, at the golf course near Griffith Park. With Joe's insightful instruction, Hal had mastered his initial lessons quickly, and Gilbert played well enough to turn pro. They were looking for a fourth man.

"I asked Lou King if he played golf," Hal said as he placed his ball on a tee at the first hole. "He doesn't, but invited us to shoot pool with him in Chinatown sometime."

"Chinatown?" Gilbert nearly shuddered at the thought. "Wouldn't that be dangerous?"

Hal laughed. "I'm sure we could play pool with Lou without becoming involved in a Tong war. They were over long ago, besides, Lou is a bail bondsman and whatever criminal element there is in Chinatown would want to stay on his good side."

"I've never shot pool," Gilbert admitted with a self-conscious shrug. "There might have been a pool table in one of the bars back home, but I never went into them. You two ought to go as often as you like, but I'll stick to golf."

"Wise choice," Joe murmured under his breath. Gilbert was an engineer, and concern for his girlfriend's motives had inspired him to call Discreet Investigations. The unfortunate episode had convinced Joe that Gilbert needed some male friends who could provide sympathetic insights into what women wanted in men. When he'd invited Gilbert to join Hal and him for golf, he discovered the shy young man played with a professional golfer's skill and had much to teach both him as well as Hal.

They walked across the course at an easy pace, and Joe told them about finding Cookie Crumble's body in an empty apartment in his building. "I should call Lou King and see what he knows about the men who hang out at Sherry's."

"Isn't that one of Mickey Cohen's hangouts?" Hal asked.

"It is. That's why Lou's insights should prove valuable." Joe and Hal stood back as Gilbert made a long drive straight up the fairway. "Nice shot."

"Thanks. I read about Miss Crumble in the *LA Times*," Gilbert remarked. "Why would anyone want to kill such a pretty girl?"

"Her looks had nothing to do with it," Joe assured him. "It was probably something she wanted to do, or refused to do, that the three of us could discuss in a civil manner with a woman. A man with more muscles than brains, however, would allow his temper to get the better of him. I hope to stop him before he kills another girl."

"Won't the police catch him?" Gilbert asked.

"I've learned not to trust the police," Hal interjected. "A detective can get the wrong man in his sights, and he won't let go despite a clear lack of evidence."

"I thought the police always caught the right man," Gilbert said. "At least they did back home, but it was such a small town, there were few criminals to catch."

"Sometimes they do apprehend the guilty party," Joe agreed. "Let's hope this is one of them, but I'm doing my own investigation too."

"Be careful," Hal warned him.

"I always am," Joe replied, but this was the first time an investigation would involve mobsters, and they weren't all that friendly. When he got home, he called Lou King and made an appointment to see him Sunday afternoon at his bail bondsman office in downtown Los Angeles.

Saturday night, Mary Margaret wore a long-sleeved black sheath dress to show off her petite figure and compliment her red curls. Her black heels added a couple of inches, but she still barely reached Joe's shoulder. Joe had picked up his navy blue suit from the cleaners, and with a white dress shirt and maroon tie, he could almost pass for a gentleman.

"Let's not stay more than half an hour," he suggested as they left her cottage in the Chrysanthemum Court. "We'll have a drink and observe the place without staying for dinner."

"Is it expensive?" she asked.

"More than the Jumpin' Plate," he responded, but he intended to list the tab on his expense account when he gave Leon Helm his bill.

"I'll be too busy observing the entertainment to taste dinner anyway, so I'll be happy to leave without running up a large bill. We need to keep an eye on our resources, Joe. I want a small wedding with our friends rather than an extravaganza like the Hollywood stars have, and we need to start saving now."

Joe hoped he'd soon be earning enough money to cover the minimal expenses his budget allowed, plus something more to save. "A frugal wife will be a great blessing."

She giggled. "I'm not making any promises for after the wedding."

He laughed with her, but turned serious when they reached Sherry's. "This is a job for me. Let's look like we're having a good time, even if we aren't."

"Yes, I understand. We want to look like a couple out for a good time. We should be engrossed in each other, shouldn't we?"

"Perfect, my pet." He handed the car keys to the valet, and held Mary Margaret's hand as they entered Sherry's. There was a display of color photographs of the featured entertainment enticingly dressed as they were at the beginning of their acts. An empty space must have held Alice Reyes's Cookie Crumble photograph.

Joe and Mary Margaret were seated at a small table in the corner and ordered a Scotch and water and a sloe gin fizz. They had chosen to come in after ten, when the place would be too busy for anyone to notice them.

Joe smiled at his beautiful date and looked around the room. The first person he recognized was Stuart Helms seated with three young men who were probably fraternity brothers. Their table was near the stage, and they clapped enthusiastically when a stripper named Ginger Snap came sashaying out on the stage. A buxom brunette, she wore a bibbed floral apron, a tall white baker's hat, and high-heeled shoes. She swung a pair of oven mitts strung together like kids' mittens in wild swirls as she strutted close to the edge of the stage, and then backed away.

Mary Margaret leaned close to be heard. "She's really pretty. Why would she be working here?"

"It pays well," Joe responded. While Ginger traipsed across the stage he checked the others in the room and spotted Mickey Cohen. A cloud of cigarette smoke hung over his table, and he and his friends were laughing over something one of them had said. Two turned to give Ginger their full-attention, but Mickey and the other three remained involved in the humorous tale.

"They're being awfully rude to Ginger," Mary Margaret observed. "Why did they come here if they don't intend to watch?"

Stuart and his friends made up for the mobsters' inattention. They hooted and called to Ginger, and snapped their fingers. She winked at them over her shoulder. Other men, and some couples, applauded the stripper's suggestive routine, but all she'd removed thus far was her baker's hat.

Mary Margaret sipped her sloe gin fizz. "I counted five

other women in the room, and they don't look as though they have to work for a living."

Joe kissed her cheek. "They are working," he assured her.

She understood and blushed almost as deeply as her hair. "And the men they're with?"

"Mobsters," Joe answered. He was more interested in Stuart Helms, who looked right at home at Sherry's, although he'd denied knowing Cookie Crumble. One of his friends had caught Ginger's hat, and plunked it on his own head.

The stripper untied the bib of her apron, but kept it in place with slow gestures beautifully enhanced by her bright red nails. An accomplished entertainer, she flirted with Sherry's patrons with every turn and shoulder dip. She promised so much more than she gave, and her audience became ever more enthusiastic.

"How long does this go on?" Mary Margaret asked.

Joe laughed. "A little longer. It's called a *striptease* for a reason." By the time Ginger had completed her routine with expertly spun tassels, he was ready to go. Mary Margaret wanted to see another act.

"That was an amazing performance," she leaned close to say. "Do you suppose if I got some tassels, I could actually master a twirl?"

He thought she was teasing, but he was never sure with Mary Margaret. "I'll buy the tassels if you'll practice." She raised her hand to promise.

In the next act, a young woman calling herself Carmella Cordova came out draped in a tiered black shirt, a low-cut red ruffled blouse, and a fringed Spanish shawl. The toes of her black high heels were decorated with red silk roses. She wore her raven dark hair in a chignon, and her vivid make-up would have been more appropriate for the dramatic expressions of a silent film star than a stripper at Sherry's where patrons were seated close.

The house band featured a guitarist to provide an authentic flavor and began "Lady of Spain." They were talented musicians and played with an impressive enthusiasm.

"Do you suppose she's ever been to Spain?" Mary Margaret asked.

"Tijuana maybe," Joe replied.

A burly young blond man stood near the stage with his arms crossed over his chest. He appeared to be asking for a disturbance to quell, and Joe wondered if he'd dated Cookie, or had wanted to. A man at Mickey's table called the young man over, but he quickly returned to his post. His mouth formed a menacing downward curve, and he observed the crowd rather than Carmella dipping her embroidered shawl to reveal a dimpled shoulder.

When their waiter came by, Joe asked the blond man's name.

The man bent down to be heard over the rhythms of Carmella's music. "That's Corky Coyne. He's here to see everyone behaves himself."

Joe smiled as if he'd only been curious, and ordered a second round of drinks. The next minute, a man seated near the stage rose and made a lunge for the long fringe on Carmella's shawl. Corky quickly responded, picked him up by his collar and the seat of his pants, and marched him out the exit to the parking lot. Corky soon returned dusting his hands, and Carmella hadn't missed a beat.

"I hadn't realized there were hazards to a stripper's job," Mary Margaret posed. "Do you suppose Corky was as protective of Cookie Crumble?"

"That's what I intend to discover." They left Sherry's at the end of Carmella's routine. She had a sultry dramatic flare Ginger Snap couldn't match, but he wished they'd been able to see Cookie's naïvely endearing schoolgirl act.

Sunday afternoon, Joe drove to Lou King's office on Los Angeles Street near the criminal courts building. The one-story concrete structure had the squat bearing of a prison facility, which might work to Lou's advantage. King's Bail Bonds in gold lettering decorated the large front window. Venetian blinds blocked the afternoon sun.

A bell chimed as Joe came through the front door into the

waiting room. A strikingly beautiful Chinese girl met him at the counter. A pale blue *cheongsam* graced her slender figure's subtle curves. She had pulled her glossy black hair into an intricate knot at her nape, and ebony chopsticks held it in place. She smiled and greeted him warmly.

"You must be Joe Ezell. I'm Lou's sister, Jade. He usually forgets to introduce me."

"A terrible oversight," Joe responded. He had the totally inappropriate thought that she could do a terrific Oriental goddess routine at Sherry's. Ashamed of himself, he quickly suppressed the exotic mental image. "Is Lou in?"

"Yes, he's waiting for you. Come with me." She led him down a corridor to the end office and rapped lightly at the door. "Joe's here."

Lou opened the door and gestured toward one of the leather chairs in front of his desk. "Come in and make yourself comfortable. May I offer you a drink?"

"Thanks, but it's too early for me." The dark brown wool rug muffled their footsteps. Joe was surprised by how handsomely the office was decorated. The walls were painted a warm beige, and dark-stained wooden bookshelves behind the desk held almost as many leather-bound volumes as an attorney would display. Lou's formidable teak desk would add gravitas to any transaction. A lush philodendron in a handsome ceramic pot sat atop a low file cabinet and added a bit of color.

The neatly kept office could have been used for a movie set, and Joe wondered if that was all it really was. "Thank you for meeting with me," he began. "A young stripper's body was found in an apartment in my building, and the owner has asked me to work on the case. Perhaps you read about it in the paper?"

"I did. Cookie Crumble had an abundance of talent and would have gone far had she not met with such a tragic end. Talk about 'cold-blooded' murder. I don't mean to make light of her death, but humor helps in this business. How may I help you?"

Lou was an attractive man. He wore his thick, black hair

slicked back, and he possessed an innate elegance Joe knew he sadly lacked. Even if he wore one of Lou's custom tailored suits, he'd merely be posing as a gentleman, and Lou looked and behaved as the real thing.

Joe played with how much to reveal. "Cookie's agent told me she had lousy taste in men. Sherry's attracts boisterous college boys as well as two-bit mobsters who love only their mother. I've got a lead on the college boys, but I'd rather not sidle up to any of Mickey Cohen's men. I thought you might have heard if one of them is rough with his women."

Lou nodded thoughtfully. "Too many to count, and they get away with it because the girls are afraid to go to the police. They're usually paid off to leave town and are glad to go."

"How about Corky Coyne? Do you know anything about him?"

"He's a conscienceless thug who circles the fringes of LA crime. He might do a favor for Mickey Cohen if asked, but it wouldn't require much thought, merely muscle. He works at Sherry's as a bouncer, so he had to have known Cookie. If she truly did have poor taste in men, he'd be at the top of the list."

In the Coast Guard, Joe had known some big guys with a gentle demeanor. Corky didn't project even a particle of gentleness, however. "Heard anything new on the Black Dahlia's killer?"

"Intriguing whispers," Lou replied. "He has to be the kind who'd stuff a girl in a refrigerator, but he'd probably do it while she was still alive."

"Cookie was strangled first. The question is how she ended up in an apartment that had suddenly turned vacant."

"A dead girl in the fridge would be a good motive for a fast change of address."

"It would, but the couple who lived there didn't seem like the type. I'm looking into them in the coming week. They could have gone to Sherry's, met Cookie and invited her home for a drink."

"And the wife got jealous and strangled her?" Lou posed.

"Maybe. They left the apartment without telling the landlord and turning in their keys. No one saw them go."

"Could it have been a *ménage a trios* that went wildly wrong?" Lou asked.

Joe felt like smacking himself in the head because a threesome gone awry hadn't even occurred to him. He played it cool, or attempted to. "It's a possibility, I suppose. I don't want to take up any more of your time. Thanks for talking with me." He stood and Lou walked him to the door.

"My pleasure. Sundays are quiet, and I get bored easily. Call me any time. Did Hal tell you I prefer shooting pool to playing golf?"

"Yes, and we'll have to get together to shoot pool sometime soon." Joe told Jade good-bye on his way out and went to his office to play around with his file of suspects.

Joe had discounted Vince and Peggy Thornton's involvement in Cookie's death because they'd struck him as such good kids. Maybe they were acting the part while they carried on private lives of an entirely different sort. Peggy might be teaching at a school somewhere in Los Angeles, but Vince had lied to Leon Helms about having a job at Disney.

Vince and Peggy could have met Stuart Helms at the apartment building, seen him at Sherry's and invited him to come home along with Cookie. Somehow Cookie ended up dead, the Thorntons fled, and Stuart could have their keys. Or maybe they'd taken their keys, and Stuart had taken his father's spare off the ring meaning to unlock the door after the Thornton's had had time to leave town.

Rather than Stuart, Corky Coyne could have been the fourth person at the late night party. Maybe Cookie hadn't wanted to leave with him, and he took it badly. The Thorntons would have been scared he'd come after them next, and high-tailed it out of town.

Or maybe Stuart knew the Thorntons had vacated their apartment for whatever reason, taken the key his father carried, and had used the place for a private party with his Kappa Sig brothers and Cookie. However, the boys would have been loud and undoubtedly awakened the other residents of the building. Joe lived right above apartment three, and he hadn't heard any music or laughter.

He wondered about Detective Lynch's investigation of the murder and reached for the telephone to call Henry Hilburn, a retired LAPD detective who still had contacts inside the department. He chatted a moment with him before he mentioned Cookie Crumble.

"I've been following the case," Henry replied. "I never saw her perform, but from what I hear, she was as cute as a bug. Most likely she didn't return an admirer's affections, and he took it badly. How her body ended up in the refrigerator puzzles me."

"Me, too. Does Jacob Lynch know anything?"

Henry laughed. "He claims to have a list of suspects, but I don't know who's on it. Most likely the people who had rented the apartment, the others who live in the building, the building's owner, maybe even the mailman. Throw in the crowd that frequents Sherry's, as well as the other strippers, and he must have a lengthy list. Personally, I'd focus on the couple who rented the apartment where the body was found."

"Makes sense to me too," Joe responded. "Call me if you hear anything new."

"Sure will. It's got all the elements I like to follow: the violent death of a beautiful dame, suspects from the darkest elements of the Los Angeles under-belly, and no clear motive for the crime, other than unrequited love or just plain lust."

Joe thanked him and hung up. Henry hadn't considered a man who simply lived to kill like the Black Dahlia's murderer, and surely that was an outside possibility. Still, someone who frequented Sherry's could have picked up Cookie the way he'd picked up Elizabeth Short. But why would he have stuffed the body in the Thornton's refrigerator?

What he needed was a large bulletin board like the ones the police used to track their cases. Unfortunately, with a small office, and a steady stream of clients coming in and out, he couldn't display one. Maybe he could get a small one and turn it toward the wall behind his desk when a new client came in. He'd stop by the hardware store and buy one first thing Monday morning.

For today, Sunday afternoon would be a good time to call on his neighbors. Maybe one of them didn't sleep as soundly as he did, or was troubled with insomnia and had seen or heard something Detective Lynch hadn't had time to investigate. He'd then have to convince Lynch to follow up on the lead, which would be another sort of challenge.

CHAPTER 4

B rett Wayne came to the door of apartment one casually dressed with a yellow pencil behind his ear. "Hi Joe, what's up?"

"I hope I'm not interrupting your work," Joe responded. He wasn't convinced Brett actually did any serious writing, but he'd let the man pretend and save face.

"No, I spend much of my time thinking. It can become tiring, so I'm glad to take a break. I'd invite you in, but screenplays are stacked on all the chairs."

"We can talk right here," Joe assured him. "Several days have passed since Cookie Crumble's body was found, and I wonder if you've recalled anything more than a chance meeting with Vince Thornton out by the trashcans. Your front door faces apartment three, did you see or hear anything that struck you as unusual before they disappeared?"

"Not a thing. I've sat out here in the patio and tried to remember the Thorntons, but I really didn't know them, and probably couldn't pick them out of a line-up. I like living here because it's quiet during the day when everyone else has gone to work, and I can concentrate on writing. In the evenings, I usually listen to the radio rather than eavesdrop on my neighbors. Although when the Kembles get started, it's impossible not to overhear."

"True. What time do you usually go to bed?"

"Most nights around ten o'clock, and I'm a light sleeper, so if Cookie had screamed for help, I would have heard her." He leaned close. "You know what I think?"

"Tell me," Joe encouraged.

"I'll bet she was murdered elsewhere, maybe even at Sherry's, and then her body was left at the Thornton's."

"I'm sure the police are considering it. The apartment hadn't been torn up as though there had been a fight."

"I don't go to Sherry's often, mind you, just once in a while; and I've heard there's stiff competition between the strippers. Cookie was very popular. Do you suppose one of the other girls killed her?"

Joe could easily imagine how a fierce argument, or catfight, between a couple of strippers could have ended with one of them dead. Stuart could have helped the survivor hide the body in apartment three. Stuart's name popped up rather often no matter where Joe's conjecture began.

"Women can be more brutal than men," Joe said, "or at least I've been told so. Thanks for talking with me."

"Anytime. I don't like the thought of a murder here and hope you'll soon find who did it." He began to close his door, but stopped and turned back. "Do you suppose Leon will rent out number three soon? I'm hoping for another quiet couple."

"He'll have to wait for the police to okay it, and after a murder, if might be difficult to find renters."

"Oh, you're right. I didn't think of that."

Joe went on to apartment two. Abby Hicks had always been friendly, but she made her living being cheerful to everyone who came through her cashier's line at the market. He rapped lightly on her door, but she didn't answer. He climbed the stairs and knocked on the Kembles' door at apartment four.

Morris answered wearing a long white apron and carrying a wooden spoon. A former chef who now worked as a food critic for a ritzy food magazine with a French name Joe couldn't pronounce, he sometimes reviewed

restaurants for the *Los Angeles Times*. He was a burly man
with white hair, quivering jowls, and piercing blue eyes.

"Hello, Joe. I'm right in the middle of making what
should be a fabulous dessert, but I have a minute. What do
you need?"

"Leon has asked me to look into the unfortunate event in
apartment three. Did you ever speak with the Thorntons, or
hear a mention of any plans they might have had to move?"

Morris leaned against the doorjamb. "Murder goes way
beyond 'unfortunate', Joe, but no, we said hello when they
moved in, but I believe they were both gone in the
mornings before we left for work."

"It's likely the murder happened last weekend. Did you
hear or see anything out of the ordinary?"

"We spent last weekend with friends who live on Balboa
Island, so we weren't here. I'm sorry to be of such little
help. Do you want to speak with Joy?"

"If I may." Joe waited while Morris returned to the
kitchen to call her.

Joy Kemble was as slender as a reed, with frizzy, blonde
dandelion hair. He wondered if she ever allowed herself to
eat more than a single morsel at mealtimes, while her
husband was clearly overly fond of food. Her black-framed
glasses enlarged her eyes to complete her startling
appearance. She worked as an office manager downtown.
She usually dressed in skirt-suits and silk blouses, and Joe
was surprised when she came to the door wearing slacks
and a sweater.

He rephrased the questions he'd asked Morris. "The
Thorntons lived here a few months, but no one seems to
have known more about them than their names. Did you
ever talk with them, or hear them mention plans to move?"

"I'm afraid not. As a young couple, they wouldn't have
been interested in spending time with us even if we'd asked
them, which we didn't. I wish we'd seen something, or
someone suspicious, and could help solve the crime." She
rubbed her arms. "It makes me anxious just thinking of
what happened to that poor girl. I've always felt safe here,

but now, I wonder if we shouldn't move to a safer building."

"This has always been a secure address, Joy, and we probably won't see another murder here before the end of the century." He planned to live with Mary Margaret in the Chrysanthemum Court after they were married, so he'd move soon himself. "Thanks again for your time. If you think of something more about the Thorntons, please let me know."

"I will." She rolled her eyes, and whispered, "Morris is making an avocado pudding. Doesn't that sound revolting?"

"I've never heard of one," Joe readily admitted.

"Neither has anyone else." After she'd closed her door, Joe went on to apartment five where Melissa and John Todd lived. They frequently greeted each other in passing, but this was the first time he'd ever knocked on their door.

Melissa answered carrying a thick novel and handful of note cards. She was slightly taller than her husband, slim, and wore her dark hair pulled back in a bun. Today curls sprouted behind her ears so her usual prim style must have been hastily made. She pushed her glasses up her nose.

"Joe? Is something wrong?" She leaned out her door to look down the walkway.

He assured her there was no reason for concern and explained Leon had asked him to investigate Cookie's death. "I wondered if you recall anything about the Thorntons. They seemed like such a nice couple, but clearly something went very wrong in apartment three."

"An understatement if I ever heard one. When they moved in, we invited them to come to the programs at the library. They weren't rude, but they claimed they had their college degrees, and were through with books. She'd introduced herself as a teacher, and it struck me as a very peculiar thing for her to say."

"Indeed it was," Joe agreed. He loved to read and couldn't imagine anyone choosing not to enjoy books, especially when libraries offered such an abundance of wonderful stories for free.

John Todd joined his wife at the door. His hair was rumpled as though he'd not bothered to comb it that day, and his shirttail had slipped out of his trousers. His rimless glasses were slightly askew, and Joe couldn't help but wonder how the pair had been occupied before he'd knocked at their door. Perhaps they engaged in wild sex games on Sunday afternoons. From what he'd seen of the world as a detective, little surprised him anymore.

"Hello, John." Joe explained the purpose of his visit. "Do you recall anything about the Thorntons?"

"They were an attractive couple," John observed with a nonchalant shrug. "I'm afraid that's all I noticed. Sounds rather shallow, doesn't it?"

"Don't apologize. None of us knew them well. What about last weekend, did you see or hear anything unusual?"

"Not a thing. We often work on the weekends, and when we're not at the library, we're in and out running errands," John replied.

Joe thanked them and went on to his own apartment. It grew stuffy when he was away all day, and he opened the windows and looked out. The apartment house across the street had a vacancy sign on a wrought-iron stand. Housing was at a premium since the end of the war, and he thought it would be rented soon. Finding eager residents for a murder scene, however, might prove difficult.

Abby Hicks called to him from the sidewalk. She wore her peach colored checker's uniform and had slung her purse over her shoulder. "Hey, Joe! Are you watching for suspicious strangers?"

"Always. I'll meet you at your door." He planned to speak with her there, but she invited him to come in.

"I've got to sit down after being on my feet all day. Would you like something to drink?" she asked.

"No, thank you. I just have a few questions about the Thorntons."

He waited while she poured a bottle of Coca-Cola into an ice-filled glass. The seating choices were the sofa, draped with a knit afghan in a rainbow of colors, or a green velour overstuffed chair by the radio. Abby had always been friendly. He'd never asked her out, but she'd given him the impression she'd be delighted if he did. She was pretty in a rather frazzled way after a day of work, and rather than give her the opportunity to sit close, he took the chair. She sat down on the sofa opposite him.

"In addition to the police investigation, Leon asked me to look into the murder in apartment three. I haven't found anyone who has exchanged more than a casual greeting with the Thorntons. Did you ever speak with them?"

"Sure, they came into the market on Saturday mornings and were always real friendly. They bought just the basics: bacon, eggs, bread, coffee, and milk. They were real fond of oranges, but sometimes bought grapes. The first time they came in, they recognized me and always got into the line at my register. I don't understand how they could have killed Cookie Crumble. Strippers like funny names, don't they? Was she real pretty?"

That was why he'd never dated Abby, she was sweet, but lacked focus. He kept the conversation centered on the murder. "Cookie was a beautiful girl, and had an agent who believed she'd soon become a big star."

"Boy, he must be really disappointed," she observed.

"Yes, he is. Did you ever hear the Thorntons mention plans to move?"

"No, but our conversations were never deep. Vince gave me some postcards with Disney characters on them. They're real cute, and I'm saving them for an eight-year-old niece."

"Really, may I see them?"

She made a quick trip into her bedroom and came back with half a dozen cards. They were the same ones drugstores sold, nothing uniquely made for Disney employees. "These are nice. She's sure to love them." He handed them back to her. "Did Vince mention what he did at Disney when he gave them to you?"

"No, he just said he worked there, but wasn't an artist."

"What about Peggy? Did she ever mention grading

papers, or make any reference to her classroom?"

"She bought a box of pencils once, and some erasers. I thought the school supplied everything, but she said she liked to have extras. Does that count?"

"Yes, of course it does." He stood. "I won't take any more of your time."

Abby turned coy. "I'm here alone most nights. Come by again if you like." She walked him to the door.

"Thank you, but I've just become engaged, and spend most of my evenings with my fiancée."

She burst into tears, and horribly embarrassed, hurriedly wiped her face with her fingertips. "Congratulations. I'm happy for you, but all my friends are married, or have boyfriends, and I'm the only one without a beau. It makes me feel pathetic to be alone on Saturday nights." She paused for a loud sniff. "The man I was supposed to love must have been killed during the war, maybe on one of the Pacific islands."

Joe was at a loss as to how to respond to such a sad assumption. He couldn't pull her into his arms to offer sympathy without giving her the wrong impression. "Just keep smiling, Abby, and love is sure to find you soon." He left her apartment at a near sprint and feared he'd sounded more like a fortuneteller than a rational private eye.

She had provided some useful information about the Thorntons with her list of their groceries, or lack thereof. Apparently the couple ate breakfast several times a day, or they ate breakfast once and ate out most nights. With a town full of restaurants, and no photo of the couple to show, he couldn't track where they went for supper. They had simply disappeared as though they'd never been in Los Angeles at all.

"Promise me you'll see the agent again," Mary Margaret insisted. "You shouldn't miss this opportunity, and it might not come again."

Joe laughed. "I promise. I'll have photos taken tomorrow at Pete's Cameras, he develops film for me, and go back to see Archibald Sutton when they're ready. But I won't sign his three year contract." It was Sunday night, and they were enjoying chocolate sundaes at Aunt Lucy's Ice Cream Parlor. Ice cream always put him in a very agreeable mood.

"The contract is definitely a sticking point," she agreed, "but he wants to represent you. Maybe he'll not insist upon the three year term if you're firm about it."

"You can always count on me to be firm," Joe promised with a sly wink.

"Stop it! This is a family place, not Sherry's." She laughed in spite of herself. "I haven't seen anything more in the *Los Angeles Times* about Cookie Crumble. We really should call her Alice Reyes. Shouldn't she have a funeral?"

"Thank you, that's the perfect excuse to go back to Sherry's to see what their thoughts are on the subject."

She licked whipped cream off her spoon. "Don't make me sorry I mentioned it."

"Never." He raised his hand to swear. "Besides, the girls should know the best place to buy tassels."

Mary Margaret caught herself before she snorted in a most unladylike fashion, but she was tickled clear to her toes. "I love that you always make me laugh, Joe."

"Thank you. I'll wait until we're back at your place to show you what I love most about you."

"I'm looking forward to it." She winked at him this time.

Joe's Coast Guard uniform was taking up space in his closet, and he was relieved to find it still fit. He wore a sports coat, dress shirt and trousers to Pete's Cameras and carried his uniform in its travel bag.

"Hi, Pete, you offered to take some photos for me. Do you have time this morning?"

"We have the place to ourselves, so come to the back with me." He locked the shop's front door and hung up the small sign indicating he'd reopen in fifteen minutes. "I did some photos for an attorney last week, and he was real pleased with them. I need to advertise this as a portrait studio as well a camera shop."

"That's a good idea. I need photos to help me pose as an actor for a case. A couple of head shots, and one in my uniform should do it."

"And you'd like them tomorrow?" Pete asked. He was a lanky, red-haired young man who'd taken the business over from his uncle after the war.

"You needn't rush the order, but Wednesday would be appreciated."

"You got it."

Joe was more amused than embarrassed by the photo session and came up with both smiles, and an expression mirroring the ruthlessness of a weary soldier or trail-worn cowboy. "How's that?" he asked.

"Are you trying to look tough? If so, you're almost scary."

"Scary is good." Joe donned his navy blue Coast Guard dress uniform and Pete whistled. "By the end of the war, I was a Chief Warrant Officer, not the captain of our ship, so don't get too excited."

"I was merely appreciating the uniform, Joe. Turn so we have a three-quarter view. This would be good for a recruitment poster."

"Let's not go overboard. I only have to look as though I can play a part."

"You've convinced me."

"My girlfriend, or I should call her my fiancée, would want these photos too. Will you make a set for her?"

"You're engaged? Congratulations! I'll bet she's a great girl. I sure wish I could meet someone nice. There are plenty of nice girls, of course, but not many come in here to buy cameras or film."

Joe couldn't resist making a friendly suggestion. "One of the young women who lives in my apartment building complained to me only yesterday that she hadn't met any nice men." He named the market where Abby Hicks worked as a checker. "Do you know where it is?"

A bright gleam of inspiration filled his gaze. "Yes, and I have to buy groceries somewhere, don't I?"

"My thought exactly. Her name is Abby, and she's

pretty. She has light brown hair, brown eyes, and a nice figure. If you make a point of standing in the line for her register, you can see if she appeals to you without having to suffer through an awkward blind date."

"Thanks, Joe. I hope to have your photos ready by tomorrow afternoon."

"Give me a call if you do." Joe thought Archibald Sutton would be suitably impressed with them. He doubted he could add the cost of photos for the agent to his expense account unless he uncovered something that led directly to Cookie Crumble's killer, but he'd save the receipt and try.

He put his uniform in his car trunk and made a quick stop at the hardware store. They had bulletin boards in several sizes, and he chose the three feet by two feet version he could easily grab and turn toward the wall if necessary. He added some thumbtacks and went on his way. Once at the office, he duplicated the information written in Cookie Crumbles' file folder on three by five cards, pinned them to the board and was grateful for the larger format. He called it a fine morning's work, and just to be on the safe side, he turned the board to the wall, and went to lunch.

Joe drove to Sherry's at one o'clock that afternoon and sat down at the bar. Mae greeted him, and he ordered his usual beer. He drew a business card from his wallet and handed it to her.

Her eyes widened. "You're a detective?"

"Why are you surprised?" he asked. "Does it seem like an unlikely profession?"

"No, not at all. I love detective movies. *The Big Sleep* is one of my favorites, but I love anything with Humphrey Bogart and Lauren Bacall."

"So do I," Joe responded, although they'd always struck him as an unlikely pair. "I'm working on Alice Reyes, or Cookie Crumble's, case for an interested party. Do you know of plans for a funeral?"

"Excuse me a second." She left him to fill orders for a waiter, and then hurried back. "No. From what I heard, there's a wait for the coroner to release her body, and then she'll be shipped home for burial there. That a person could be *shipped,* like a crate of oranges, sounds awful, doesn't it?"

"It does. Do you know her hometown?"

"Kansas City, Missouri. She used to laugh about the fact her family believed she was employed as a model and studying acting. She said she was lucky no one from Kansas City ever came in. Stripping involves acting as far as I'm concerned, but not everyone agrees."

"Her friends aren't planning any sort of a memorial for her here?"

"No. I liked Alice a lot, but the strippers here aren't good friends. Alice made it plain stripping was simply a way into the movies, not something she intended to do much longer. Quite naturally, the other girls were insulted."

Joe sipped his beer. "Would you say she looked down on them?"

Mae grabbed a towel and polished a glass to look busy while they talked. "She was more proud of herself than rude, and she had big dreams."

"Thank you, Mae. What time do the strippers come in?"

"Six o'clock at the earliest. They spend a lot of time on their make-up and their costumes. Natalie Ryan, she performs as Ginger Snap, is already here working on a new routine. Shall I call backstage and see if she'll speak with you?"

"Thank you." Joe crossed his fingers as Mae made the short call, and it sounded good from her end.

Mae smiled as she hung up. "Natalie says come on back. She's here early, so the owner can't complain she's wasting time on his dollar, but it wouldn't be wise to stay too long."

Joe doubted Corky Coyne got up before four o'clock in the afternoon, so even if the owner did complain, he wouldn't have the muscle to throw him out. He walked up the stairs at the side of the stage and found Natalie behind the curtain.

She was a very pretty girl even without her seductive, theatrical make-up. She was dressed in navy blue shorts, a red halter-top, and ballet slippers. She read Joe's card and slipped it into her back pocket.

"Are you looking for the truth about Cookie Crumble?" she asked.

"Yes, the better I know her, the easier it will be to find who killed her. Please don't censure your thoughts." They sat on a couple of bent back chairs on the side of the stage.

As she spoke, Natalie fluffed her dark brown hair with her fingers. "Her name was Alice Reyes, Alice, of all things. Doesn't that sound too sweet to be believed?"

"Maybe. What else about her annoyed you?"

"Strippers all play into men's fantasies, but her naughty schoolgirl act was popular with men who really would like to have a cute little girl sit on their lap. The whole number nauseated me."

"I've heard her act described as 'cute.'"

"Oh it was cute all right, but every move she made was calculated to titillate. That's our job, of course, but she enjoyed it more than any of the rest of us. Men sent her big bouquets, and she'd pass them along to the rest of us, like we were poor orphans who'd never seen a rose. I'm sorry she's dead, but she was one of my least favorite women in the world."

Joe leaned forward. "Could I see her dressing room?"

She covered her mouth to muffle her giggles. "This isn't a movie studio, and we share a single room, but come on, I'll show it to you."

Joe followed her off stage and down the stairs to the basement. The dressing room was at the end of the hall, and not much wider than the outer hallway itself. The air reeked of perfume, and not the expensive kind. Lighted mirrors covered the long wall above a counter cluttered with jars of makeup, hairbrushes, and combs. Bent back chairs sat at each station, giving the effect of a beauty parlor struck by a hurricane. Stockings hung over the backs of several chairs and rolling racks held a colorful variety of costumes. He recognized Natalie's Ginger Snap apron and hat.

"Is Alice's costume here?" he asked.

"No, the police took everything of hers. Her spot was on

the end, and it's been wiped clean."

"You said she passed along flowers, did you save any of the cards?"

"Someone else's love notes? No, I'm not that desperate for attention." She walked to her place and plucked a card from the mirror frame. "See, here's one written to me."

Her name was scrawled at the top. The message read, "I'd love to eat what you're cooking." It was the signature that impressed Joe: *Brett W.* "Do you know this man?"

"Brett, yeah, he comes in here often. Nice fellow, but my dad's age and not my type anyway. I'd never say that to a man's face, mind you. I flirt with everyone while I'm on stage, but not on my own time."

"I understand completely, although some men might not be able to separate the performer from the young woman off the stage." Brett had mentioned going to Sherry's occasionally, but Natalie pegged him as a frequent visitor. "May I keep this?"

"Sure, I don't know why I kept it. Just to have something to put on my mirror when Cookie had so many cards she could barely see her reflection."

"The police took them all?"

"Yes, they were very thorough. The detective wasn't nearly as nice as you, Joe."

She was flirting with him for sure, whether on her own time or not. "Thank you. Do any of her fans stick out in your memory?"

"Too many to name. I had the same conversation with the police detective on the case. He warned me to keep my thoughts to myself rather than alert any of our regulars to the investigation. You're a detective, even if a private one, and you claim to be discreet, so I figure it must be all right to talk with you."

"It is, and you've been very helpful," he insisted. "Did any of Cookie's regulars stop coming in last week before her body was found?"

She pursed her lips with the effort to recall. "Frankly, when I'm on stage, I don't really look at the audience but slightly above them. I also make it a point to forget every catcall and whistle the minute I exit the stage. I've not struck up friendships with any of the men who come here. Maybe one of the other girls will be more of a help to you."

"Have any suggestions?"

"Luisa Miller, she calls herself Carmella Cordova, lives to gossip. She may know all sorts of incriminating things about Cookie and her fans. She usually comes in just before six. Do you want me to tell her you'll come by?"

"That would be great." The cluttered dressing room was making him claustrophobic, and he needed a breath of unscented air. He left Sherry's through the exit at the back of the stage and checked the time. With four hours to spare, he needed to return to his office, update his bulletin board information, and hope for more business.

At three-thirty, he heard a faint tap at his door. He quickly turned the board to the wall. "Come in," he called.

A blonde girl in a starched white blouse, plaid skirt, and saddle shoes, clearly her school uniform, glanced in the door. She projected a true schoolgirl's innocence rather than a stripper's polished naiveté, but for her to turn up at his door today struck him as a very odd coincidence.

He stood. "How may I help you, miss?"

She edged only a single step inside his office. "It says Discreet Investigations on the door."

"Yes, it does. Have you lost something you'd like to have found?"

"No, I've found something I shouldn't have, and I need to know what to do."

"Please take a chair by my desk, and tell me what concerns you." He hoped it wasn't anything too serious, because he couldn't charge a child more than her weekly allowance.

She came in, sat down on the edge of her chair, and hugged her schoolbooks to her chest. Joe opened a new file folder and picked up a pencil. "Let's begin with your name."

"Lacy Fitzgerald." She looked around the sparsely furnished office, but there wasn't much to see other than the desk and file cabinet.

"How old are you, Lacy?"

"I'm fourteen and in the eighth grade at Saint Veronica's."

"What is it you've found?" he asked.

She took a deep breath and let it out slowly before beginning in a rush. "Well, last Sunday afternoon, I took my little brother, Tommy, to the movies. When we came out, I saw our father across the street walking with a woman I didn't know. He was carrying a little boy in his arms, and they were all laughing. They went into The Pepper Mill Café, and if Tommy hadn't been with me, I would have followed him in and asked to be introduced."

She was sitting up very straight, the way the nuns at Saint Veronica's must insist upon. "Could you have been mistaken?" he asked.

"I know my own father, and he's supposed to be in San Francisco. He's an architect and working on a hotel being built there. He'll spend a week home with us, and then go up to San Francisco for a few days. Or at least that's his story."

Joe nodded thoughtfully. She was a very smart girl and had drawn the most obvious conclusion from what she'd seen. "What is it you'd like me to do?"

"Don't you follow people around and take photos?"

"Yes, if the case requires it, not all do. If I took photos for you, what would you do with them?"

"I'll show them to my mother so she'll have grounds to divorce him."

He leaned back in his chair. "Has it occurred to you that your mother may already know where your father actually is?"

Lacy shuddered at the thought. "She has principles and wouldn't stay with him if he were seeing another woman. Walking down the street in board daylight with her sure wasn't being discreet about it either. That the little boy he held might be his son is doubly nauseating."

Joe couldn't believe he was having this conversation with a fourteen-year-old and felt way out of his depth. "Even if a husband or wife strays, couples are often able to work things out and put it behind them."

"You don't know my mother," she insisted. "Will you take my case?"

He wanted to help her, but he foresaw serious complications and only one possible answer. "I'm so sorry, Lacy, but I really can't work for a minor against her parents' best interests. If your mother came to see me, I'd take the case."

She leaped to her feet. "You think I'm just a little kid who doesn't know anything! Well, you're wrong!" She ran out of his office and nearly collided with the building custodian.

CC looked in the door. "Goodness gracious, she was sure in a hurry."

"She was disappointed I couldn't take her case."

He came in to empty the wastebasket. "Why would a sweet little girl need a detective?" he asked.

"I won't betray her confidence, but she saw something upsetting and thought I could put things right."

"Poor child. I'm afraid too many children see things they shouldn't."

"You can say that again, CC."

The custodian went on his way, and Joe closed Lacy's folder and set it aside. He doubted he would meet her mother, but Lacy might be underestimating her. He got up to stretch, and then left the building to take a brisk walk around the neighborhood. Exercise kept him awake in the afternoon, and while he had no employees at present, he wanted to cultivate the habit and set a good example.

At six o'clock, he parked on the Sunset Strip near Sherry's. Mae worked only the lunch shift, so he bypassed the bar and went backstage. He'd discovered early that few interfered with a man who walked with purpose, and no one stopped him. He found his way to the dressing room. The door was open, and Natalie waved to him.

"Come on in," she called. "Everyone wants to talk with you."

He and Mary Margaret had seen only two acts, Natalie, and Luisa, or Carmella Cordova's. He recognized the other two women from their glossy photographs at Sherry's entrance. They were in varying stages of undress, but smiled at him and welcomed him warmly.

"Good evening, ladies. I'd like to speak with you one at a time if I may. Luisa, would you step out in the hall with me, please?"

She wore a red silk wrapper she might have bought in Chinatown, and fluffy white feather mules. Rather than spit out her chewing gum, she blew big pink bubbles as she followed Joe down the hallway. Her jet-black hair glistened in the light from the overhead bulbs, but without thick layers of dark mascara and eyebrow pencil, it was plain she was no more Spanish than he was.

"From what I've heard, Cookie Crumble was very popular with Sherry's clientele. Can you tell me something about her?"

She rolled her eyes, and then stuck her gum in her cheek. "It's hard to know where to begin. She borrowed a scarf from me one night when it was raining, and I never saw it again. It was always, 'Oh, I'm so sorry, but I forgot it at home and will bring it tomorrow.' But she never did. She always needed something someone else had, but she kept treating loans as gifts, and we learned not to trust her.

"Men would send her flowers, and she'd make sure we all saw they were prettier than whatever we got. She claimed the applause was louder after her numbers. She sometimes wore expensive jewelry she swore a devoted fan had given her, but she'd never wear it twice. Maybe she pawned gifts from men, but she made sure we all saw them first."

"It sounds as though she took advantage of everyone," he remarked.

"I'll say. We'd all had more than enough of her, but she kept telling us she'd be leaving soon to appear in a movie. We couldn't wait to throw her a good-bye party."

"How do the rest of you get along?"

Luisa paused to blow a bubble. "None of us are best friends. We'd all like to be the headliner here, but we don't fight about it. I suppose you could say we try to outdo one another, but the competition is good. It keeps our routines fresh. I'm trying to figure out how to do a mermaid, but I don't know what to do with the blasted tail."

Joe gave it some thought. "What if the stage were lit with blue and green lights? You could begin as a sleeping mermaid, reclining on a chaise decorated to look like a reef, and then dreaming, you could turn human, discard your tail, and rise to dance?" Calling what she did a dance was generous he supposed, but he wanted to be kind.

"I love it!" She grabbed him for a bubblegum flavored smack on the lips and stepped back to speak in a whisper, "This has to be our secret. Please don't give anyone else an idea. It's all I can do to stay ahead of them."

"Agreed." He'd never thought of himself as having a talent for choreography, but she'd had the original idea.

Patty Poleto talked to him next. She was a blue-eyed bleached blonde. "You must have seen my photo on display out front." She folded her hands beneath her chin and batted her false eyelashes at him.

"I'm the Southern Belle, and have layers and layers of lace-trimmed slips and bloomers beneath the near endless yards of my gown. It takes almost as long to squeeze into my costume as it does to shimmy out of it. Speaking of which, our 'dressing room' is little more than an old broom closet, but whenever I suggest hiring a maid to help us dress, the manager says he'll be happy to deduct her salary from mine. I ask you, is that fair?"

"Certainly not," he agreed. The top of her floral robe gapped open to provide a tantalizing view of her ample charms. He focused on her eyes. "What can you tell me about Cookie?"

She bit a hangnail. "Nothing good. I couldn't wait for her to finally land a movie role and leave. The rest of us are just trying to earn a living, but she'd drone on about how she'd win an Oscar for her film debut. I refused to listen to her prattle rather than tell her to shut up, but I was tempted to slap her silly a time or two."

"Did you say that to Detective Lynch?" he asked.

"Are you kidding? Of course not, or he'd have me on his suspect list."

"Good thinking. Do you know anything about the men she dated?"

"She liked college boys, but she wasn't particular about which one. I think she was more careful with some of the other men who frequent Sherry's, you know what kind I mean. They might have plenty of money to spend on a girl, but they keep real scary company."

"I understand, and I plan to avoid them too."

Bernice Ross was Lily Montell for her act, and the last of the strippers being featured at Sherry's. In her late twenties, she had an elegant routine where she dressed as a 1920s heiress featured in Erte's art deco prints with slinky lily-patterned gowns, black satin gloves, and a long cigarette holder. Her dark hair was cut in a short bob, and she was the most subdued of the women Joe had met that day.

"Let's just say Cookie was as relentlessly annoying as a mosquito whining in your ear. None of us shed a tear when we learned she'd died. That sounds rather harsh, doesn't it?"

"I find an honest opinion refreshing," Joe countered. "Who do you think might have killed her?"

She shrugged. "I've no idea, but what's happened to the people who rented the apartment where she was found?"

"Excellent question. I haven't found them, but the police may have better luck."

"I didn't care for the detective working the case. He's the type who'll go to a strip joint three nights a week and still swear he's never been in one."

"Clearly you're an excellent judge of character," Joe replied. He handed Bernice his card. "If anything more occurs to you, please give me a call. On the off-chance someone is out to murder a whole string of strippers, I'd like to stop him at one."

"Good luck." She walked away with a seductive sway, and then paused to turn back. "Thank you."

"You're welcome." Joe wasn't sure how he'd sparked that show of gratitude, but he smiled as though he were pleased. He couldn't wait to tell Mary Margaret how he'd spent the afternoon, but he'd make it about the case, and not the assortment of half-clothed women.

CHAPTER 5

Mary Margaret was in a subdued mood that night. "We lost a favorite patient, and I feel sick about it. Please tell me something at least amusing if you've nothing side-splitting to share."

They were in her cottage snuggled together on the couch. "I'm sorry about your patient. I know you're fond of them all. Let's see, I did help a stripper choreograph a new routine, and that has to strike you as oddly amusing."

She sat up, more keenly interested than amused. "What were you doing with a stripper, may I ask."

"I'm working on Cookie's case, and went to Sherry's to speak with her co-workers."

"Co-workers is a flattering term." She relaxed in his arms and covered a wide yawn. "Don't worry, I'm not jealous. I haven't the energy for it tonight."

That she worked with handsome physicians and surgeons all day, to say nothing of recuperating young veterans who might have enormous charm, wasn't something he cared to concentrate on either. "I'd never want to make you jealous, sweetheart. Besides, without their stage makeup and costumes, they aren't nearly as pretty."

This time, she nearly jumped from his arms. "You saw them without their costumes?"

He laughed, even if she wasn't in the mood for humor.

"They weren't as naked as they are at the end of their acts. They were wearing street clothes or light robes, and we spent our time standing in a hallway talking about Cookie."

"We only saw a couple of girls on the night we went to Sherry's. How many did you talk to today?"

"The two we saw, plus two more, but we were talking about a young woman who had been murdered, not flirting away the afternoon."

"Except when you were choreographing a routine?"

"That was a serious effort at creating art, Mary Margaret, not mindless flirting. I don't flirt, except with you. Is there any more of your luscious apple pie?"

She slipped from his arms to rise. "I see right through your ploy, Mr. Ezell. You're trying to distract me, but I might be able to find a couple of pieces if I look real hard. I'll make coffee."

He watched her nearly skip into the kitchen and figured he was out of trouble, if he'd been in any, which was unlikely with such a delightful fiancée.

She liked to call her one-bedroom cottage cozy, but when he moved in after the wedding, it would be a challenge not to constantly bump into each other. That could be nice though. Being careful not to crowd her in the kitchen, he remained on the sofa and thought about Lacy Fitzgerald.

He'd been wise not to take her case, but he still felt bad about having to disappoint her. Apple pie would help, of course, but he couldn't eat his way out of a case like Cookie's, and he wouldn't even try.

The next afternoon, Joe got a call from Mae, the noontime bartender at Sherry's. "Cookie's brother, Max, is here. The police won't tell him anything about their investigation. He seems like a real nice kid. May I send him on to your office? Please."

He heard the slight catch in her voice, a clear sign of distress. "Sure. Do you still have my card with the address?"

"Yes, and I'll draw him a map, so he'll be there soon."

"Fine." Joe opened his case folder on Cookie. He'd typed his notes from yesterday's interviews with her fellow strippers, but shifted the pages to the bottom of the stack. None had wept a tear over the murdered girl, but her brother didn't need to know how little she'd be missed.

By the time Max finally arrived, Joe had thought he might have decided against coming to see him. He stood to greet him. "Max? Come on in and sit down. Would you care for coffee?"

Max was a tall, lanky kid, who only his mother would describe as handsome, but he might one day grow into his oversized features. He had the same thick brown hair as his sister, with an unfortunate cowlick he reached up in a futile effort to tame.

"No, thank you, Mr. Ezell, I'm sorry I'm late. I know how to get from one place to another at home, but here I keep getting turned around and go in the wrong direction every time."

His apologetic smile gave him a charm Joe hadn't expected. "You needn't apologize, and call me Joe. I'm so sorry you had to visit California for such a sad reason."

Max waited for Joe to take his seat before he sat down. He had to move the chair a couple of feet away from the desk to accommodate his long legs. "Alice and I talked about my coming for a visit, but she wanted me to wait until she had a role in a movie so she could show me around the set." He swallowed hard. "That's not ever going to happen now."

"Everyone who knew her remarked on her talent," Joe replied, which didn't stretch the truth too far. Her agent had praised her, and her many fans loved her act. "Where are you staying?"

"The rent's paid until the end of the month at Alice's apartment, so I'm staying there. The police made a mess of it searching for clues, but they didn't find anything and said I could move in."

Joe wondered if Cookie—he'd have to remember to call her Alice—had just been a lousy housekeeper. "You and I might find something the police missed. Would you mind taking me there?"

"You really want to go?"

"Yes, I do."

Flustered, Matt blushed a deep red. "I don't have the money to pay you. Alice sent money home for mother, but we don't have enough in the bank to hire a private detective."

"I'm being paid by another interested party, so you've no need to worry over my fees. My services are covered."

His expression brightened. "Really? I don't want to say anything bad about the Los Angeles police force, but they didn't seem very interested in finding who killed Alice."

"They're careful not to make promises they can't keep," Joe replied. Something he needed to learn. "Give me Alice's address, and I'll follow you there."

"I rented a car so I wouldn't have to pay taxis to get around town, but it would be a whole lot easier for me to follow you so we both don't get lost. Alice's apartment is on a side street near Sherry's." He handed over the address on a scrap of wrinkled paper. "She wrote to Mom about modeling, so I was surprised to learn she'd been waitressing."

"Waitressing?" If his sister had had such a job, Joe hadn't heard about it.

"At Sherry's. It's a real nice restaurant. The girl bartender sure was friendly. I guess she and Alice were good friends."

Max reminded him of a big puppy, and he could understand why Mae had shielded him from Alice's true employment. He doubted the kid could leave town without learning she'd worked as Cookie Crumble, a favorite stripper with Sherry's clientele, but it didn't have to be that afternoon.

Alice Reyes's apartment was in a stark concrete building built in what passed for an ultra-modern style before the war, but the architect posed no competition for Frank Lloyd

Wright. Pale aqua glass bricks framed the wide entrance, creating a disorienting blur as Joe and Max entered.

Max led the way to the elevator. "She's on the third floor, so she had a nice view."

"I'm sure she enjoyed it," Joe responded.

They stepped out of the elevator. "Hers is the first one on the right. It's convenient, but must be kind of noisy when the elevator runs late at night. I guess it didn't matter to her." He unlocked the door and reached in to turn on the light.

"Will you need help packing her things?" Joe asked.

"She didn't own much except her clothes, and I'll give them to the Salvation Army rather than send them home. Mom would be too sad to open the boxes, so they'd just sit in Alice's bedroom catching dust."

"That's very thoughtful of you."

"Thanks, but it's what seems right. I just got into LA this morning, so please excuse the mess. I wanted to see what the police knew, rather than spend my time cleaning up."

The door opened into the living room, with a small kitchen to the left, along with a hallway to a bath and bedroom. It was a small apartment by any standard, and Joe felt an almost uncontrollable urge to open the refrigerator.

"Do you mind if I get a glass of water?" Joe asked.

"No, go right ahead. There must be clean glasses in the cupboard."

Joe had expected the sink to be full of unwashed dishes, but it was empty and sparkling clean. The burners on the stovetop were without a single crumb or drip. Maybe Alice preferred not to cook meals for one. He found half a dozen mismatched glasses and turned on the tap to fill one. He now had a reason to open the freezer compartment on the refrigerator, but all it held were the two empty ice cube trays. He filled them.

It was lunacy to expect to find a dead body after the police had searched the apartment, but Joe still held his breath as he pulled open the door. There was a bowl of oranges on the top rack, and a jar of grape jelly in the door.

That was it. He closed the refrigerator as softly as he could.

"It looks as though your sister ate her meals out," he called to Max.

"Mae, she's the nice bartender at Sherry's, told me Alice ate her meals there. It's a good thing, because she was an awful cook. Mom tried to teach her, but she'd always insist movie stars didn't have to prepare their own meals."

Joe joined him in the living room. "Her determination should have paid off."

"Well, sadly, someone thought different." Max gathered up movie magazines strewn over the sofa. "Back home, Alice always had a library card, but it looks as though she only read magazines here. I guess she wanted to keep up with show business." He stacked them on the coffee table.

"In her letters home, did Alice mention dating anyone?"

Max sat down on the sofa and leaned back. The afternoon sunlight streamed through the large window behind him giving his dark hair a golden shimmer. "Never, which was odd because she was always chasing boys back home. She was homecoming queen and real popular, but if she wanted a boy who hadn't thought to chase her, she'd go after him."

Joe folded the sweater hanging off the back of a chair and sat down with him. "How would she go about it? Did she have any special tricks?"

"She'd dress extra cute and show up wherever he worked. She'd just walk by and say hello. She usually got his attention."

"She didn't leave anyone special when she came to California? Someone who might have followed her?"

"You think someone from home killed her?" Max shook his head. "No, sir, that just wouldn't have happened. The man who killed her has to be someone she met here. How are we going to catch him?"

"You're a nice kid, but it would be best if you accompanied your sister's body home and let the police, with whatever help I can provide, solve the crime."

"You've no idea who did it, do you?" Max countered. He

stood and began to pace the small living room in a frantic circle.

Joe spoke in a soothing tone, "It's likely the murderer is someone she knew from Sherry's, someone who was infatuated with her, while she had no interest in him. He must regret becoming so violently angry with her, but he can't bring her back to life."

Max shoved his hands into his pockets. "She knew how to take care of herself."

"She may have been drinking, and didn't realize she was in danger until the murderer's hands were wrapped tightly around her neck." She would have seen the specter of death in the man's narrowed gaze, and Joe hated to think how terrifying her final moments must have been.

"You think he was a man she trusted, until it was too late?" Max asked.

"Yes. It's possible he gave her expensive gifts. Have you looked through her jewelry?"

"Haven't even looked for it."

Joe stood and nodded toward the hallway to the bedroom. "It would probably be in a jewelry box on her dresser. Do you mind if I help you search?"

"No." He led the way. "Looks like she left in a hurry and didn't have time to make the bed."

"The police might have thrown back the covers." Joe opened the drapes to let in the light. The room was painted a pale pink. There was a pink blanket on the bed, and a white chenille bedspread pooled on the floor beside it.

Teasing bits of lingerie peeked out of the dresser drawers, and Joe continued to let Max believe it was the police's doing. There were some necklaces hanging from the mirror frame above the dresser, but they were costume jewelry, not expensive tokens from someone who'd adored Alice. Max looked through the top drawer and found a red leather jewelry box, but it contained only a pair of small gold hoop earrings.

"Mother gave her these for her birthday one year. She said every woman ought to have at least one pair of gold earrings." He closed the lid and set the box on top of the dresser. "Mom would like to have those, so I'll take them home." He continued to search the dresser drawers, but found no more jewelry.

"Did the police say anything to you about Alice's purse?" If she'd pawned expensive gifts, the tickets might have been in her wallet. Joe wanted to follow up on them, but it looked as though he'd have to make the rounds of nearby pawnshops and hope to find one Cookie, no, Alice, visited.

"No, they didn't find it with her. Do you suppose the murderer has it?"

"Probably, or he might have tossed it in a convenient trashcan. Let's just assume it's lost." He checked his watch. "Let's take a quick look through the closet."

Max opened the door to find it stuffed with colorful dresses in the latest styles. "She always loved clothes. Do you suppose the Salvation Army will take her things still on the hangars?"

"Yes, it will save them the trouble of unpacking boxes. Let's check the hat boxes for cards or letters a man might have sent."

There were three round boxes on the shelf and Max took them down and placed them on the bed. The first two held cute little hats, the third had letters tied with ribbon. "She saved Mom's letters." He thumbed through them before setting them on the dresser with the red jewelry box. "I'll take those home with me."

Joe had hoped to find something to link Alice to the man who'd killed her, but it just wasn't there. Of course, if the killer had her purse, he would have had her keys and could have beaten the police there and removed photos of them together, or anything with his name. He could also have taken whatever expensive jewelry he'd given her so it couldn't be traced to the store and buyer.

He doubted they'd find anything important in Alice's makeup in the bathroom, so he walked right by. "Come with me to pick up my fiancée, and we'll treat you to dinner."

Max hung his head. "You don't need to do that."

"You already have dinner plans?"

"No, but…"

"You'll like Mary Margaret, and she's helping me with your sister's case."

"Oh, well, then, I guess if she knows about it, I could come along."

Joe had a difficult time thinking of this shy young man as Alice's kin. Apparently she's inherited the lion's share of looks and charm in the family.

He drove with Max to the hospital and left the car to greet Mary Margaret.

He kissed her cheek and whispered, "I've invited Cookie's brother to join us for dinner. He believes she was a waitress, don't tell him otherwise."

"Are you kidding?"

"No, I'm not. Please be as sweet as I know you can be. Cookie's name was Alice. Remember to call her that."

Swept along, Mary Margaret didn't argue, but when Max Reyes stepped out and insisted she ride in the front seat, she understood Joe's concern. "I'm so sorry for your loss. Brothers and sisters share a special bond, and I know you'll always miss Alice."

Tears filled Max's eyes, and he quickly brushed them away. "Thank you, but rather than sympathy, what I really need is help to solve Alice's murder."

"We're working on it," she assured him. "You're too tall to ride in the back. Please take the front seat." She slipped into the backseat before he could argue. "Have you two decided where we're going?"

Joe waited for Max to get into the car before he climbed in behind the wheel. "What do you feel like Max, barbecue or hamburgers?" Joe asked.

"We have plenty of barbecue restaurants back home, but if that's what you want, it's fine with me."

Mary Margaret leaned forward to give Joe's shoulder a squeeze. "Let's go to the Jumpin' Plate."

Max looked over his shoulder at her, and she smiled

invitingly. "They have the best hamburgers, and their onion rings are beyond description. Do you like them?"

"I'm more of a French fry man myself," Joe interjected.

"Me too," Max offered.

The Jumpin' Plate had a homey décor reminiscent of a grandmother's kitchen. The walls were a pale blue, and the chairs had thick cushions covered in blue and white gingham. The paper placemats showed colorful farm scenes. It was a popular restaurant with families as well as couples on dates.

They were shown to a half-circle booth, and Mary Margaret slid over the blue vinyl seat into the middle. The waitress was a petite blonde named Sonia who rattled off the day's special: a hamburger patty smothered in chili and cheese.

"Give us a minute, please," Mary Margaret asked.

"Sure, take your time, honey. We want everyone to be deliriously happy with their dinner." She walked away in a bouncy strut.

Max watched her. "I don't believe I'll be 'deliriously happy' ever again. Isn't that a bit much to expect from a hamburger?"

Mary Margaret patted his arm. "It certainly is, but you need to eat. Aren't you hungry?"

He studied his menu hurriedly as though preparing for a pop quiz. "I can't remember eating today, so I guess I must be."

"I like the old-fashioned cheeseburger with onion rings," she said.

Joe nodded. "Always a good choice, but tonight I'm going with the bacon bleu cheese burger and fries."

Max closed his menu with a fast slap. "I'll have that too."

Sonia came back to take their orders and quickly returned with coffee for Mary Margaret and Joe and a chocolate milkshake for Max. "Your order will be up in just a minute."

"We're in no hurry," Joe assured her.

Mary Margaret spoke before the silence at the table grew awkward. "Tell us something about what you do at home, Max. Are you working or in school?"

"This is my last year of high school, but I have an excuse to miss classes for a week or two. I work on the weekends at a body shop. I'm good at pounding out dents if not much else."

She shot Joe a quick frantic glance. "I thought you were older. It must be your height that fooled me."

"I'm eighteen. I could have joined the Navy at seventeen, but it was too late to get into the war so I figured I might as well wait and join later. That was my plan until this awful thing happened to Alice. Now I'd hate to leave Mom alone. That just doesn't seem right."

Max appeared to be a real responsible soul with a well-developed sense of what was right and wrong, and Joe hoped he could get him on his way home before he learned the truth about his sister. At the same time, guilt ate at him for not revealing it.

"I'm sure your mother is proud of you, but it's better to find your own way rather than live to please her," Joe advised.

"Alice was always her favorite, and Mom believed she'd be a big star so she didn't mind her coming out to Hollywood. Now she's blaming herself for not moving to California to look after her." He leaned back as Sonia served his plate. His eyes widened at the size of the bacon bleu cheese burger and the veritable mountain of fries. He grabbed for one. "These are good."

"Of course they are, honey," Sonia exclaimed. "This is the Jumpin' Plate, and everything that comes out of our kitchen is the best you'll ever eat."

Max took a bite of his burger rather than reply. He'd not realized how hungry he was until he had the delicious burger in his hands. "I'm sorry, I don't mean to eat too fast. My mom always tells me not to gobble my food, but this is awfully good."

"Go ahead and gobble," Mary Margaret urged. "It's

encouraged here." She reached for an onion ring. "I keep saying I'm going to fry up some of these myself, but haven't gotten around to it yet."

The background conversation provided a cheerful hum and tunes from the "Your Hit Parade" radio show added a musical lilt. It was a wonderful dinner, but Joe kept worrying about their young guest. He had assumed Max was of age, but an eighteen-year-old kid wasn't prepared to think or act like an adult.

When Max finished his dinner down to the last French fry and sip of milkshake, Mary Margaret and Joe had barely begun eating. "Would you like to order another burger?" she asked. "Or maybe you'd like pie. They have a wonderful selection here."

Max's shiny plate looked as though it had been licked clean. "No, I'm stopping here." He sat back and smiled for the first time that evening. "Thank you. It was a really good dinner. Are there lots of these places?"

"No, this is the one and only Jumpin' Plate," Joe answered. "It's so popular, one day they might expand."

"I like to cook, but running a restaurant must take an awful lot of work and plenty of money."

Mary Margaret assured him it must. "I also love to cook, but I want to keep it fun. I'm happy being a nurse for the time being."

"Aren't you sad when people die?"

"Yes, but there's really no time to grieve when the other patients deserve our best care. We have to simply press on, be as cheerful as we can possibly be, and cry at home."

"Alice wanted to be an actress to make people happy. Do you suppose I could meet her agent, Mr. Ezell, Joe?"

Joe hadn't expected his request, and it threw him for a moment. "His name is Archibald Sutton, and I planned to see him this week. To get people to talk, I must often pretend to be something I'm not. He believes I'm an actor looking for movie roles. I told him I knew your sister, so you could come with me. To encourage him to talk, you might have to convince him you're also looking for acting work."

Max drew in a deep breath. "Lie to him, you mean?"

"Oh, not at all," Mary Margaret insisted. "It's undercover work, what detectives do all the time. Joe is working on your sister's case, and any ploy he has to use to discover the truth is acceptable."

The young man looked decidedly skeptical. "Couldn't I just be Alice's brother who's come from Kansas City?"

"Yes, if you'd feel more comfortable with that. I hope Mr. Sutton has remembered something more than what he told me about Alice the first time we spoke. Sometimes the smallest crumb of information can lead to the solution of a crime." He pulled a business card from his wallet and handed it to Max.

"Call me in the morning, and we'll make our plans then."

"Fine, but I don't mean to make trouble for you."

"You're no trouble at all," Joe responded. He savored the rest of his hamburger and hoped he could keep Max from discovering too much tomorrow.

Mary Margaret held her tongue until after they'd dropped Max in front of his sister's apartment building, and then she moved to the front seat and got straight to the point. "It isn't right not to tell him Alice stripped for a living. It has to be central to the crime, doesn't it?"

"It is, but he's just a big kid, Mary Margaret, not someone with your experience of the world."

"That really isn't the point. You should sit him down and explain the facts before he stumbles across them. What if there's another article in the *LA Times* about Cookie Crumble?"

"He wouldn't recognize the name. I know, this will probably blow up in my face, but I don't want to damage his sister's memory. It won't hurt him not to know how popular Cookie Crumble was, and he'd be embarrassed clear down to his toenails if he knew. He'd surely hide it from his mother and suffer for keeping the secret from her."

"Oh, all right, have it your way, but you better hope he's leaving town real soon."

"I'll hold that thought."

* * *

Joe picked up his photographs from the camera shop and called Archibald Sutton as soon as he'd sat down at his desk. "I want to come in this morning and bring Alice Reyes's brother with me. He's a sweet kid and doesn't know anything about Cookie Crumble. Can you help me keep that a secret?"

"Sure, I got it. Mum's the word."

Max called Joe around ten o'clock, and Joe picked him up for the drive to Archibald Sutton's office. He'd thought he'd cleared the way with the agent, but he'd forgotten about his vivacious secretary.

Charlotte rose to greet them. "You're Cookie's brother? You look nothing like her, but you're the type needed for war films, isn't he, Mr. Ezell? There's always a kid everyone looks after."

"I'm Max Reyes, Alice's brother, but who's Cookie?"

"Cookie Crumble, that was Alice's stage name," Charlotte explained. "You didn't know she used it?"

"We're in a hurry," Joe interjected. "Would you please see if Mr. Sutton could speak to us now?"

"Sure thing." She knocked on her boss's door and ushered them in.

Archibald took a long look at Max. "You're Alice's brother? Glad to meet you. You'd also be perfect for the cast of the war film I'm sending Joe on. You have that gangly kid look, and it's in high demand. Do you have acting experience, son?"

Max appeared more startled than flattered. "I've been in school plays, but I came with Joe to see if you remembered anything more about my sister. Cookie Crumble doesn't sound like a serious name for an actress. Didn't she plan to go by Alice?"

"Yes, of course she did." He sent Joe a questioning glance.

Joe shook his head and handed the agent his photos. "Max is hoping his sister's murder can be solved while he's in town."

Archibald gestured for them to sit and hurriedly went through Joe's photographs. "These are terrific. I like the scowl, that's good. No one would be smiling through a battle scene. As for Alice, our relationship was strictly professional. I didn't know her as well as the girls at Sherry's must."

Sherry's wasn't somewhere Joe wanted mentioned, and he slid down in his chair. "I'm sure the police must have questioned them. Haven't they been here?"

"Oh yes, they've been here. A Detective Lynch, the guy knows how to dress, but that's the only nice thing I'll say about him. He thought I might have arranged more than movie roles for Alice. My agency is on the up and up. He should have known my reputation before he came here."

"What did he accuse you of?" Max asked, his features crimped into a puzzled frown.

The agent leaned back in his chair. "How should I put this? There are places that provide pretty girls for parties. They might call themselves starlets, but they haven't done anything more challenging than a lingerie ad for Frederick's of Hollywood. I was working on getting Alice a role in a fine movie people would be eager to see. However, no one is getting any work sitting here in my office. Did you bring the contract, Joe?"

"I did, but my attorney advised against signing on for three years."

"Oh great, like lawyers know anything about show business. What did he recommend?"

Joe spoke his first thought. "Six months. Then if you're getting me lots of work, I'll sign on for a year."

Archibald drew in a deep breath. "Oh, all right, but I'm only doing this because I know I can get you plenty of work. Don't tell anyone else that we made this deal. Understood?" He took the contract and wrote in the new six-month limit for Joe to sign. He handed Joe his copy of the contract, his photos and a notepaper with a typed address.

"Take these with you and see the casting director, Charlie

Goode. You go along Max, because he's likely to hire you too."

Archibald shook their hands, and Joe got them out of the office as fast as he could. "I'm sorry we didn't learn anything useful."

"Yeah, it's a shame. Aren't we going on the audition?" Max asked.

Joe had promised Mary Margaret he'd go, and it would distract Max from pursuing the Cookie Crumble alias. "If you'd like to go, we will. They'll probably treat us as though we're as insensitive as department store mannequins, but actors grow thick skins. Can you handle the rejection if they tell us we're not what they want for the parts?"

"But Mr. Stafford said they'd like us."

The kid looked as though he'd be crushed if they weren't hired. "Of course he did, but that's his job, and it doesn't mean it will be true."

"He just wants us to like him?"

"Exactly," Joe agreed. "He wants the actors who sign with him to believe with his representation they'll get a big break soon."

"Didn't he mean it with Alice?"

"I'm sure he did." Joe checked the casting director's address and tried not to laugh out loud as they checked in at his office. He couldn't see himself as a serious actor, but a case was a case, and he threw himself into solving it.

CHAPTER 6

Charlie Goode was a balding, overweight man, and the suspenders holding up his baggy trousers were extended to the very last inch. A smoldering cigar hung from his lips and kept his office in a perpetual smoky haze.

Joe took an immediate dislike to the man. Unfortunately, Charlie took one look at them and beamed widely showing off a mouthful of yellow teeth. "Archibald told me you two were exactly what I wanted. Did I believe him? No, of course not, but you two fit half the roles I have open today. I assume you can read?"

"Fluently," Joe promised.

Max shrugged. "Sure, learned how in the first grade."

Charlie shuffled through the scripts on his desk to find the pages he wanted. "Take a chair. Here, you play the sergeant's part, and you're the private, kid. You've been cut-off from the rest of your platoon, and things look grim."

"How grim?" Max asked.

"Just read. You won't die here in my office," Charlie chuckled to himself.

Joe scanned the pages they'd been given, and when Max looked up, he began. "Keep your head down, Rogers. We don't want the lieutenant believing I can't keep my men alive. Besides, your body would be too damn heavy to carry."

"You could drag me by the boots, sergeant, that's what I'd do with you." Max laughed and looked up. "Do soldiers dare talk like that to a sergeant?"

"Just read the part, kid," Charlie encouraged.

"I'd hate to bounce you along," Joe read. "It might spoil your looks."

"Can't spoil looks as good as mine." Max couldn't help but laugh now.

It worked to Joe's advantage. "I warned you too late. You must have already sustained a head wound." He was actually getting into the part, and Max sounded convincing as well. When they'd finished the pages they'd been given, they waited for Charlie to respond.

Charlie picked up his pencil and made some quick notations. "You've got the parts as far as I'm concerned, but the director will want to see you this afternoon at MGM."

"That's a big studio," Max exclaimed.

"Where are you from, kid? West side of the sticks?" Charlie asked.

"That's uncalled for," Joe warned. "If he's right for the part, it shouldn't matter where he's from."

"Well, excuse me," Charlie shot back at him. "It was a rhetorical question, not meant as an insult." He wrote the director's name and told them to call him from the gate. "I'll let him know you're coming."

Joe stood, but Max stayed seated. "How does the scene end?"

Charlie rolled his eyes. "This is a war movie and soldiers get killed. The sergeant is protecting the private, see, but he's the one who is shot, and the private picks up his body and carries him away in his arms. There shouldn't be a dry eye in the theater."

"That's good to know," Joe responded. "Let's go."

"Now I wish I hadn't asked," Max admitted once outside Charlie's office.

"You would have read the script before the scene was filmed, so it wouldn't have come as a surprise," Joe pointed out.

"Maybe not, but that's just sad, you know?"

"Of course, it's sad. That's the whole point of the scene, to tug on people's hearts. For some reason, people love to cry in movies. Don't ask me why."

"Well, at least I didn't get killed, you did."

"Only on paper." Joe took Max to lunch at a deli with low prices and huge sandwiches. He hoped to keep Max eating until he forgot all about his sister having used a most peculiar stage name. He failed.

"Why didn't you tell me Alice called herself Cookie Crumble?" Max asked. He'd eaten half his pastrami sandwich on rye and paused to take a long drink of his soda. "That's an awfully silly name, isn't it?"

"Do you really want to be in a movie?" Joe asked.

"Sure, but what's that got to do with it?"

"Let's finish lunch, go talk to the director at MGM and then talk about Cookie."

"Like she was a separate person from Alice?"

"Yes, you could look at it that way. Now eat. I want to buzz through MGM and get back to my office."

Max finished his sandwich, but he kept eyeing Joe as though he could see something he'd previously missed. "I may be from the west side of the sticks, but I'm not stupid."

"Certainly not. If you're finished, let's go." He turned up the radio in his Chevy sedan to discourage conversation and headed down Washington Boulevard to the MGM studios in Culver City. It was a huge facility that turned out a film every week. They were waved through the gate and given directions to the director's office.

After meeting Charlie Goode, Joe didn't know what to expect, but the director, Casper Green, was a tall, slim fellow in a gray suit. He was as handsome as the stars in his films, but preferred directing to playing a part.

"Come in and sit down. Charlie told me you two had the look of real soldiers, but he sometimes exaggerates so I didn't believe him until now. You are exactly what I want for a pair who'll have minimal screen time, but be impossible to forget. You've got memorable faces."

"Is that a compliment?" Max asked.

Casper laughed as though Max had been intentionally funny. "We'll have to get you into a comedy. The film, *The Hell of War*, or whatever, we've yet to decide on a title, is set to begin filming right after Halloween. Keep your schedules clear from November 1st through the 15th."

"I could come back to LA," Max whispered to Joe.

Joe nodded. "Great. But we like to keep busy, Mr. Green. Do you have a film that's short a couple of actors that's shooting before then?"

"You two ever do a Western?" Casper checked his calendar. "We're beginning one tomorrow, *Arizona Sunrise*, and I can always use a couple more cowboys in the saloon. Maybe I'll write you some lines." He made himself a quick note. "Just the usual grumbling at the bar that sets the tone for the scene. Come in at seven o'clock tomorrow morning and go straight to wardrobe. They'll get you suited up, and we start shooting at eight."

Max leaned forward. "Do we get to ride horses?"

Joe touched his arm. "They don't usually serve horses in a saloon."

Casper laughed and leaped from his chair. "I can see it now, you two could be arguing over who owns the fastest horse. Maybe you've had fifteen races and one man has had eight wins."

"Shouldn't we use fourteen races so we could be tied?" Max asked. He stood and took a step toward the door.

"Yes, I see where you're going. A tie it will be. See you first thing tomorrow. The gate will have your names."

Joe led the way out the door and hurried them to his car. "I really need to get into my office this afternoon. Can you use the time to arrange for a pick-up from the Salvation Army?"

"Sure, right after you tell me about Cookie Crumble." He stood as though looking for a fight with his hands resting on his hips and his feet firmly planted on the asphalt.

A parking lot wasn't an ideal spot for such a revealing conversation when Max might take a swing at him, and Joe didn't want to have to hit him back. Anyway, it always paid to be cautious. "Let's get some ice cream, and I'll tell you what I know while we eat."

"Promise?"

"I do," Joe swore, and he used the ride to Aunt Lucy's Ice Cream Parlor to think of half a dozen ways to describe Alice's work at Sherry's. None were particularly appealing, but he was out of time. When they arrived, they were shown to a booth where they could talk without being overheard. He hoped the chill air would help Max hang onto his temper.

"I usually order ice cream or a sundae, but the milkshakes are good."

As soon as they'd ordered, Max leaned close. "Go on, tell me the whole story. I can take it."

It sounded like a dare, and Joe nodded thoughtfully. "They have entertainment at Sherry's. Did you notice the poster with photographs of the girls dressed in costumes in the entrance?"

"No, I was looking for someone who knew Alice. What sort of entertainment does Sherry's have?"

Joe drew in a deep breath. "They have some very talented striptease artists. Alice was among the most popular."

"She took off her clothes!" Max cried, and a woman with a small boy seated nearby turned to hush him. His cheeks flushed a bright red, and he took a quick gulp of his water, and lowered his voice. "Alice would never have done that."

"Of course not," Joe agreed, "but Cookie Crumble did. The people who knew Cookie Crumble didn't know her as Alice Reyes. Cookie was a performer, while Alice pursed an acting career."

"The police should have told me that in the beginning." The waitress brought his strawberry milkshake, and Joe's scoop of chocolate ice cream. Max waited for her to turn away before he continued. "Mae should have told me, and you should have told me yesterday. Does Mary Margaret know?"

"Yes, she does, and she was provoked with me for not

telling you the truth in the first place. I hope you won't think any less of Alice."

"She was my sister," he hissed. His eyes began to fill with tears, and he comforted himself with a long swig of his milkshake. "What am I going to tell our mother?"

"Your mother has suffered a tragic loss. Does she really need to know about Cookie?"

"You want me to lie to my own mother? Is that all anyone does in this town?"

"Some people, yes, but if the truth will hurt someone, isn't it better to avoid telling it? Archibald Sutton had faith in Alice's talent. He would have found her a movie role soon."

"And then what would have happened to Cookie?" Max asked. "Would she just have disappeared?"

"That's the way to think," Joe encouraged. "When Cookie was no longer needed to pay Alice's rent, she would have quietly retired and disappeared."

"Who was the murderer killing, Cookie or my sister?"

"I believe he was someone she met at Sherry's. Someone who fell for Cookie and it ended very badly."

Max finished his milkshake and set the tall glass aside. "Will you take me back to Alice's apartment? I don't want to talk about this anymore."

"Of course, I will." Joe finished his ice cream and paid the bill. When they reached Alice's place, Max got out of the car, turned and then bent down to look at Joe.

"What about tomorrow? Are we working at MGM or not?" he asked.

"I'll pick you up at 6:30," Joe responded. "It will be a great story to tell your mother."

"If I can manage the truth," Max answered, and he walked away, his hands shoved deep in his pockets.

Joe waited a minute before leaving. He'd managed what could have been a dreadful scene pretty well, at least in his view, and hoped he could say the same thing after tomorrow.

* * *

Joe stopped by his office to check his mail and found
nothing but bills he shoved into the top desk drawer. He
kept telling himself he needed a plant or two to give the
room some class, but before he could leave to run the
errand, someone knocked at the door.

"Come in," he called.

An elegantly dressed brunette edged the door open and
looked in. "How long have you been in business?" she
asked.

He stood and gestured for her to come in and be seated.
"About a year, and I have the necessary experience to
handle whatever problem you might have."

She came in, but obviously unimpressed, she swept the
stark office with an impatient glance before sitting down.
"I'll be quick about this. I'm Florence Fitzgerald, my
daughter, Lacy, spoke with you recently with some wild
tale of seeing her father with another woman when he's
supposed to be in San Francisco. If he's cheating on me, on
our family, I swear I'll take his head off with a can opener."

It was such a bizarre threat, Joe needed a moment to
respond. "I can't accept a job if there's a chance it will end
in violence."

"Don't take many jobs, do you?" Her green eyes had a
slight slant, and held a fierce sparkle of disdain.

He could well understand why Mr. Fitzgerald might
choose to spend as much time as possible in San Francisco.
"That's not really the issue, is it? If you'd like for me to
investigate your husband's whereabouts, I'll need your
promise he won't come to any harm."

She responded with a hollow laugh and dismissive wave.
"Merely an idle threat, Mr. Ezell. Phillip has to remain
alive to support us in the fashion to which we've grown
accustomed. When he's away, he telephones nearly every
night to talk with the children. Of course, he could be
calling from Salt Lake City for all we know."

He had seldom disliked a client more, but he thought of
Lacy, and forced a smile. "I'll need the basic information,
your husband's workplace to begin."

Mrs. Fitzgerald removed a business card from her sleek leather bag. "Here you are. The firm is Fitzgerald, Finegold and Sloan. It's a well-respected architectural partnership, but if Phillip is not where he's supposed to be, his partners will know and lie about it. Don't trust them to be sincere no matter how nice they might appear."

"Do you have a photo of Phillip?"

She handed him a small one. "This is the formal pose they display in their office. It's only a couple of years old."

Phillip was a strikingly handsome man with thick black hair and blue eyes. He had an engaging smile with a dimple in his left cheek, but Joe had met more than one handsome man with a thoroughly corrupt spirit.

"Do you have a number for where he stays when he's in San Francisco?"

"No, he works long hours and doesn't wish to be called there. If I need him before he calls us in the evening, I telephone his office. They give him the message, and he phones us early."

"Lacy reported seeing a man resembling her father as she left a movie theater. Which one would that have been?"

"I dropped them off at the El Capitan on Hollywood Blvd. You must know it."

"Yes, of course I do. Did you also pick them up after the show?"

"I did, and met them at the corner. My son, Tom, loves Roy Rogers's movies with all the horses and cowboys. I can't abide them myself. He told me the whole story on the way home, but Lacy was very quiet. I assumed she'd simply become bored with cowboys."

He made a few last notes, placed the business card and photo in Lacy's folder, and asked Florence for her home address and telephone number. She looked as though she could afford more than his usual fee, so he raised it twenty dollars per hour, and she didn't even blink. She paid his retainer in cash and left without saying good-bye, leaving a noticeable chill behind.

The custodian must have passed her in the corridor and

looked in. "A new client?" he whispered.

"Yes, but hopefully our association will be brief."

"She reminded me of my second wife," CC said. "Gorgeous on the outside, but without a speck of heart on the inside."

"I hope you weren't with her long," Joe sympathized.

"No, sir. We parted company when she met a man with more money than sense. I bless that day every year." He emptied the trashcan. "You have a good afternoon now."

"Thank you, CC. See you tomorrow." He'd wait until he'd actually worked at MGM before telling the story, but he knew CC would enjoy it.

He reached for the phone, called the number on Phillip's business card, and a secretary answered. "Good afternoon, is Phillip Fitzgerald in?"

"He's working on one of our projects in San Francisco this week. May I take a message?"

"This is Joe Ezell, and I'm following up on a conversation I had with Mr. Fitzgerald on a project that interested him. Would you give me his number in San Francisco, please?"

"He prefers to return calls, and I'll be happy to forward your message."

"Fine, give him my name, and number and tell him I'm a dear friend of Florence's. He'll know why I called."

Joe gave her his number, hung up and leaned back. If Phillip sat at his drawing board in his Los Angeles office, he'd call back within fifteen minutes or so. If he actually were in San Francisco, it would probably take him until tomorrow. After he'd waited half an hour, he gave up on speaking with Mr. Fitzgerald for the day and left to finally buy himself a colorful houseplant.

After work, Mary Margaret had a meeting with the nurses managing the scholarship honoring Georgia Dixon, a nurse who'd been murdered, and Joe cooked his own dinner that night. He made an incredibly good grilled cheese sandwich, and made notes as he savored it.

He'd wanted more business, but now he needed to focus on how to handle it. Focus was one of his favorite words, and he printed it and underlined it twice. He could justify pretending to be an actor to gain access to the same circle of folks Cookie might have known. He'd certainly not charge Leon Helms for what would surely be a brief excursion into the movies, however.

Max had asked if everyone in town lied. What if the people he'd questioned hadn't spoken the truth? He often came home late from Mary Margaret's, so he might not have been in his apartment the night Alice Reyes died. Brett Wayne had said he'd not heard anything that weekend. What if he'd lied? Maybe Alice had called for help, he'd gone to her rescue, and then strangled her when she didn't appreciate the gesture as he'd expected her to?

It was logical, and Brett would be sure to hide his guilt behind an innocuous interest in the next tenants in apartment three. In Joe's view, no one else in the building looked suspicious. Unless the librarians weren't as square as they seemed. If they really were into sex games, they could have picked up Alice at Sherry's. Maybe their tastes had been too extreme for Alice, and John or Melissa had strangled her in an angry fit.

Bernice Ross, who vamped it up as Lily Montell , had asked about the residents of the apartment building where Alice had been found. Was she merely steering the suspicion away from herself? What if she'd taken Alice along to the type of parties Archibald Sutton had sworn he didn't send his pretty clients to?

Then again, maybe Archibald Sutton had lied through his teeth, and he did have a tie to mob run parties where beautiful girls were at a premium.

Joe couldn't overlook the other girls at Sherry's. They might have been better friends with Alice than they admitted. Maybe the whole bunch were guests at private parties. What about the bouncer at Sherry's, Corky Coyne? He could have strangled Alice with one hand. There were also the nameless men who showered Alice with flowers and gifts.

One of them could have taken a rejection very badly, but why would they have stuffed her body in the Thornton's refrigerator? He kept getting stuck on that point.

He hadn't had time to question Stuart Helms, but there was a frat house full of possible suspects there. After filling several pages with notes, he was satisfied he'd spent enough time on Cookie Crumble and set them aside.

The mystery novel he hadn't finished called to him, but now that he'd become a detective, mysteries weren't nearly as enjoyable to read as they once were. He could spot the murderer too quickly, which didn't actually happen in the real world.

The next morning, Max Reyes stood in front of his sister's apartment house, and Joe greeted him warmly, "Good morning. Sometimes scenes are cut from films, so even if we're paid for the day, it doesn't mean our faces will get on the screen."

"Every Western has a fight in a saloon though, doesn't it?" Max asked.

"I believe so, but the fights aren't real. Or at least I hope they're not." He kept the conversation centered on the film as they rode to MGM. Once there, Max was too busy to get in a word about his sister.

At wardrobe, there were a couple dozen other guys pulling on jeans and pearl button shirts. Most had outfits already set out for them, and Joe and Max had to hurry finding boots and hats that fit.

A whiskered older gentleman gave them some advice. "Most of us have our own boots. You'll want to get your own if you plan to work more Westerns. No use hobbling around all day in a pair of uncomfortable boots, and believe me, wardrobe has some excruciating pairs."

Joe quickly found what he meant. He finally went with a pair a size larger than usual and advised Max to do the same. He stomped around a bit, but the boots still felt strange. "We'll be leaning against the bar, so maybe no one will see us walking around."

"Didn't you ever dress up like a cowboy when you were a kid?" Max asked. He'd been lucky with the first pair of boots he'd tried, and walked as though he'd always worn them.

"Sure, had holsters with a pair of cap pistols too, but that was a long time ago." After hurrying to get dressed, they rode a tram to the set and sat for an hour while Casper Green and the male leads of the film discussed the script. What there was to discuss about a fight in a saloon Joe couldn't imagine. He was grateful Max appeared to be lost in his own thoughts and remained silent by his side.

Joe enjoyed movies, but before that day he'd not considered how much technical expertise they involved. There were cameras, cables, lights, microphone booms, and the men to run them and make everything appear real. There were make-up artists ready to touch up the star's splendid tan, but the extras didn't get any such attention. By the time they finally did a run through of the fight scene, it was nearly noon.

The whiskered gent led the way to the food trailers. "The big stars eat in the commissary, but all we'll get are sandwiches. I'm glad for them anyway."

Joe took a ham sandwich and Max took turkey. There were sodas to wash down their lunch, and then they went back to work, such as it was. They did a slow walk through the fight, and despite Casper Green's offer to write lines for them, they weren't given any. All he and Max had to do was lean against the bar, and then back out of the way once the fight began.

When they were released for the day at three o'clock, they returned their clothes to wardrobe, and put their names on them for tomorrow. Joe was ready to go home and take a long nap. "I swear there's nothing worse than standing around doing nothing all day."

"Riding home on the train with my sister's casket will be a lot worse."

"I'm sorry. That was thoughtless of me," Joe stressed.

When they reached Alice's apartment, Max turned to Joe.

"I found a good café around the corner, so you needn't worry about taking me to dinner. See you in the morning?"

"Sure thing."

Joe headed for his office rather than home, and pushed himself to use the rest of the day looking for Phillip Fitzgerald. He and Mary Margaret went to the Jumpin' Plate often enough to be recognized, and he wondered if the owners of the café across the street from the El Capitan Theatre might recognize Phillip.

Thinking it was worth a try, he washed up in the restroom and drove to Hollywood Blvd. He found The Pepper Mill Café located across the street from the El Capitan Theatre, and entered wearing a congenial smile. He showed the cashier Phillip's photo and used his inheritance story without mentioning Mr. Fitzgerald by name.

"This looks like Fred from the barber shop down the way." She called to the manager.

"Yes, that's Fred Cooper, although I've never seen him wear a suit. You say he's won an inheritance? Lucky guy. None of my worthless relatives has anything to leave the rest of us."

Joe thanked them, took the photo and slipped it into his shirt pocket thinking Lacy Fitzgerald must have seen a barber who resembled her father and worried herself silly over nothing. Certain he'd solved the case, he went on to the barber shop. The barber at the first chair turned and smiled at him.

"Sit down. I'll be with you in a few minutes."

Joe had studied Phillip's photo and didn't need to remove it from his pocket to check, but the man didn't merely resemble Phillip Fitzgerald, he was the man down to the dimple in his left cheek.

CHAPTER 7

Joe sat down as directed and gave Fred Cooper's startling appearance some thought. It was extremely doubtful Phillip Fitzgerald led a double life spending half his days as an architect, and the other half running a barber shop. Florence Fitzgerald hadn't mentioned her husband had a twin. Sometimes cousins looked very much alike, and it was logical Fred and Phillip were somehow related. If Florence hadn't made the connection, it was possible Phillip and Fred didn't know about it either.

The case was becoming a different mystery altogether, and when Fred's client paid and left, with a very nice haircut, Joe approached him. "I don't know what I was thinking. I'm an extra in a movie we're shooting tomorrow, and I shouldn't get a haircut today. I'll come back another time."

He turned away, and then stopped, as though he'd had a sudden thought. "You remind me of the architect working on my sister's new house. Is Phillip Fitzgerald a relative of yours?"

Fred shook his head. "No, and I don't believe we have anyone named Fitzgerald in the family. I'm here Tuesday through Saturday. Come back whenever you can."

"I will." Joe was positive he'd be back and soon.

It was too late in the day to call Florence when he might interrupt her dinner. God forbid!

* * *

Mary Margaret felt like having lasagna so they went to their favorite Italian place. It had red and white checked tablecloths, and a container of breadsticks on every table. Joe ate three before he tasted anything more than confusion.

"Is being in a movie anywhere near as exciting as you thought it would be?" she asked.

"Not yet. We'll see how tomorrow goes, but once the chairs start flying in the saloon, I intend to keep out of the way and see Max does too." They'd had a long talk on the telephone last night, so she knew how poorly Max had taken the news of Alice stripping as Cookie Crumble.

He reached for another breadstick. "I've a new case that started out looking fairly simple, but it's taken a weird turn."

"I love weird turns," she responded with a delighted smile. "Tell me all about it."

"I was hired to follow one man, and found another who looks exactly like him. They don't appear to be acquainted, but they could be twins. I can answer my client's question as to whether or not her husband is cheating on her, but there needs to be a lot more sorted out if the men are brothers and don't realize it."

"That is definitely a weird turn all right. Maybe the men are twins. Sometimes twins are separated if they're put up for adoption. Maybe that's what happened in your case, and the boys went to different homes."

"That's one possibility. Maybe the mother was overwhelmed with the thought of raising twins, and gave one away."

"Ouch," she replied. "I know you feel obligated to tell your client the truth, but do you feel you ought to also tell the other man he may have a twin?"

The waiter brought their meals, and Joe paused to savor his ravioli. "I'm an only child, and I'd love to have a brother. That only confuses the issue."

"Well, I have two brothers and two sisters, but if there

were another sibling wandering about, we'd all want to meet him, or her. Of course, asking our mother to explain might embarrass her to tears, and none of us would want that. Suppose the twins were born before a young couple married? The girl might have hidden the pregnancy and left the babies on a church doorstep. Or she could have gone to a home for unwed mothers, and the staff there found homes for the boys."

"There are multiple possibilities, but they're grown men now, and they may not know they were adopted. People used to hide that fact from their children. There's certainly no shame in it, but some wanted it kept private."

"Secrets can be dangerous," she observed. "Are both men pretty well established?"

"Yes, one is an architect, and the other owns his own barber shop."

"So they took completely different paths," she mused. "There are all sorts of intriguing twists to this case. I'll leave them to you to handle as beautifully as I know you will."

"Thank you," he responded. "I'll try not to feel abandoned."

"I haven't abandoned you, Joe. Don't be silly. I'm simply leaving the case in your capable hands."

"So, how was your day?"

She sighed. "No one has been hired to take Georgia's place, and we're all overworked as a result."

"Is there a shortage of nurses?" he asked.

"Not if you look only at the numbers, but at the end of the war, many went back to being wives and carrying for their families, rather than continue to work in the VA hospital. Other young nurses have married returning vets and moved out-of-state with them."

They had talked about combining their incomes after they married, so he knew she intended to continue nursing. She also wanted a couple of kids, but he sure hoped that day wouldn't come too soon.

* * *

Joe found Max no more talkative Friday morning than he had been yesterday, and they drove to MGM in a somewhat strained silence. At wardrobe, they found their western clothing where they'd left it and hurriedly dressed for the saloon scene. They were ready, but the star of the film, a handsome man Joe had never heard of, required more time to prepare.

"What does he need?" Max asked. "Someone to hold his hand through the fight, that isn't really a fight?"

Joe turned his back to the others standing nearby. "Keep your voice down. We're being paid for the day, and it doesn't matter if we're doing nothing, or not doing much with the cameras rolling."

Max briefly remained silent, and then took a new tack. "Wouldn't Mr. Sutton have sent Alice to audition for small parts? Isn't that where most actresses begin?"

"It is, but Archibald thought your sister was really special, and he wanted her to have a chance at a lead."

"Or so he says."

With Max's cynical view, Joe continued to wonder about everyone involved in Alice's case. "It's possible she did work as an extra. I'm going to amble on over to the saloon girls at the end of the bar and ask. Stay here."

Joe walked behind the bar to reach the three girls, a blonde, a brunette and a redhead. They were dressed in colorful costumes with full skirts, low cut tops and tightly cinched waists. As a finishing touch, they had tightly curled upswept hairdos.

"Good morning," Joe whispered. "Alice Reyes was the sister of a friend, and she did some extra work. Did any of you ever meet her?"

The redhead hid her laughter behind a gracefully placed hand. Her nails were polished a deep wine red, which might not have been authentic for the old West. "Cookie Crumble you mean?"

"Yes, she also went by that name. Did you know her?"

The blonde produced a silk fan and waved it to accent her words. "Honey, everyone knew Cookie."

Joe was glad Max had stayed put. He lowered his voice, "You met her on a set?"

"No, at one of Casper Green's parties. Frankly, his parties are better than his Westerns. He ought to film them and promote them as comedies."

"Hush," scolded the brunette. "Don't you dare insult Mr. Green. I need this job even if you don't."

"Don't we all," the redhead echoed.

"When does Mr. Green hold these parties?"

"After the film wraps, but they aren't for everyone, the stars, producers, and he invites a few others, mostly pretty girls. He owns a big home in Beverly Hills with a gigantic pool. There's live music for dancing, and plenty of booze, so everyone has a good time."

"Do you remember when he held the last party?" Joe held his breath, but naturally, things didn't fall into place.

"It must have been a month ago now," the redhead replied, and the blonde nodded.

"It was the middle of August and really hot, so everyone wanted to get into the pool," the brunette added.

"Did you see Alice there?"

"Yes, she was one of Casper's favorites. She came with another girl from Sherry's, Lily something or other. She was elegant and aloof. Just the type many men can't resist."

"Lily Montell?" Joe asked.

"Yes, that's her. She's been to Casper's parties before, but that night they came together."

"Did they leave at the same time, or did Alice leave alone?"

The three laughed, then quickly hushed. "She never left alone," the redhead whispered.

"You don't either," the brunette scolded.

Joe looked over his shoulder, but Casper still wasn't ready to shoot the scene. "Tell me something about the men at the parties."

"Most were movie people with lots of money, and they left their wives at home. It was all in fun and no harm done," the blonde insisted. "Why are you so curious? Did you date Cookie yourself?"

"No, we never met." Joe had put a handful of his business cards in his hip pocket and gave one to each girl. "I'm a detective working on the case. Call me if you think of anything more about Alice." He tipped his Stetson, and made his way back to Max who'd been talking with the actor playing the bartender.

"None of the whiskey is real," Max announced. "The bottles are filled with colored water or soda."

"That's real disappointing to hear," Joe responded, getting into character as best he could.

Casper Green came up to them with a couple of sheets of the script. "Here are your lines. Read them a time or two, and when you're ready, we'll begin." He directed one of the cameramen into position behind the bar.

"I got it," Max said after scanning the page. He folded the page and shoved it into his pocket. "You ready?"

"Better slouch over the bar," Joe suggested. He also pocketed the page with their lines and got into the pose himself. He waved to Casper, and heard the whirl as the cameraman began filming.

"I'm sick of racing you," Joe began. "With only three legs my horse could beat yours."

"Don't waste your breath bragging. I'm challenging you to another race."

"I'm sick of racing you," Joe repeated, and the action moved to the center of the saloon where the leads were facing off with challenges of their own. He kept his head down and when the staged fight broke out in a raucous swirl, he shoved Max down the bar, and they stayed out of the way.

"Cut!" Casper yelled. "That was great. This next time, girls, pick up your skirts and show more leg as you dash to hide behind the bar. The cowboys at the bar were terrific. Do it again just the same." He continued with small criticisms for the actors involved in the fight, and once the tables and chairs were picked up and set in place, they repeated the scene.

Joe and Max were thoroughly tired of the few lines

they'd been given by the time Casper called a stop for lunch. "Is this all there is to acting?" Max asked. "Just doing the same scene over and over until the director is sick of it too?"

"I'm afraid so," Joe agreed. The afternoon was a repeat of the long morning, but at last, Casper Green called it a day.

The director walked over to Joe and Max. "You two were as convincing as I knew you'd be. Be here on November 3rd when we begin fighting the war all over again."

"Will there be sets like this one?" Max asked.

"A few, but we're shooting on the back lot where we'll have plenty of dirt and mud. We want to make it look authentic." He walked away whistling after a good day.

"Authentic," Max whispered under his breath.

"You expect him to fly us all to Germany?" Joe asked.

"I had no expectations at all."

"That's probably best."

They picked up their pay for the two days. At the minimum wage, forty cents an hour for two six-hour days, they earned close to five dollars each. "We should get more for the war movie," Joe hoped aloud.

"Sure we will. Can we go to get ice cream again?"

"Now that you mention it, I'm hungry for ice cream myself." Joe never tired of Aunt Lucy's and had a chocolate sundae while Matt ordered a chocolate malt. He had learned something valuable that day, and was prompted to share it.

"Casper Green holds an occasional party, and the saloon girls told me Alice used to go. There was music, dancing, swimming in the pool."

"Could someone she met there have killed her?" Max asked.

"I'll investigate the possibility. One of the other girls at Sherry's goes, and I'll question her, and convince her to invite me along to the next party."

Max was quiet until he'd finished his shake. "I wish I could stay, but the mortuary has Alice's coffin crated and ready to go. I need to get her home so Mom can have the funeral. The church will be crowded with people who watched Alice grow up. Everyone loved her."

"I'm sorry I didn't know her," Joe responded. "Let's keep in touch. Would you like to join Mary Margaret and me for dinner?"

Max gave Joe his home telephone number, but refused the dinner invitation. "I'd rather be by myself tonight," he explained. "You've been a good friend, Joe. Thank you."

Joe felt sad to drop him off at Alice's apartment. He liked the kid, and intended to solve Alice's murder no matter how many Hollywood parties he had to attend.

Saturday morning, after playing golf with Hal and Gilbert, Joe went by his office to catch up. First thing, he gave Florence Fitzgerald a call. She planned to take the children to the movies that afternoon, and promised to come to his office then.

"While I have you on the phone, Mrs. Fitzgerald, what is your husband's birthday?"

"November 11, 1911. What's that got to do with anything?" she asked.

"It may be pertinent. Did he serve during the war?"

"No, he was married with children, and he has a heart murmur."

"Thank you, I'll see you later."

What Joe needed now was a haircut, and he returned to Frank Cooper's shop. He had to wait while two other men went before him. He picked up a *National Geographic* magazine and read an interesting article on sharks and counted the time well spent.

When Fred called him to his chair, Joe let the barber begin with small talk, and then posed a question of his own. "I'm thinking of studying astrology. Would you mind telling me your birthday?"

"That's a lot of hocus pocus as far as I'm concerned, but it's November 11, 1911. I'm only thirty-six, but 1911 sounds like ancient times now, doesn't it?"

"It's all in your perspective I suppose. Did you serve in the war?"

"Yes, in the Army, but I spent most of my time up at Fort Ord giving haircuts to recruits, or supervising other barbers who gave them. How about you?"

"I served in the Coast Guard off Greenland. We handled weather reports that were used to make command decisions in Europe."

They continued to discuss the war until Fred finished and brushed the stray hairs off Joe's jacket. "Thanks, this is one of the best haircuts I've ever had."

"That's because I take the time to look at how a man's hair grows. Some barbers cut hair the same way no matter who the client is. It works for some men, but for others, they either find a new barber or get used to bad haircuts."

Joe paid, tipped him, and also handed him his business card. "If you ever have need of a detective, give me a call."

"I've never met a detective. I sure like Humphrey Bogart movies though."

"They're movies," Joe reminded him. "My life is seldom as exciting."

He stopped for a quick sandwich at the drugstore counter downstairs in his building, and was seated in his office when Florence Fitzgerald arrived. She looked no more pleased than she had on her previous visit. He smiled anyway.

"I've good news," Joe began. "The man Lacy saw wasn't her father, but another man who resembles him closely. They could be twins, in fact. Both were born on November 11, 1911. Has Phillip ever mentioned having a twin?"

"A twin? What nonsense. He's an only child."

Joe weighed his words carefully. "We still have two men with identical looks and the same birthday making it highly likely that they are brothers. Was Phillip adopted?"

"No, of course not."

Clearly she had no interest in pursuing it, but he couldn't

resist pressing the issue. "Fred Cooper owns a barbershop across the street and down a way from the El Capitan Theatre. Before you pick up your children, you might want to stop by and ask if he cuts children's hair."

Her gaze grew absolutely frosty. "You want me to see for myself, is that it?"

Joe nodded. He handed her his bill, and she paid in cash. "I've answered Lacy's question, but whether or not your husband is really in San Francisco is another matter. I left my telephone number with his firm, but he didn't return the call."

"He was probably too busy. Let's stop while we're ahead," Florence exclaimed, and saw herself out.

Joe rocked back in his chair. He thought Florence would be too curious not to go by Fred's barbershop, but she'd probably be too proud to call him and admit it.

He spent the afternoon checking the pawnshops near Alice's apartment. He took the photo from the *LA Times*, and while many a shop owner recognized her as Cookie Crumble, she hadn't pawned anything with any of them. That didn't mean she hadn't pawned expensive gifts elsewhere, but it would take weeks to canvas every pawn shop in the greater Los Angeles area, and he couldn't devote the time.

He stopped by Sherry's on his way to Mary Margaret's. He slipped into the corridor to their dressing room without being stopped and waited outside the open door for the girls to notice him.

"Good evening, ladies. May I speak with you a minute Bernice, or do you prefer to be called Lily?"

She tightened the belt on her robe and followed him out into the hallway. "I chose Lily because I love the flower. Bernice was my grandmother's name, and she may have been a wonderful woman, but I've never cared for it. Do you like your name?"

"I prefer Joe to Joseph, so I understand what you mean. Tell me about the parties at Casper Green's home."

"You heard about those?" She dipped her head, but couldn't hide an incriminating blush.

"Yes, I did. If you went with Alice, although she was as annoying as a mosquito, why didn't you tell me?"

She kept her back turned to the open dressing room door. "Casper is a fan of mine, and he asked me to bring Cookie, or Alice, along to his next party. She was so popular with his male guests, he insisted I bring her to the next party and the next."

"And that annoyed you?" Joe asked.

"Promise this won't go any further?"

"I'm discreet, remember?"

"So you say, just keep this to yourself. Casper has a nice friend, and I go to see him. He's married, and you needn't tell me this is shameful, I already know it is. He has small children and can't leave his wife, and I don't want to be married anyway, so that's simply the way it is. It wouldn't matter who came with me, I go to see him."

Joe had learned long ago not to be judgmental. "So you and Alice didn't stay together at the parties?"

"No, Casper has a son who's in college, and after Alice flirted with every man present, she'd usually jump into the pool with him. I'd wander off with my friend, and when I'd be ready to leave for home, she'd already be gone."

"Do you know where Casper's son goes to school?"

"USC, Casper's a big fan of the Trojan football team and mentions them often."

"When was Casper's last party?"

She licked her lips as she tried to recall. "It was on one of those really hot nights in August, but I don't know the date off-hand."

"But you could look in your diary," Joe suggested.

"I could, but it wasn't the weekend Alice died, so what does it really matter?"

"Right. Did any of the other ladies here attend the parties?"

"I love the way you refer to us as ladies. No. They've probably seen Casper here, but I never mentioned his parties and Cookie didn't either."

"I have another source, but will you call me the next time Casper invites you to a party at his place? He'll never know you told me, so there's no risk for you." He handed her another of his cards, and she slid it into her robe pocket.

"His parties are catered. You could sneak in wearing dark pants and a white jacket and not be noticed," she suggested.

"Thanks for the idea." He doubted Casper would recognize him if he were circulating carrying a tray of canapés so he just might do it.

That night, Mary Margaret baked pork chops with stuffing and steamed asparagus. Joe enjoyed every single morsel. "Absolutely delicious, as always. Do you ever tire of hearing me say so?"

"Not yet." She checked her watch. "We've plenty of time before the movie starts if you'd like more."

"You like me lean, remember? And I have to keep my figure for upcoming movie roles." He laughed, and she giggled with him.

"I was afraid appearing in a B-movie Western might be a complete waste of time, but I learned Alice attended the director's wrap parties. I'm definitely making progress on the Cookie Crumble case by tracing where she went and who was also there.

"Alice knew at least one young man who attends USC, and she may have known several others, including Stuart Helms. We saw him at Sherry's, so he knew her from there. This is just another possible link." He told her about his new bulletin board. "It makes it easier to add information and see how the contacts line up. Leon Helms will expect a report, but I'll hedge the details."

She nodded thoughtfully. "Are you afraid he'll call off your investigation if he fears it might incriminate his son?"

"Yes, that's why I won't give him any details."

"But you won't quit, will you?"

"No, as you well know, I like to finish everything I begin, to everyone's satisfaction."

She knew exactly what he meant and kissed him soundly.

* * *

Monday morning, Joe called Leon Helms to recap his investigation. "Cookie, Alice Reyes, hoped to become a movie star and may have met the man who killed her at a director's wrap parties. I'll continue working on that angle."

"Fine, just get the matter solved so it can be forgotten. I need to rent apartment three, and every month it's vacant is money lost I can't afford to lose."

"I'm doing my best, Leon," Joe promised. He had the number for the Kappa Sigma fraternity house at USC, and today might be a good time to meet with Stuart. He had just reached for the telephone, when Florence Fitzgerald knocked at his door and looked in.

Her eyes were red, and clearly she'd been crying. He'd not thought her capable of such a depth of emotion. "Come in, Mrs. Fitzgerald. Would you like coffee? I just made a fresh pot."

"I don't suppose you have cream and sugar?" she asked, and sniffed loudly.

"I'll get some from the drug store downstairs if you'd like them."

She settled into a chair, her slack posture as droopy as her mood. "Could you, please?"

"Give me a minute." He rushed downstairs, and asked the girl at the counter for cream and sugar. "It's an emergency," he explained.

"Here, just take these." She gave him a sugar container and small pitcher of cream. "You'll need a spoon," she added. "It's on the house."

Joe thanked her and returned to his office. He had grabbed some napkins and set them down on his desk with the cream and sugar. "Here you are, Mrs. Fitzgerald." He poured coffee into one of the cups he had for clients, and was grateful he always kept them clean.

She poured sugar into her coffee, stirred until it dissolved, and then added the cream. Her hands shook as she raised the cup to her lips. "I'm amazed, Mr. Ezell, but this is actually a decent cup of coffee."

That was the Florence Fitzgerald he knew. "Thank you. Now tell me what's wrong." He removed her folder from the file cabinet and picked up a pencil to take notes.

"Well, against my better judgment, I went by Cooper's Barber shop on Saturday afternoon. To say I was shocked by what I found is a gross understatement. I was flabbergasted. Fred Cooper has to be my husband's identical twin, but how can that possibly be?"

"Would you like me to investigate the matter?" he asked.

"Of course, why else would I be here? My husband comes from a well-to-do family, but they've never told him he's adopted. Do you suppose my in-laws didn't realize they'd had twins? Perhaps they were told one of the twins had died. When, in fact, he'd been stolen and adopted by someone on the hospital staff. Babies are kidnapped. Look at the poor Lindbergh baby."

Joe nodded. "Thank God it's rare, but it does happen. I'll begin with the birth records. Was Phillip born in Los Angeles?"

"Yes, I brought a copy of his birth certificate. He needed it for a passport he hasn't applied for as yet."

She opened her purse and removed a white envelope. "It lists Pearl and Douglas Fitzgerald as his parents."

After a brief survey of the document, Joe found it had been a home birth attended by a mid-wife named Bertha Lloyd. "Would your in-laws be open to questions about Phillip's birth?"

"Good lord, no!" she exclaimed. "They are an extremely private and proper pair. They wouldn't be open to questions about anything personal, let alone their only son."

"Perhaps Fred Cooper's parents would agree to meet with me. I'll be discreet, but clearly someone has to know how the boys were separated."

"They're thirty-six. Maybe the people who knew are no longer living." She finished her coffee and placed the cup on his desk. "I didn't notice the plant the last time I was here. Dresses up the office, doesn't it?"

He'd bought a brass pot for the showy philodendron and

placed it on the file cabinet. "Yes, indeed it does."

"Some art wouldn't hurt," she added.

"It's also on my list. You're right, delving into what happened so long ago won't be easy, and especially not if it involves family secrets, but I'll do my best. Fred Cooper seems like a nice man."

Florence rose. "He might be a veritable prince, but the Fitzgerald's will never welcome a barber into the family. They'd die first."

"It's an honest trade," Joe reminded her.

"That's just it. They've not had a tradesman in the family in multiple generations."

He asked for a retainer. She had come prepared to pay, and he gave her a receipt. He opened the door for her, gave her time to leave the building, and then returned the cream and sugar containers to the lunch counter downstairs.

He'd wanted more interesting cases, and he sure had them now. He began where he'd been interrupted and called the Kappa Sigma house at USC and asked for Stuart Helms. He had to hold the phone away from his ear as the young man who'd answered yelled for Stuart. Several minutes past before Stuart finally came on the line.

"This is Joe Ezell, I live in your father's apartment building."

"Sure, I remember you."

"Good. I'm a private investigator, and I'd like to buy you lunch and talk to you about Cookie Crumble."

Stuart hesitated. "I didn't really know her."

"You know more than you think." Joe named *El Vaquero*, a popular Mexican restaurant near the USC campus, and Stuart agreed to meet him there at noon.

After he'd said good-bye, Joe rocked back in his chair. Stuffing a dead woman into a refrigerator was demented, of course, but it had always struck him as something scared college kids might do.

CC looked in the door. "How are things going this morning, Mr. Ezell?"

"Surprisingly well. A simple case of mistaken identity

has developed into a much more complex investigation. It should take some time to unravel, and I welcome the challenge."

"I understand, yes, sir, I do," CC responded. "My imagination keeps me from growing bored."

"You're a smart man, CC. If you have a minute, I'll tell you how I ended up in a Western movie last week."

The custodian glanced down the hallway, saw no one coming his way, and stepped into Joe's office. "Did you get to ride a horse?"

Joe laughed. "Not this time, but maybe one day soon." He related his adventure with Max at MGM, and they shared a good laugh. "I'll never star in a movie, but I saw how one is made. It's a lot more work than shows up on the screen."

"I'll bet it is. Have yourself a good day now," CC replied and left to continue his work.

While Joe arrived at *El Vaquero* early, he was surprised to find Stuart Helms already seated in the restaurant. Maybe the young man was anxious to get something off his chest. He joined him at the table and scanned the menu. "Is everything still good here?" he asked. He'd found talking about food put people at ease.

"It sure is." A waiter brought Stuart a plate with three beef tacos, rice and refried beans. Joe asked for the same.

The detective let Stuart enjoy his first taco before he asked another question. "What was Cookie Crumble's real name?" He did his best to appear confused.

"Alice Reyes, but she liked to introduce herself as Cookie."

Joe's lunch appeared, and he savored his own food for a moment. "There's a Hollywood director named Casper Green. Do you know his son?"

Stuart wiped his hands on his napkin, and picked up another taco. "Sure, Tom Green. He's a fraternity brother."

"Did he ever bring Cookie to a frat party?"

"Are you kidding? No. He liked her at Sherry's. We all

did, but she wouldn't have fit in with sorority girls."

"They're a more refined type of young woman, I assume?" Joe asked.

"I'll say. Tom's father throws big parties, and there would be starlets there. Tom talks about them, but he never brings any to the house." He paused mid-bite. "None of us has actually met any of the starlets, so maybe it's all just talk and nothing more."

"Are you and Tom good friends?"

Stuart shrugged. "Not really. He's a couple of years older and runs with a different crowd."

"Is it my imagination, or are these especially fine tacos?" Joe asked.

"They're the best in LA. They barbecue the beef, and it makes the difference."

Stuart was nearly finished when Joe asked, "Who do you think killed Cookie?"

He had a prompt answer. "Mickey Cohen and his men hang out at Sherry's. Everyone knows they're violent, and it has to have been one of them."

The answer sounded well rehearsed. "It's likely, but how did Cookie's body end up in a refrigerator in one of your father's apartments?" Joe asked.

"Beats me," Stuart responded. "Maybe the couple who'd lived there was involved with the mob. Have you talked to them?"

"Not yet."

Stuart checked his watch. "I have a class. Thanks for lunch."

"You're welcome." Joe let him go and enjoyed the rest of his meal down to the last grain of rice.

The waiter came with the bill, hovered over the table, and whispered, "I heard you mention Cookie Crumble. She's been here with the boy you were with."

"Really?" Joe wiped his mouth on his napkin.

"Yes, she was with that boy and one of his friends. They all laughed together and had a good time."

"Do you remember the last time they were here?"

The waiter shrugged. "This is a busy place. I can't keep track of everyone."

"I understand." Joe left him a big tip, paid, and took the receipt to document his expenses. Leon Helms wouldn't be pleased to learn he was questioning his son, but Stuart knew how to lie with a straight face. He probably lied to his father as well.

CHAPTER 8

Fred Cooper's barbershop closed at 6:00 p.m. and Joe waited for him as he locked the door. "Afternoon. If you aren't in a hurry to get home, maybe we could have a cup of coffee and talk."

"That sounds serious," Fred replied. "Don't like your haircut?"

"No, my haircut is fine." He pulled Phillip Fitzgerald's photo from his jacket pocket and showed it to Fred. "Do you recognize him?"

Stunned, Fred shook his head. "I'd swear it's me, but I don't recall anyone photographing me in a suit."

"He's an architect named Phillip Fitzgerald. You must have some questions about him. Let's go down the street to The Pepper Mill Café and talk. I won't keep you long."

"Fine, let's go." Fred led the way and waved to the cashier as they entered. "We're just having coffee, Irene."

"Take any table, honey. I'll bring your coffee."

Joe found they served a very smooth brew. He'd planned what he wanted to say, but he couldn't control both sides of the conversation, and that's where things usually went astray. He told Fred about Lacy Fitzgerald's worries about her father, and that Mrs. Fitzgerald had hired him to investigate what she regarded as a preposterous case of mistaken of identity.

"I showed Phillip's photo here, and Irene thought it was you," Joe explained.

Fred asked to see the photograph again and studied it closely. "This is either an odd coincidence, or we're related somehow. When's his birthday?"

"November 11, 1911." Joe took another sip of his excellent coffee. "Same as yours. Have your parents ever discussed your birth?"

"Not really, but I do know my aunt Ida was the midwife. She worked with our family doctor, Percival O'Dowd. He's the only Percival I've ever met."

"Do you have brothers and sisters?" Joe asked.

Fred sighed and leaned back in his chair. "Two younger sisters, Kate and Sue. My aunt Ida delivered them too." He checked his watch. "My wife will worry if I'm not home soon. Could we talk about this again tomorrow after work?"

"Yes, of course. Are your parents still living?"

"Only my mother, but she's had a stroke, and her memory isn't clear. She lives with Ida in Pasadena. Ida was the baby of the family, and is in her sixties. She ought to know the truth."

Joe rose with him and picked up the check. "The question is, will she tell you?"

"I hope so. Let's meet at my shop after work tomorrow, and we can decide how to approach her. Maybe ease her into it."

"Good plan." The conversation had gone better than Joe had expected, and he couldn't wait to talk with Aunt Ida. He hoped she was a woman who loved an audience for her memories, rather than a fidgeting spinster who'd want them out of her house.

Joe took Mary Margaret to Clifton's Cafeteria that night. This time, he had the chicken potpie, and she had the meat loaf. He waited until they'd taken the edges off their appetites before he told her he'd spoken to Fred Cooper. "He's a nice guy, and seems open to an investigation of how he and Phillip are related."

"Can you work with him if Florence Fitzgerald is paying you?"

"I'm not charging two clients for the same case, although I suppose there might be such a case someday. I'm questioning Fred to get answers for her."

"Still, you've brought him into it. Won't he expect to be in on the answers?"

She had the most beautiful mouth, and he watched her lick a stray bit of mashed potatoes from her lower lip. "I don't see the Fitzgeralds and Coopers getting together for Thanksgiving this year, but if the men are related, both ought to know how it came about."

"I agree. How long will Phillip be in San Francisco?"

"His wife didn't say. I'll call his firm tomorrow and ask. I left a message for him, but he didn't call back. Maybe he knows the whole story and never told his wife."

"That's doubtful," she mused. "I don't believe he's aware of anything more than Fred Cooper is. If Lacy hadn't mistaken Fred for her father, the men might have lived their whole lives and never learned they had a twin."

"I'm hoping Fred's aunt Ida knows the truth of the situation."

"But will she tell?"

"That, my dear, is the question."

Leon Helms was on the apartment patio watering the plants when Joe left for his office Tuesday morning. He turned off the water, and gestured to bring Joe close. "No use sharing this with the other tenants," he whispered. "Have you learned anything since yesterday?"

Joe jumped right in. "Did Stuart tell you I'd talked with him?"

"No, what did he say?"

"Not much, but one of his frat brothers partied with Cookie at a Hollywood movie director's house parties."

Leon turned his back to the patio. "Casper Green's son, you mean? I've seen a couple of Green's Westerns, but they don't measure up to what Roy Rogers produces."

"In what way?" Joe asked, relieved Leon hadn't fired him for questioning Stuart.

"He has all the necessary components, wild towns with noisy saloons and over-worked sheriffs, plenty of dusty cowboys, and a greedy rancher, or maybe a banker, who's causing trouble. There has to be a man who'll stand up to the villain, and a beautiful young woman, usually the schoolmarm. But the stories lack heart, and are easy to forget."

Joe feared he'd been part of just such a trite film. He'd wait until the movie came out and Leon recognized him before he'd admit it though. "I know what you mean. There's plenty of action, but not much real content."

"Exactly, and I'm afraid that's what Brett Wayne writes," Leon added.

"Probably. Anyway, I'm working on several promising angles."

"Keep me posted. I've left messages for Detective Lynch, but he doesn't return my calls."

"The police have their own methods, but they aren't chatty about them. They have the resources to find the Thorntons. Let's hope they use them soon."

"I'll say." Leon bent down to turn on the hose, and Joe went on his way.

Once at the office, Joe studied his bulletin board. If Brett Wayne had written scripts for Casper Green, he might have attended wrap parties and recognized Alice Reyes as Cookie Crumble. She wouldn't have gone in her schoolgirl costume, but she wouldn't have hidden it when it was her one claim to fame. It was an intriguing thought and placed the writer on the growing suspect list.

Staring at the telephone had never prompted any calls, so he drove to the Salvation Army thrift store to look through their art. Perhaps "art" was too generous a term to use, but at the back of the store where the paintings leaned against the wall, he found a California desert scene complete with a towering eucalyptus in the foreground. The frame was battered, but there was an amateurish portrait of a clown in a simple gold frame that would do fine. He carried both works to the cashier.

The cashier made no comment on his purchases, and Joe carried them both to his car. He opened the trunk for a space to work, and switched the frames. He made sure no one was looking, and chucked the garish clown and battered frame in the trash where they surely belonged.

CC produced a hammer and a picture hanger from his utility closet, and held the painting up for Joe to decide where to place it. In such a small office, there weren't many possibilities.

Joe went out into the hall and came back through his office door. The file cabinet and philodendron were to his left. He had posted his private investigator license beside the window behind his desk, and the bare wall to his right called for attention.

"Let's place it in the middle of the wall, at eye level." He took the painting while CC placed the brass hanger, and then hung it with pride. With the new attractive frame, the painting looked to be worth far more than what he'd paid. It was signed by someone he'd never heard of, but that didn't mean it might not grow in value over the years.

"Looks good, Mr. Ezell," CC said. "Brightens up the place. It's almost like having another window facing the desert."

Joe stood beside him. "It does. I need another hook on the wall behind my desk to hang a bulletin board." He moved to pick it up. "This is just for me, I don't plan to leave it up when clients are here."

CC pulled another picture hook from his pocket. "What about right here even with the window?"

"That's good. Thank you."

The custodian hung the bulletin board on the new hook. "You're welcome. I'm here every day to help, Mr. Ezell. You have a nice day."

Once alone, Joe sat down at his desk and enjoyed simply

observing the soft greens, tans, and ambers of his new painting. The artist had added a wisp of cloud in the clear azure sky, and he liked the idea of pretending it was another window into a completely different world. It was the first bit of artwork he'd ever owned, and it gave his office a real touch of class. Inspired, he decided a rug would be nice to have under the two chairs there for clients. He'd have to return to the Salvation Army soon and see what they had that would complement his new painting. He laughed knowing he wasn't the only one relying on the thrift store for their decorating needs.

Fred Cooper met Joe at the door of his barbershop, invited him in, and locked the door behind him. "I called my aunt Ida and told her it had been too long since I saw her and Mother, and she invited me to come over tonight. I know the way, so I'll drive."

"Fine. From what I've found, if I broach a subject, and then remain quiet, people will rush to fill the silence with information they wouldn't have volunteered had I questioned them."

Fred kept his Ford sedan in the small parking lot behind his shop, and they exited through the shop's rear door. The car was newer than Joe's Chevy, but that was no surprise. A barber could count on a steady income, and he couldn't. They made their way through the downtown traffic and took the Arroyo Seco Parkway to Pasadena.

Ida Sparks lived in a neighborhood filled with the bungalow homes made popular by the Arts and Crafts movement at the turn of the century. Built of wood and natural stone, her home sat nestled in a slightly overgrown, but welcoming front garden. Fred led the way up the walk and rang the bell. They could hear the musical chime from deep within the house.

Ida came to the door smiling widely and gave Fred a quick hug. She was a slender woman with gray hair, blue eyes, and a lovely pale peach complexion. "So nice to see you, honey. Even if your mother doesn't always remember you, I do. Who's this you've brought with you?"

"I'm Joe Ezell, a friend of Fred's, and he invited me to come along."

"Good. We love to have company. Come right in, the both of you. Your mother is in the living room looking through magazines, something she loves to do. It fills the time for her. You'd probably rather have a beer than tea, but we don't serve alcohol in this house."

Her home was beautifully furnished with fine examples of Stickley furniture, one of the Arts and Crafts movement's most celebrated designers who stressed simplicity, honesty, and truth in his construction and materials. He built solid oak furniture and with the proper care and attention, it might last several centuries. Unfortunately, it wasn't what people were buying after the war when there was a fierce craving for the new and modern.

Fred bent down to give his mother a kiss on the cheek, and her eyes twinkled as she looked up at him. "Is that you, William? It's been much too long since you came to see me."

"William was my father's brother," Fred whispered to Joe. He took a place on the sofa beside his mother and kept her hand in his. "I'm Fred, Mama. Have Kate and Sue been to see you?"

His mother looked to Ida. "Have they been here? I can't seem to recall."

"Yes, they have, Lillian. They like to come by on Sunday after church when they can. I have the tea all ready for us."

As she turned toward the kitchen, Joe offered to help and followed her down the hallway. An array of family portraits were displayed along the wall, weddings, christenings, and graduations were all remembered. Joe stopped in front of a photograph of a man who closely resembled Fred. "Is this Fred's father?" he asked.

Ida stopped and came back to him. "That's his uncle William. This is Fred's father, Paul, here." She tapped her finger on the frame of a photo showing a man with the same black hair and blue eyes, but he wasn't nearly as handsome as his brother.

"I know what you're thinking," Ida remarked. "Clearly William got the looks, but Paul was the better man, and my sister knew it. Paul loved being a family man, and William, well, he never did settle down."

"Is he still living?" Joe inquired.

"Haven't heard from him in a couple of years. At Christmastime, he used to send us delicious fruitcakes filled with pecans and cherries. I miss those, but not him."

Joe followed her into the kitchen, and carried the tea tray out to the living room. Along with the teapot and cups, a plate of lemon cookies beckoned, and Joe waited for Fred to take one first before he sampled them.

"These are delicious!" Joe exclaimed. "My fiancée is a fantastic cook, but she doesn't bake many pastries."

"Everything my aunt bakes is delicious," Fred agreed.

"It's all in how I mix the ingredients," she explained. "Some people are in too big a hurry, and the flavors need to be coaxed to be their best. I'll send both you boys home with some cookies."

"Thank you," Joe replied. "I'd love to share them with my fiancée."

"I always try to get home with your treats Aunt Ida, but I usually eat them on the way," Fred confessed.

"Well, put them in the trunk of your car and you won't be tempted," she exclaimed.

"Why haven't I thought of that?" Fred laughed, and talked about his sisters for a while with his mother. She recalled how much they'd loved going to school. "I made all their pretty dresses."

"You were a fine seamstress, and they always looked real cute." He waited for his mother to swallow the last bite of a cookie before he mentioned meeting a man who looked just like him. He nodded to Joe and took the photograph the detective offered.

"His name is Phillip Fitzgerald, and he's an architect. He was also born on November 11, 1911."

His mother studied the photo. "Are you sure this isn't William?"

"Positive. Do you remember the night I was born, Mama?"

Lillian turned to Ida who was seated on her left. "He was such a beautiful baby."

"Yes, he was," Ida agreed. "Don't press your mother for anything more." Her tone was pleasant, but her stern expression made it a curt order rather than a polite request. "All your babies were beautiful, but Sue was especially cute with all her curls."

Joe sat back in his chair. They needed to speak with Ida alone, but it would probably be a waste of time. The pride in her posture had stiffened, and she'd keep whatever she knew to herself. Clearly she knew something Fred ought to know.

They stayed nearly an hour, and Fred and Joe left with bags of cookies to take home. Fred promised to come back soon and bring his family. "I should be a better son," he murmured as he started his car.

"My parents died before the war, and I'd love to be able to visit them."

"I'm sorry, I didn't mean to complain. My aunt Ida knows more than she's telling."

"I got the same impression. Would she talk with you if you came alone?" Joe asked.

"Probably not. If you're wondering about my uncle William, he more closely resembled my grandfather than my father did. So while I might be said to look like my uncle, it's really my grandfather looking back at me in the mirror. I heard jokes about it growing up, but I've always known which man was my father."

Joe wondered if he really did.

CHAPTER 9

M ary Margaret prepared an incredibly tasty potato leek soup for dinner with freshly baked cornbread. They saved the lemon cookies for dessert. "Let's say you were a midwife and delivered one of your sister's babies," Joe began. "Would you recall details of that night years later?"

"Of course, I would," she insisted. "Emotion-charged events cling in our memories. That's why soldiers have such a difficult time forgetting bloody war battles. Were you interviewing a particularly forgetful midwife today?"

He told her about his visit with Fred to his aunt Ida. "She was very warm and charming until Fred asked about the night he was born. She closed up like the proverbial clam, as though she'd been insulted. To add to the fun, Fred looks more like his uncle William than his father, but he calls it merely a family resemblance."

"Oh, this is getting exciting," she exclaimed. "Will you please pass the butter? Thank you. I'll bet Ida recalls everything about Fred's birth, the time of day, the weather, how difficult or easy the birth might have been, and how Fred's father behaved. Some men are thrilled by the prospect of having a son, other men faint dead away. That means the midwife has two patients, not one."

"The birth of twins would be doubly difficult to forget, wouldn't it?" he asked.

"Yes, indeed. What are the chances Uncle William could have had an affair with Fred's twin's mother? It might be possible, but unlikely the boys would be born on the same day and resemble each other so closely."

"Highly unlikely," he agreed. He had a second bowl of soup and another piece of cornbread. "What makes the food you prepare taste so good?"

She reached for his hand. "It's the love you're tasting, my dear. Every delectable bite is a taste of love."

He squeezed her fingers and grew certain he'd died and gone to heaven.

Wednesday morning, Leon Helms ran up the stairs to knock on Joe's apartment door. He gasped and sputtered, "Stuart has been arrested for Cookie Crumble's murder! What should we do?"

Joe had been ready to leave for his office, and was fully dressed this time. "Come in. I'll call a bail bondsman I know. He's an expert at this sort of thing."

"How can you be so calm? Detective Lynch arrested Stuart for murder!"

"Do you believe he did it?" Joe asked.

"No, but he's my son. Who's going to believe me?"

"I believe you." Joe assured him. In his view, Stuart was a possibility, but a dim one when there were so many other suspects. An hour later, they were seated in Lou King's office. They'd stopped at Leon's bank on the way, and he had a thousand dollars cash in his wallet.

The bail bondsman exuded a quiet strength. In a bespoke gray suit, a white dress shirt, and a colorful silk tie, he proved himself to be a successful businessman without uttering a word.

"But Stuart would never have strangled a woman, let alone stuffed her into a refrigerator in one of our apartments!" Leon exclaimed. "That's just absurd."

Lou nodded sympathetically. "I made a call soon after you contacted me, and Stuart's bail has been set at five thousand dollars. I charge ten percent for the bond, and it's not refundable. Do you need time to think about it?"

"What's the alternative?" Leon asked, nearly in tears.

Lou flashed a disarming smile. "Stuart will remain in jail until the arraignment, Friday afternoon, and the judge could decide he'll stay there throughout the trial."

"His mother wants Stuart home, and so do I."

"Then we'll go ahead with the bond." Lou had the paperwork readied, and Leon signed with a shaky hand. He counted out five hundred dollar bills, and laid them on Lou's desk.

Lou swept the money into his top drawer. "You'll need to have an attorney at the arraignment. Do you know a criminal attorney?" he asked.

"No, of course not. No one in my family has ever been arrested, not even for unpaid parking tickets." He turned to Joe. "What should we do?"

"Gladys Swartz did an excellent job for one of my clients. Let's call and see if she's available," Joe suggested.

"Mrs. Swartz is a fine defense attorney," Lou agreed, "but she's very particular about the cases she accepts. I have a list of other excellent attorneys should she not be available."

"Do you mind if we call from here?" Joe asked.

"Not at all. Use the first office down the hall." He stood and led the way to an office slightly smaller than his own. It was decorated with pale blue walls and a navy blue carpet that imbued the room with a peaceful sense of calm.

Joe waited until Lou had left to close the door and call his friend Hal Marten. "I hate to bother you at work, but my landlord's son has been arrested. Would you give me Gladys's office number?"

"Is this the Cookie Crumble case?" Hal asked.

"Yes, and Detective Lynch has gone for an easy arrest rather than search for the actual killer."

Hal described the detective with some well-chosen words before supplying the telephone number. "That's Gladys's office. If she can't take the case, perhaps someone else in her firm can."

"Thank you, Hal."

Joe drew in a deep breath. Leon wore khaki slacks and a lavender Hawaiian shirt with lime green palm trees. "That's a terrific shirt, but you'll want to wear a suit to meet with an attorney and whenever Stuart has to be in court. Judges are big on respect, and they might regard it as too casual for the courtroom."

Leon looked down, noticed his buttons were misaligned and quickly fixed them. "I grabbed the first shirt in the closet, but I understand. I should look like an upstanding citizen to emphasize Stuart comes from a good home."

"That's it." Joe dialed Gladys's number, a secretary answered, and he had to wait for the attorney to come on the line. He and Mary Margaret had gone to dinner with her and Hal, so they had met. He reminded her he was Hal's golf buddy before he explained Leon Helm's desperate need for an attorney.

"The need is always desperate," she responded, a sly smile in her voice. "Thank you for thinking of me. Arrange for bail today, and I can meet Stuart and his father Friday morning. We'll plan for the afternoon arraignment then."

Joe put his hand over the phone to check with Leon, who said he would be available whenever necessary. "Fine, we'll be there. Thank you." Joe hung up and leaned against the desk. "How is Doreen taking this?"

"Not at all well, as you may imagine. She's lying on the sofa with a cold compress on her eyes. Do you think you can find who really killed Cookie before Stuart has to go on trial?"

Joe thought of his bulletin board. He had plenty of suspects, but doubted anyone would confess spontaneously. "I'm closing in on them, Leon."

"Good. I'm trying not to cry because it would be so unmanly, but I sure feel like it."

"I understand." Joe gripped Leon's shoulder. "Stuart will be released soon. Think about how happy Doreen will be to see him."

"Yes, that's a good thought. Thank you."

* * *

Stuart joined them after having spent only one morning in jail, but he looked much the worse for the wear. "Did Detective Lynch or one of his men give you that black eye?" Joe asked.

"No, sir, it was a man in the holding cell with me. He took exception with his fists to the fact that I'm a college student. His name was Eugene something or other."

"I have my camera in my car. Let's get a photo of your eye before we leave with the jail in the background," Joe offered. "Not only were you wrongfully arrested, but you were also abused by other prisoners."

Once the photos were taken, Stuart climbed into the back seat of Joe's Chevy. "Are you studying law, Mr. Ezell?"

"No, but I recognize the need to document every single thing for your attorney. Before you meet her on Friday, we're going to sit down and have a very long talk, Stuart. You're going to tell me the truth this time." Joe glanced at him through the rear view mirror so he wouldn't mistake his meaning.

Leon turned to face his son. "Do you know who killed Cookie Crumble?"

"No, sir, I don't."

"Ignorance isn't an effective defense," Leon warned. "That's right, isn't it, Joe?"

"Yes, unfortunately, it is."

Joe had known Leon must have a spacious home, but the white colonial house was even grander than he'd imagined. They came in the front door and walked by the living room, dining room, and den to reach the kitchen. Elated, Doreen fussed over her son, and shed a few tears over his black eye. Stuart backed out of her arms saying he needed to shower and change his clothes. He ran up the back stairs before she could argue.

Leon gave Joe a cup of coffee, and they sat together in the breakfast room while Doreen prepared the hearty breakfast she insisted Stuart needed. Joe recognized her flurry of activity for the frantic fear it masked, and hoped she'd fry up a few extra pieces of bacon for him. He took out his notebook and spoke softly so only Leon would hear.

"When Cookie's body was found, Detective Lynch thought Stuart a possible suspect because he had access to the Thornton's apartment keys. Maybe they left their door unlocked, and the keys could have been on the kitchen counter where anyone could have found them. Stuart admitted he'd seen Cookie at Sherry's, but she'd had lots of fans, so that's a flimsy link. Tom Green bragged about entertaining 'starlets' at his father's parties, which included Cookie, but he didn't invite his fraternity brothers to join him."

"There's a closer tie to Tom Green and Cookie than to my son, is that what you're saying?"

"Yes, and I need to ask Brett Wayne if he wrote any scripts for Casper Green. If he did, he would probably have been invited to the wrap party. He also sent flowers to Cookie at Sherry's, so he went there more often than he admitted."

Leon sat back. "Could he have killed her?"

"Maybe. We're thinking of what's possible. I'll talk to him today about writing scripts for Casper Green. He loves to talk about his writing, and he won't suspect why I'm asking. We need to add whatever Stuart knows that he's not telling. If he's protecting one of his fraternity brothers, he needs to think of himself first, not them."

"I don't know what to think," Leon moaned.

"What you need is a good breakfast," Doreen announced as she brought him a plate heaped with scrambled eggs, bacon and toast.

"Would you care for some breakfast, Mr. Ezell? There's plenty."

"In that case, I would love to have breakfast with you. It smells too good to miss."

"There's nothing like the aroma of bacon in the morning, is there?" she nearly chirped on her way into the kitchen.

"She's so happy we got Stuart out of jail, she's not thinking past this morning," Leon whispered.

"Let's join her and enjoy the moment of quiet while we can," Joe urged. Doreen brought him a plate, and the eggs were scrambled and seasoned perfectly, and the crisp bacon was beyond perfection. "I can't recall ever having a better breakfast, Mrs. Helms."

She came to the table with a single strip of bacon and one piece of toast for herself. She slathered the toast with butter and strawberry jam. "Thank you. You've got to catch the murderer, Mr. Ezell. Clearly the police have gone off on completely the wrong track. I didn't like that detective when I met him. What was his name?"

"Lynch," Joe replied. He'd always considered the name a bad omen. "I'm not impressed with him either."

Stuart joined them with his hair damp from the shower and ate more than Leon and Joe combined. "Do you think I can go back to USC?" he asked. "I don't want to get behind in my classes."

Leon and Doreen looked to Joe for an answer. "It might be a good idea to miss the rest of this week and see what your attorney advises when you see her on Friday."

"All right. I just want out of this mess."

Doreen had left the table to return to the kitchen, and Joe suggested they go into the den to talk. "I'm not telling you to hide things from your mother, but you'll probably speak more freely if she isn't with us."

Stuart rose from his chair to lead the way and Leon and Joe followed. The room was painted a deep forest green and the bookcases on three walls were filled with reference books as well as bestselling fiction. The windows on the remaining wall had shades to diffuse the morning light and gave the room a cheerful warmth. Leon gestured for Joe to take a comfortable leather easy chair, pulled his own chair out from behind his desk, and nodded for Stuart to take the wingback chair.

"We need to get serious," Leon began. "You may be fond of your Kappa Sigma brothers, but if you have even an inkling one of them is guilty of murder, you need to protect yourself rather than him. Do you understand what

I mean, Stuart? Murder is no college prank."

"I know that, and if I knew anything at all, I'd tell you rather than risk spending another hour in jail. I wouldn't wish that on anyone, except that brute Eugene."

Joe leaned forward. "Maybe you know more than you think you do. Where were you on the weekend three weeks ago when Cookie Crumble died?"

Stuart focused on the rug beneath his feet rather than meet his father's gaze. "I go to class and study during the week, and on the weekends, there are football games and parties. People are coming and going, and I wasn't paying attention as to who was where on that weekend, or any other. I don't keep a diary the way girls do."

"You were at Sherry's the Saturday night after Cookie was found and appeared to be in very high spirits," Joe recalled.

Stuart's head snapped up. "You were there?"

"I was. Did you spend any time with the strippers after Sherry's closed that night?"

"No, I never did, but I already told you Tom Green knew Cookie better than the rest of us." Stuart drew in a deep breath. "I'm not accusing him of anything. All I know is that during her act, Cookie used to wink at him like he was someone special. But it has to be more likely one of Mickey Cohen's men killed her. They spend more time at Sherry's than my friends and I did. They probably all have records. Why didn't the police arrest one of them?"

"Cookie's body was in a refrigerator in our apartment building," Leon responded in a hoarse whisper. "There's no link to Mickey Cohen and our tenants."

"Maybe there is, and you just don't know it," Stuart argued. "I'm tired. May I go up to my room?"

"Wait a minute," Joe replied. "Tell me about having lunch at *El Vaquero* with Tom Green and Cookie, or Alice Reyes."

Caught, Stuart sat back in his chair. "We were together there only once. I think she'd spent the night at Tom's family home after one of his father's parties. They saw me crossing the street near the restaurant, and picked me up. She loved talking about movies, and thought now that she'd met Casper Green, she'd be starring in one of his films soon. Tom didn't disabuse her of the idea, but he teased her about taking acting lessons so she'd be ready. After lunch, I left for an afternoon class and Tom drove her home."

"How was she dressed?" Joe asked. If the waiter had recognized her, he wondered if she went around town in her private school getup.

"In a sweater and skirt I think. She only wore pigtails on stage, and had her hair down in curls."

"Yet some people recognized her?" Joe continued.

"Men who'd been to Sherry's would have. She was too pretty to forget, and she flirted with everyone, even the waiters. It was as though she couldn't turn off the charm. Now may I be excused?"

"You may," Joe replied. "But you need to stay real close to home."

"I understand. I won't go to Sherry's tonight."

"See that you don't," Leon stressed. He waited for Stuart to close the door behind him before he spoke. "I don't believe he understands the seriousness of this."

"He's a kid, and of course he doesn't, but we do." Joe stood. "I need to get to work. Would you like me to go with you to meet Gladys Swartz on Friday?"

Leon walked Joe to the front door. "Would you please? I want to make certain we ask all the right questions, and I'm not sure what they are."

"See you Friday morning."

Still on Stuart's case, Joe knocked on Brett Wayne's door, and the writer greeted him with a wide grin. "What's up, Joe?" He stood in the doorway and as before didn't invite the detective to come in.

"I'm trying to earn some extra money for my honeymoon, and ended up playing a very small role in a movie Casper Green is currently shooting."

"Was it *Arizona Sunrise*?" he asked, his face aglow. "I wrote it!"

"Did you? That was just what I'd come to ask. Alice Reyes's brother came with me, and we played a couple of cowboys in the scene with the fight in the saloon. We just stayed out of the hero's way, and probably won't even be noticed when the movie is released."

"I'll look for you. *Sunrise* is the third picture I've done with Green. I like writing Westerns with plenty of action, and he likes filming them. I'm working on another script for him right now."

"Good for you," Joe responded. "I heard Green throws great parties after his films wrap. He doesn't invite extras, so even if I do another film with him, I won't see one."

"Casper hosts wonderful parties it's true, but he limits the invitations to the stars, a few friends, and pretty girls."

"Have you been to one?" Joe leaned forward as though eager to hear about it.

"Yes, I have." Brett's satisfied smile bordered a sly smirk. "We don't see any beautiful girls in swimsuits around here, but Casper's pool teems with them. They aren't interested in me, you understand, no one tries to impress a writer, but I enjoy watching them."

"Any man would," Joe agreed. "Did Cookie Crumble attend the parties?"

"I saw her there, but I'm not invited to all the parties, only the ones where I wrote the script."

"Did she come alone that night?"

"No, the bodyguard from Sherry's brought her after Sherry's closed. His name's Corky, I think. He sat in a dark corner, kept his eye on her, and sulked. He doesn't appear to be the friendly sort, and I didn't approach him."

Lily Montell, or Bernice Ross, had failed to mention Corky when she'd told Joe she'd brought Cookie to the parties. While the idea appalled him, he really needed to interview Corky.

Joe backed away. "I stopped by to ask if you'd written *Arizona Sunrise*. You won't see my name in the credits, but

I'll look for yours. I'll let you get back to work."

"Sure, come by anytime."

Brett didn't offer to sneak Joe into the wrap party, which would have saved him the expense of renting a white jacket to pass for one of the catering crew. He needed the truth, however, and that meant another trip to Sherry's to check in with the ladies, and to ask Lily or Ginger Snap to introduce him to Corky.

Brett's neighbor, Abby Hick's, called to Joe as he started up the stairs to his apartment. "Joe! I've only a minute before my shift begins at the market, but I wanted to tell you I've met a really nice guy. His name is Pete, and he owns a camera store."

"Isn't that what I told you?" he asked. He'd never admit he had anything to do with their meeting.

"Yes, you did, but it actually happened!" She waved as she left, and her delighted smile would last all afternoon.

Joe told Mary Margaret he had some business to attend to that night rather than tell her he was going to Sherry's. He felt guilty for not including her, but if things went as he feared they might, he didn't want her to be involved in the resulting brawl.

Lily saw him coming down the hall and waved him on into the strippers' crowded dressing room. "Did you hear a college student has been arrested for killing Cookie?" she asked.

"Yes, but he didn't do it, and I helped his family arrange his bail. I came by to ask a couple more questions."

Ginger Snap was already in her apron costume and primping in the mirror above her place on the long make-up counter. "Sorry, but I'm all out of answers," she explained.

"I understand." Joe lured Lily out into the hallway. "Did Cookie ever go to a party at Casper Green's with Corky?"

She frowned trying to remember. "There was a time I left before she was ready to go, and he might have taken her that night. I wouldn't want to be alone with him, but Cookie treated him like a pet, and she adored her."

Joe looked over her shoulder. "Are the other ladies wary of him?" He watched her eyes widen, and when someone clamped a firm hand on his shoulder, he knew who it would be before he turned to face him.

Corky's expression was as threatening as his grip. He had cold blue eyes that reminded Joe of the icy waters of a swimming pool where nobody swam. As Corky withdrew his hand from Joe's shoulder, a fresh tattoo of the letters CC showed clearly on his wrist. It was unlikely he'd have his own initials tattooed there, so there was a good chance he'd gotten it to honor the late Cookie Crumble. Touching.

"You don't belong here," Corky stated in a low, rumbling growl.

"He's a detective working on Cookie's murder," Lily quickly responded. "Leave him alone."

Joe slapped a business card into Corky's hand. "I'd hoped to speak with you tonight. Do you have a minute?"

Corky frowned, clearly confused. "Sure, and I'll use it to throw you out."

"Let's talk as we go," Joe suggested. "I'm investigating the wrap parties the director Casper Green throws at his home. Were you there with Cookie last summer?"

"Maybe." The hallway wasn't wide enough for them to walk abreast, and he gave Joe a push to hurry him along.

"He makes Western movies, and Cookie wanted to star in one. Did she ever talk to you about him?"

"That's no business of yours," the bouncer responded, his voice still threateningly low.

"Oh, but it is. Someone who went to the parties may have killed Cookie. I want to see him caught."

"I want to see you out of here," Corky replied. He swung open the rear exit door and with a forceful shove, sent Joe stumbling out into the parking lot.

Catching himself, Joe expected a sharp jab to the chin, and held his breath, but Corky slammed the exit door behind him and remained inside. The valets laughed, but now that he had their attention, Joe thought it a good time to question them too.

He walked up to the valet stand. "I'm a detective working on Cookie Crumble's murder. Were any of you still on duty when she left Sherry's at the end the show? Did you see a man pick her up?"

The three young men exchanged amused glances. "Yes," answered the one who appeared to be in charge. "She had boyfriends. All the girls do."

Joe pulled several bills from his wallet. "Names would be appreciated."

"We park cars, and we're not good with names," the spokesman insisted.

"Cars will do for a start," Joe encouraged.

The valets conferred briefly. "There was a young man with his daddy's Cadillac. He took her home sometimes. One man drove a Lincoln, a couple of others had Chevy's, but we didn't see them that often."

Joe waited, but the men offered no further information. Joe tipped them all and handed each one his card. "If anything more occurs to you, give me a call. A lot of men may have loved Cookie, but we need to catch the one who caused her death." He strode off the parking lot and returned to his car parked down the street.

The evening had gone better than he'd hoped, and he'd call Mary Margaret when he got home to wish her a good night.

CHAPTER 10

Joe heard his office telephone ringing as he came up the stairs. He yanked his keys from his pocket, opened the door, and grabbed for the telephone before the caller hung up. "Discreet Investigations."

"This is Phillip Fitzgerald. I hear you've been looking for me."

Joe fumbled with the phone. "Yes, I am, Mr. Fitzgerald. Did your wife tell you why?"

"She claims there's a barber who closely resembles me. Why should that be any concern of mine?"

He had Joe there. He'd believed Phillip would be as agreeable a man as Fred, clearly a mistaken notion. "He shares your birthday, Mr. Fitzgerald, and is most likely your twin. Did your parents ever discuss your birth?"

"No, why would they?"

"Some families enjoy telling those stories. Do you recall the name of your family physician when you were small?"

"Percival McDowd, but he's long dead. I've gotten along as an only child my whole life, and I sure don't need a brother now. If he's asking for money, he's out of luck. Tell him I won't give him a cent."

Joe held onto his temper and withheld Fred's name. "He's a honorable man, Mr. Fitzgerald, and would be a credit to any family."

"Not mine. Good-bye."

Inspired to go to the restroom to wash his hands, Joe brought back a wet paper towel and wiped off his telephone. He'd seen CC coming up the stairs, and opened his door to speak with him. "I'm taking a quick poll. How would you feel if you discovered you had a twin brother?"

CC burst into a joyous smile. "Well, now, I'd love to have a twin. Maybe we could go fishing together, or whatever twin brothers do. I sure wouldn't trade places with him to fool our wives. No, sir, that would be playing with dynamite."

"It sure would, and there's always the possibility the wives would enjoy the switch, and you'd have an even bigger mess. Thanks for your answer."

"Anytime, Mr. Ezell. You have a nice day now."

"You too."

The phone rang again before Joe had a chance to sit down. "Discreet Investigations."

"I love that name," the woman giggled as though highly amused. "You gave me your card when we were filming *Arizona Sunrise*. I'm the red-haired dancehall girl."

"Yes, I remember you. How may I help you?"

"I called to help you. The wrap party is tonight. I have Casper Green's address if you want it."

"Sure do, thank you." He wrote it down and got the directions. "What time does it start?"

"Usually around 10 o'clock. That's the time we always get there. The caterers must arrive earlier because the food is always laid out."

"Fine. I'll be there, and if you see me, don't let on that we know each other."

"I got it, you'll be working undercover."

"I will. Give me your name and telephone number in case I need them." He held his breath and hoped she wouldn't doubt why he needed them.

"It's Pamela Smyth, with a y," she responded and also supplied her number.

"Thanks, good-bye." Joe pumped his fist in the air.

Sometimes, too seldom, unfortunately, help came from an unexpected source, and he always followed up on it.

Now he needed a white coat like caterers wear. He checked the telephone book, called a local costume place, and reserved one such jacket. He had dark slacks and shoes, so he was all set.

Mary Margaret wasn't nearly as thrilled with the idea as Joe was. "You think the man who murdered Cookie will be there. How do you plan to approach him? Good evening, sir, would you like a shrimp, and by the way, did you kill Cookie Crumble?"

Joe picked her up and swung her around in his arms. "I'll be more discreet. I'm going to watch how things play out. Tom Green, Casper's son, wouldn't talk with me if I knocked on his frat house door, but he'll be his usual self tonight. All I have to do is pass hors d' oeuvres, watch, and listen."

She stepped out of his arms. "And ask a few questions, I'll bet."

"Sure, but not provocative ones. I mainly want to see who's there."

"What if Casper recognizes you?"

"He'll know I need the money, and won't suspect anything underhanded. What's the worst that could happen? The catering crew might tell their boss I don't belong, but I'll bet they're hired from job to job and won't know who's part of the crew and who isn't."

"You're depending on everything going your way," she argued. "If Casper Green invites pretty girls, I could slip in with the starlets. No one would know the difference."

"True, you're awfully cute, but I'd worry about you drowning in the pool, and then I'd not get anything done." He gave her a quick good-bye kiss and left her cottage before she could insist he take her along. He hadn't given her the address, so she wouldn't be able to show up on her own. Unless Casper Green's address was in the telephone book, and he sure hoped it wasn't.

* * *

While Beverly Hills had wide streets hugging the hills, Joe drove slowly to avoid a crash with anyone coming downhill. Douglas Fairbanks and Mary Pickford had built their mansion, Pickfair, on Summit Drive, and Casper Green lived not too far away. So many celebrities had moved to Beverly Hills, Joe could probably knock on any door and find a movie star who'd not want to know him.

Casper Green's home had a wide circular driveway, and the caterer's truck, with Hollywood Catering in fancy script decorating the side, was parked near the gate to the patio and backyard. Joe dodged the valets and parked on the street. He pulled on his white coat as he neared the truck, and his plan worked even better than expected.

"So you finally decided to show up, did you?" a large man in a white jacket and chef's hat yelled. "We're short a man tonight and need all these trays out on the patio now. Grab a cap and take the crab cakes and get moving!"

"Yes, sir." Joe placed the paper busboy's cap at a jaunty angle, lifted the tray from the rack, and followed the path to the patio with a brisk step. Casper stood near the dimly lit pool house ready to greet his guests. He held a drink and took a sample from each tray passing by. Joe kept his head down and slowed as he came by him.

He lowered his voice, "Care for a crab cake, sir?"

"Sure, these are my favorites." Casper was distracted as the next man came into the patio, and Joe placed his tray on the long table and returned to the truck for another.

Once the hors d' oeuvres were on display, the chef stationed his men on the far side of the table to refill or remove the trays when needed. It was an easy job, and Joe kept his eye on the partygoers as well as the food.

The proportion of pretty girls to the male guests was as lopsided as Lily Montell had described. The men were casually dressed in sport shirts and slacks, while most of girls wore one or two-piece bathing suits. It was a warm September night, but he wondered how they dressed for the winter parties.

He slipped an empty tray under a filled one and rearranged the spacing on the table. The chef saw him and came over.

"Good work, you've got more initiative than most."

"Thank you," Joe called as the chef walked down the long table guiding other men to keep pace with the guests' appetites.

Pamela Smyth, the red-haired dancehall girl, wore a black polka dot two-piece bathing suit, and looked much prettier than she had wearing thick make-up for the movie. He kept his head down when she came over to say hello.

"I'm just tempted by the crab cakes, I won't give you away," she whispered. "What do you think of the party?"

"It's terrific, but are you interested in any of the men?" he responded.

"Not the ones who could be my father's friends, although the smell of money turns other girl's heads. I'm more sensible." She winked at him and drifted away toward the pool.

Joe saw Lily Montell talking with a nice-looking man who smiled and touched her arm when he spoke. They entered the main house through a side door and weren't followed.

A fair-haired young man joined the girls in the pool, splashing, dipping, and diving beneath them. With no other young men present, he had to be Tom Green. He came out of the water long enough for Joe to judge just how handsome a young man he truly was. He had a sleek, muscular build, and a wicked grin he used often. When he returned to the pool, several of the swimming 'starlets' clustered around him.

Joe kept an eye-out for Brett Wyatt, but he didn't arrive until the party was well underway. He took a few hors d' oeuvres from the far end of the long table and didn't come close enough to recognize Joe. He chatted with others, but kept turned to watch the girls cavort in the water.

Tom Green left the pool holding hands with a pretty brunette in a green bathing suit. They entered the pool house, and stayed there. Joe wondered if that was his usual pattern. Maybe he romanced a different girl at every party, and Cookie had mistakenly believed his flattering lies. A lover's quarrel could have grown violent, and Tom could have called Stuart Helms to ask for his help stowing the body. Maybe both of the young men had been too drunk to think past a refrigerator in a vacant apartment. It was plausible, and he'd add the possibility to his bulletin board when he got to the office in the morning.

There was no sign of Corky from Sherry's. Then again, Cookie wasn't there either. If she'd been the only reason he'd been invited, the bouncer wouldn't come again.

They were nearly down to the last crab cake and bacon-wrapped chicken liver when Joe saw Edwin Mooney, a man whose brother, Curtis, had been a patient at the VA hospital where Mary Margaret worked. Crystal Cavanaugh, a beautiful young woman who knew many of Los Angeles's wealthiest men had described Edwin as a mean drunk. Edwin could have met Cookie there, and Joe would add his name to the bulletin board.

The chef came by to collect his men. They left the remaining food on plates Casper Green supplied, carried the empty trays out to the truck, and slid them into the racks made for them. The chef paid them all two dollars for three hours work, which was generous.

"We've got work for you any time you want it," he told Joe, and slipped him an extra dollar. "Call the office and Sylvia will tell you where we'll be."

"Thank you, I'll do that," Joe replied. He removed the cap and white coat and climbed into his car laughing. It was too late to call Mary Margaret, but he'd take her to dinner tomorrow night and describe every minute detail.

Friday morning, Joe drove Stuart and his parents to Gladys Swartz's office. Doreen began to complain soon after she got into the car. "I just don't feel right about hiring a woman, Leon. Is she any good?"

"She's an excellent attorney," Joe assured her. "She'll

argue her clients' cause effectively in court or on the police station steps. Wherever it's needed. Ask her if she wins most of her cases. I'll bet she does."

"Wouldn't a man be more forceful?" Doreen asked.

Leon's patience grew thin. "Let's meet her before we make any judgments, dear. I agree we need the best attorney we can afford, and she may be the wisest choice."

"Well, I hope so," Doreen murmured under her breath.

Striving to appear professional, Joe had dressed in the navy blue suit he saved for weddings and funerals. Gladys Swartz's firm had an impressive set of offices in a building in downtown Los Angeles, and he wanted to look as though he belonged. The receptionist welcomed them warmly and showed them to Gladys' office.

The attorney rose to greet them, and gestured for them to take seats. She was a stunning blonde who wore her hair pulled back in a clip at her nape. Had she worn it falling free, she could easily have been mistaken for Veronica Lake. Her black suit showed off her shapely figure, and her smile disarmed the Helms' family completely.

Joe provided her with the few known details of the crime. "I've found no trace of the Thorntons who'd rented the apartment. If the police have found them, they haven't told us, and there's been no mention of the case in the newspapers."

"So the authorities appear to be stymied," she mused thoughtfully. "Tell me about your arrest, Stuart. Were you taken off the USC campus?"

Stuart and his father had worn their best suits. The younger man sat up in his chair, and adjusted his jacket for a better fit. "Yes. They were wearing LAPD uniforms, and I've never been so scared. I know nothing about Cookie's death, but how can I prove it?"

Gladys kept the surface of her desk free of clutter and took no notes as they spoke. "Do you have an alibi for the weekend she died?"

"That's the problem," Stuart complained. "Cookie performed last at Sherry's on Saturday night. Her body was found the following Wednesday. Because her time of death isn't certain, I need alibis for several days. My fraternity brothers will swear I was at the house that weekend, but all of us come and go, and that's not good enough, is it?"

"You're assumed to be innocent, Stuart, and the prosecution must prove you're guilty. Is the location of the body all they have?"

"I don't know," he exclaimed. "If they arrested me, they must know something I don't."

"I sincerely doubt it." Gladys sat forward. "I'll go with you to the arraignment this afternoon, and you'll plead, 'Not Guilty.' That's all you'll say. During the discovery phase, the DA must let us see all of his evidence. Detective Lynch is involved in the case?"

Joe answered, "He is. After what he did to Hal, I'd hoped to never see him again."

"We'll collapse him like a folding chair," the attorney responded. She pulled a sheet of paper from her desk drawer and handed it to Leon. "These are my rates. Would you care to study it a minute? My fees are comparable to other attorneys handling criminal cases."

Leon scanned the sheet hurriedly. "This isn't the time to scrimp. Thank you for offering to represent my son. We can't bear the thought of him spending another hour in jail, let alone serve time in prison for a crime he didn't commit."

"Wait a minute," Doreen asked, sitting forward. "How many of your cases have you won?"

Understanding her concern, Gladys smiled rather than be insulted. "All of them, because I'm always thorough and well-prepared."

"All right then," Doreen responded. "Where do we sign?"

Joe bit his lip rather than laugh out loud, but Gladys Swartz had easily convinced them of her interest and concern for their son. He'd had the photo he'd taken of Stuart developed at Pete's Cameras, and handed it to Gladys in a brown envelope.

"Stuart was assaulted by one of the other men in the holding cell. If he's not safe for an hour in the central jail, then he shouldn't be forced to return there and face further abuse while he awaits a trail."

Gladys studied the photo. "Excellent shot with the jail in the background. Your black eye is evidence of the altercation, Stuart. May I assume you didn't start it?"

"Of course, he wouldn't," Doreen exclaimed.

"I can answer for myself, Mom. Yes, you may. Eugene made some snide remark about having to share a cell with a college kid and socked me in the eye before I could dodge out of the way."

"I'll use this," Gladys assured them.

"Do you think I can go back to my classes at USC?" Stuart asked.

"Yes, if you live at home, and don't hang out at the fraternity house. You must look like a serious student, not one who loves to party. I hope to have the charges dismissed, and you shouldn't lose a whole semester because you weren't in class for a week or two. Why don't you go to lunch, and I'll meet you at the courthouse at two o'clock."

"I don't think I can eat," Doreen responded.

"Then we'll go to Bullock's, and do a bit of shopping," Leon suggested. He took her hand as they left their chairs, and guided her toward the door. Stuart followed.

"Thank you," Joe paused to say, and Gladys responded with one of her beautiful smiles. He didn't need to spend any time shopping, and told Leon he'd go to lunch and meet them later.

"May I go with you?" Stuart asked. "I don't care how scared I get, I'm still hungry."

"Be at the courthouse early," Leon warned.

"Of course, I will," Stuart promised.

Joe intended to see that he did. He took Stuart to a deli nearby and ordered corned-beef on rye. Stuart went with pastrami. The place was crowded, and they had to sit at a small table placed against the wall.

Joe waited until he'd taken several bites of the delicious sandwich before he spoke. "You come across as a clean-cut kid, and Mrs. Swartz will make a good case for your remaining free on bail."

Stuart nodded and continued to eat his savory sandwich.

"Last night, I went to Casper Green's wrap party for *Arizona Sunrise*. There were lots of pretty girls, but Tom was the only young man there. What kind of car was he driving when he and Cookie picked you up to go to *El Vaquero*?"

Stuart had to take a swallow of water before he replied. "He had his father's Cadillac. The studio sends someone to pick-up Mr. Green when they're shooting a film, so most days he doesn't need the car, and Tom drives it. Why do you ask?"

"Cookie was often picked up at Sherry's by a young man driving a Cadillac; it's likely it was Tom."

"So? That doesn't mean he killed her," Stuart argued. "Why would he? There are plenty of girls vying for his attention."

"Because his father is a director, or for his looks and charm?"

"Probably both. If you've seen Tom, you know how good-looking he is. He's a Kappa Sig at USC, and his father is a movie director. What's not to like?"

"Good point. If he finds girls easy to get, how does he treat them?"

"How should I know? I've never been on a date with him."

"Cut the attitude, Stuart," Joe cautioned. "Your father hired me to solve Cookie's murder, and if I have to look under every rock to do so, I'll head out to the Irwindale Quarry and get busy."

Stuart regarded Joe with a befuddled look. "It all comes back to the refrigerator, doesn't it? Shouldn't Mrs. Swartz pin the crime on the Thorntons? Why haven't the police found them?"

"An excellent tactic I'm sure she'll use." Joe glanced at

his watch, and finished the last bite of his sandwich. "Let's wash up in the restroom so we don't look like we ate as well as we did for lunch."

Stuart came along, took a glimpse at his shiny chin, and saw the need to clean up. "I hope I don't throw up in court," he murmured.

Joe slapped him on the back. "You'll do fine."

They met his parents outside the assigned courtroom, and Gladys Swartz joined them soon after. She carried a black briefcase and with her easy confidence, looked thoroughly at home in the courthouse.

"Just listen, Stuart, and don't react to whatever the prosecutor says," she reminded him.

"I understand," he promised.

Joe held the door, and their small parade entered the courtroom with Gladys leading. She whispered, "Don't worry, this judge likes to grant bail when the case calls for it." When Stuart's name was called, she stood beside him.

"The charge is murder in the first degree," the judge announced. "Good afternoon, Mrs. Swartz, it's always a pleasure to see you in our courtroom. What is your plea, Mr. Helms?"

Stuart swallowed hard. "Not guilty, sir."

The prosecutor was a chubby young fellow, who wiped the perspiration from his brow with his handkerchief, and shuffled the papers in front of him. He described Stuart as a serious threat to the community and requested bail be denied.

"What are your thoughts, Mrs. Swartz?"

"Stuart Helms's home and family are in Los Angeles. He is a student in good standing at USC. He has no previous arrests, and the bail already set is appropriate. May I approach the bench?"

"Of course."

She handed him the photograph showing Stuart's black eye. "The defendant was assaulted within minutes of his arrest by another man held in detention. He should not be placed at further risk by a return to a jail where clearly he isn't safe."

The judge showed the photograph to the prosecutor, but didn't allow him time to comment. "I agree, Mrs. Swartz, defendant is released on the current bail bond." He checked his calendar to set a preliminary hearing several weeks away. "You understand you must be here, Mr. Helms?"

"Yes, sir. I will be."

As they left the courtroom, Gladys hesitated and spoke softly to the prosecutor. "You don't have a case, better drop it now rather than look like a fool at the preliminary hearing."

The man's eyes narrowed. "You'll be the one looking foolish, Mrs. Swartz."

She smiled. "Not even possible."

Joe had heard what she'd said and tried not to laugh as the prosecutor waddled by again whipping his brow.

CHAPTER 11

Joe became so involved in telling Mary Margaret about the last couple of days, he ate most of his French fries before he tasted his hamburger. The Jumpin' Plate was crowded on a Friday night, but they were in a booth where they could talk without having to shout.

Mary Margaret had eaten half of her dinner before Joe stopped to take a breath. "With movie roles and catering jobs, do you think you'll have time to continue working as a detective?"

He laughed. "Sure, I'll have plenty of time. They won't be asking for my footprints at Graumen's Chinese Theatre anytime soon, and I doubt I'll ever have another reason to play a busboy. Although, it's a good ploy to get into celebrity parties, so maybe I should keep it up."

"It will look good on your professional résumé," she countered. "Gladys Swartz impressed me as an extremely intelligent woman, but do you really believe she can get the charges against Stuart Helms dropped?"

"Yes, because the tie between him and Cookie is too thin to merit prosecution."

"I keep thinking about the refrigerator," she mused. "Could someone have chosen it to throw the blame on Stuart?"

Joe stared at her a long moment. "That's an angle I

hadn't considered, but you're right. The killer might have wanted Stuart to be blamed."

"Or, what's the writer's name who lives in your building?"

"Brett Wayne, which can't be his real name."

"Would anyone have stashed the body where they did to throw the suspicion on him?"

His hamburger was too good to let grow cold, and he thought about her question while he ate. He took a drink of coffee to wash it down. "Brett is an innocuous soul. He keeps to himself and writes, with an occasional visit to Sherry's. At the wrap party, he watched the girls, but he didn't approach any. I don't see him as any kind of threat."

"When the police catch a murderer, aren't they often loners who keep to themselves? If he is such a solitary individual, he could be harboring murderous thoughts."

"He could be. I've never seen the inside of his apartment, but he's never been in mine either."

"There's still no trace of the couple who rented apartment three?"

"None that I could find. That they vanished is reason enough to believe they were involved in the crime, and Gladys will use it, but it just doesn't feel right. Let's enjoy our dinner and leave the detective work in my office."

"If you insist," she teased, and batted her eyelashes. "Have you been too busy to shop for tassels?"

She had timed the question so he'd not have a mouthful of food to choke on, for which he was grateful. "Not yet, but I'll put it on my list for next week."

"Good, I'm anxious to start practicing. It might put some spice in our honeymoon."

"Our honeymoon will be plenty spicy with or without tassels," he promised, but he still had a pitiful amount in his savings account making the day trip to Catalina still the best possibility.

Saturday morning, Joe met Hal Marten and Gilbert Werner for golf. It was a bright sunny morning, without any hint of fall in the air. They'd played several holes before Hal asked him about the refrigerator case.

"Gladys doesn't discuss her work with me, other than to mention she took your landlord's son's case. How's it going on your side?"

"I've plenty of suspects, but no proof any of them did it."

"No possibility of getting incriminating photographs?" Gilbert asked. Joe had gotten some for him.

"Taking photographs of men going in and out of a mob haunt might get me in more trouble than it's worth. Let's concentrate on improving our golf game for the rest of the morning."

"That's fine," Gilbert responded, "but I like hearing about your cases. My engineering job pays well, but there's nothing in the way of excitement."

"I do have another case that's puzzling." Joe told them about the twins who hadn't known a brother existed. "It looks as though their mother raised the barber, and the architect was adopted by a much wealthier family."

"Is there any way you can help them reach an accord?" Hal asked.

"I don't see how. I reported the facts, and it's up to the brothers to deal with them, or not. The architect's wife is paying for my investigation, which tickles me, as he doesn't want anything to do with it."

Gilbert turned toward Joe. "Maybe the architect needs more time to adjust to the shift in his family. If he hadn't been told he was adopted, it must be a difficult thing to accept. Makes me wonder how the mother chose which son to keep and which one to give away. That's the real story right there."

"True. The doctor is the link between the two families, and perhaps he made the choice for her," Joe surmised. "Private adoption is legal, but money may have changed hands, and that's another story."

"A wealthy family may have been eager to pay for a son," Gilbert added.

"They could have, but they'll never admit it," Joe replied.

"Whatever the family secrets involved in the boys' birth, apparently they'll stay secret."

The men continued playing the front nine holes, and Hal soon changed the subject entirely. "Are you dating anyone, Gilbert?" he asked. He placed his ball on a tee, and followed with a forceful swing to send it flying down the fairway.

"No, not anymore," Gilbert admitted as he teed his ball. He kept his head down as he lined up his shot. He was the best player of the three, and they all knew it. He made yet another excellent drive before he admitted more. "I just don't meet any women where I work, and I've already dated the other guys' sisters."

"There should be plenty of attractive nurses at Joe and Mary Margaret's wedding. That would be a great opportunity to meet them," Hal encouraged.

Joe hadn't thought about the guest list, but Gilbert was a man he could count on to behave himself. He slapped him on the shoulder. "Plan to be there, and I'll introduce you to every unmarried nurse Mary Margaret knows."

Gilbert blushed at the thought. "Okay, I guess it couldn't hurt to go."

Hal laughed at his lackluster response. "I'll see you have a good time. Now we need to keep walking rather than block the party following us on the course."

Relieved to have the attention swing again to golf, Gilbert led the way.

Monday morning, Fred Cooper telephoned Joe. "I'd like to see my brother, and thought I'd meet him after work the way you met me. Would you come with me? I'd like to have a witness in case he wants to make a point with his fists."

Joe turned his attention to the serenity of the new painting and drew in a deep breath. "I had a brief conversation with Phillip last Thursday. He wasn't eager to meet you then, but maybe his view has softened over the weekend. I've got the address of the architectural firm, so why don't I pick you up?"

"I'll close early, and meet you out front."

"See you later, Fred."

It was a terrible idea, Joe already knew it, but Fred had the right to make the choice on his own. Maybe the brothers would shake hands and each go his own way. Or, Phillip could be as obnoxious in person as he was on the phone. Either way, he'd be there and get to see the consequences of one investigation at least.

He hung his bulletin board on the wall behind his desk and devoted an hour to thoughts of Cookie Crumble. He wondered how Max was doing at home in Kansas City, and hoped his sister's funeral had been respectful and well-attended. Too many pretty girls came to Los Angeles bent on making it big in the movies. It was a shame Alice hadn't lived long enough to play a single part.

Fred wore a nice shirt, sports coat and trousers to meet Phillip. "I doubt we have anything in common, but I do want to shake his hand at least once. Do you suppose he'll ask about our mother?"

"I doubt it." Joe had tried not to hold his breath the whole way to the Fitzgerald, Finegold and Sloan office, but it had been an effort. "Let's wait in the parking lot for the firm to close for the day. If we walk in the front door, I'm afraid Phillip will walk out the back, and drive away."

A sly smile tugged at Fred's mouth. "Oh no, I want to use the entrance and meet everyone I can so Phillip can't deny he has a twin."

"Throw caution to the wind and involve the whole staff? That does have a certain appeal," Joe admitted. He parked in the firm's lot and followed Fred through the front door.

The receptionist looked up from her desk to smile, and then stared. "Mr. Fitzgerald? I thought I saw you at your desk just a moment ago."

"It is confusing, isn't it?" Fred asked. He smiled warmly. "I want to surprise my brother. Will you ask him to come to the front without telling him why?"

"I had no idea he had a twin. What fun that must have

been growing up." She reached for the desk intercom. "Mr. Fitzgerald, I have something that needs your attention. Will you please come to the front for a minute? Thank you."

Fred and Joe moved to the side of the receptionist's desk so Phillip wouldn't see them until he reached her. It took only a minute before the architect appeared. Startled, he looked Fred up and down, and ignored Joe.

"What is it you want?" Phillip asked rudely.

"Just stopped by to say hello. This is Joe Ezell. We'd like to buy you a cup of coffee, or a drink if you'd rather."

"No, thanks." Phillip focused a menacing gaze on the receptionist. "You ever pull another stunt like this, and it will be your last day here. Do you understand me?"

Her eyes filled with tears. "Yes, sir."

Phillip returned to his office without a backward glance, and Fred laughed. "We both got the looks, but I'm the only one with any charm. I'm sorry if I got you in trouble."

She grabbed a tissue and dabbed at her eyes. "I thought he'd be happy to see you."

Another of the firm's architects, Noel Sloan, a tall sandy-haired man, came in the front door carrying a roll of blueprints. "Hey, Phillip, could you take a look at these before you call it a day?"

Fred extended his hand. "I'm Phillip's brother, Fred, and this is Joe Ezell, a detective friend of mine. How do you do?"

"Noel Sloan." He juggled the blueprints to shake each man's hand. "I had no idea Phillip even had a brother, let alone an identical twin. Does he know you're here?"

"Yes, he does."

After being introduced, Joe stayed out of the way and enjoyed their conversation as Noel described how fortunate he felt to be working with such a talented architect. He called Phillip the genius of the firm, and mentioned the address of a building of theirs under construction on Wilshire Blvd.

"What sort of work do you do?" Noel asked.

Fred handed him a card. "I own a barber shop. It's been the family business."

"Really?" Joel appeared confused. "Isn't your father an attorney?"

"Phillip's is. We didn't grow up together."

The receptionist was leaning forward in rapt attention, but drew back in alarm when Phillip reappeared.

Noel spoke first. "Fred just told me you two were raised apart. That's got to be a fascinating story, and I'd love to hear it. Why don't we all go and have a drink before going home?"

"Drink yourselves into a stupor," Phillip answered. "I don't care. I'm leaving."

Fred stepped aside as Phillip shot by him and nearly ran out the front door. Badly embarrassed, Noel looked at Fred.

"I don't understand. Are you two involved in some sort of a family feud?"

"It's entirely one-sided," Fred replied. "We'd love to have a drink with you, wouldn't we, Joe?"

"Sure would." Joe understood Fred wanted Phillip's friends to make their own judgment about him. They walked a half-block to a bar that drew businessmen at the end of the day, and sat in a red leather booth.

When Noel realized Fred knew only his own story and not Phillip's, he understood why he needed a detective. "My family is so uninteresting, a detective would fall asleep listening to my background, but I can see why you need one."

Joe immediately seized the opportunity to learn more. "How did you and Phillip meet?"

"We were fraternity brothers at USC. I began as a math major, but Phillip pulled me into architecture, and I've never regretted it."

"What sort of a man is he?" Joe continued.

Noel sat back. He'd ordered a martini and turned the glass in his hands. "The first word that comes to mind is difficult, but his ideas are so original and clever no one objects to his surly attitude. He doesn't just think of what would garner attention for the firm today, but what would build our reputation over the next twenty years, and we hope even longer."

"Does he play golf?" Joe asked, with no intention of inviting Phillip to join him and his friends.

"Are you kidding? No, his idea of fun is to work on a project to suit his own tastes rather than a client's. He goes up to San Francisco to oversee our work there, and he uses whatever spare time he has to sketch Victorian buildings. He's very modern in his thinking, but he's fond of the Victorian era for some reason."

Fred checked his watch. "Thanks for talking with me. I appreciate your time, but I don't want to make you late getting home."

Noel finished the last drop of his martini. "I enjoyed meeting you, and will readily admit to being too curious to let you walk away." He handed Fred one of his cards. "If you're ever inspired to build a home or new shop, give me a call."

"I wouldn't want to cause trouble at your firm," Fred replied.

"It might be good for us," Noel answered.

Joe made it a point to give Noel one of his business cards. "Someday you might have need of a detective."

Noel laughed. "I just may, and I'll keep your card." He slid it into his jacket pocket.

Joe drove Fred back to his shop. "I'm sorry Phillip wasn't open to knowing you."

"You warned me. It's a shame we can't talk to Percival McDowd. Do you suppose his medical records could be in storage somewhere?"

"They might be. Why don't you call your aunt Ida and ask if the doctor's widow is living somewhere close? She might know, and I won't have to charge you to make the call."

"I'll call her when I get home."

After leaving Fred, Joe drove home. He called Mary Margaret after he'd enjoyed a can of soup, and asked about her day.

"It was the usual," she complained, "not nearly as exciting as yours I'm sure."

"It's nice to have a reputation for excitement, but today was nothing special." He'd wait until they were having dinner to tell her about Fred and Phillip, but he was sorry the story didn't have a happier ending.

Fred Cooper called Joe about ten o'clock on Tuesday. "The police called me at home at six this morning. Someone tossed a brick through the shop's front window. They asked who might have done it, but I couldn't offer Phillip's name without proof. As for anyone else, not liking a haircut is one thing, but such a person wouldn't have vandalized my building. Phillip could have been mad enough to have done it though. What do you think?"

"Give me a minute, and I'll call Phillip's wife. She won't offer an alibi if she doesn't realize he needs one." Joe got out her number, and made the call.

"Mrs. Fitzgerald? It's Joe Ezell. We need to settle my bill. Can you come into my office this morning?"

"Not before eleven-thirty. Will that do?"

"Yes, see you then." Joe rocked back in his chair. He hadn't been drawn to her when they met, but now that he knew her husband, he was prepared to give her a mile of slack.

He had hot coffee with cream and sugar waiting for Florence. He presented his bill with the additional hours and sat back while she studied it. "Is your husband back at home?" he asked.

"Yes, but he's been leaving at dawn to stop by the Wilshire construction site before he goes to the office."

"He did that this morning?"

"Yes." She crossed her legs and gave her skirt a tug to cover her knee. "Phillip isn't pleased Fred Cooper discovered they were twins due to my meddling in his life. I don't regard it as a mistake though." She gazed at him over her coffee cup, which was an oddly flirtatious gesture. "Lacy is too embarrassed to admit that when she first saw Fred, her uncle Fred I should say, she assumed her father was cheating on me, on us."

Joe recalled that meeting well. "Even if your husband doesn't want to know Fred, the investigation showed there were two men, rather than one unfaithful one. That has to be considered good news."

"Yes, indeed." She set her coffee cup on his desk, and placed what she owed him in cash beside it. "I have a terrible feeling this isn't over yet, but I hope I won't have to call you again anytime soon."

"It's been a pleasure, Mrs. Fitzgerald," he responded. He closed the door behind her and returned the cream and sugar dispensers to the drugstore counter. When he got back to his office, he called Fred to report Phillip had been leaving home at dawn.

"He must have done it then. Do you remember the address of the construction site Noel Sloan mentioned?"

"Yes, I do. It might be worthwhile to stop by and see if they are using bricks."

"He threw an old brick through the window, not a new one. Maybe he took one from rubble left from the previous building."

"I'll take a look. Were you able to talk to your aunt Ida?"

"We had a long chat last night. She won't admit a thing about the night I was born. But she's kept in touch with Dr. McDowd's widow, Rebecca, who lives in Monrovia. I'll give you her address and telephone number. Do you have a pencil?"

Joe had his notebook ready and took them down. "You realize I earn my living doing detective work," he began.

Fred interrupted him, "I expect to pay you, Joe. Just pick up a brick if you can, and see if Mrs. McDowd will speak to you in person. If her husband arranged adoptions, she has to know about it. Wasn't there a midwife's name on Phillip's birth certificate?"

"Yes, a Bertha Lloyd. I might be able to find her."

"Let's concentrate on Rebecca McDowd first," Fred suggested.

"Will do. What are you doing about your window?"

"It will be replaced today. I own the building, and have insurance."

Impressed, Joe said good-bye, but before he left to search for used bricks, he called Henry Hilburn to ask if he'd learned anything new about the police investigation into Cookie's murder.

"You don't believe the boy who's out on bail did it?" Henry asked.

"No. Has Det. Lynch found the Thornton's? They couldn't have simply vanished."

"I'll check on it for you. When people leave town, jurisdictions can get all tangled up, but Lynch ought to at least know where they are."

"Thanks, Henry."

Joe drove down Wilshire Blvd. to the address Joel Sloan had given them. From what he could see of the construction project, it would be a five-story building with lots of glass. He kept his distance from the men working, walked the perimeter of the site, and sure enough, he found a pile of old bricks heaped by the outdoor chemical toilets. He picked up one, but before he could hide it under his jacket, the burly foreman shouted at him.

"Hey, what are you doing there?" he called.

Joe was blessed with a fluent supply of believable prevarications and chose one. "Good morning. My wife makes doorstops by covering bricks with felt she embroiders so they look like cute little cottages. I thought you were throwing these away, and picked up one for her. I'll give you fifty cents for it."

"Doorstops? Take it and get out of here, and don't come back."

"Yes, sir, I'll do that." He carried the brick to his car and headed for Monrovia, a suburb nestled against the foothills of the San Gabriel Mountains.

CHAPTER 12

Joe drove to Mrs. McDowd's home and found a cute yellow cottage with a white picket fence and a colorful flower garden out front. A woman wearing a cotton housedress, straw hat, and garden gloves stood on a path curving through the flowers. She held a watering can, and appeared to be speaking to her favorite plants.

Joe hadn't called first to avoid giving her the opportunity to refuse to meet with him, and he had a story prepared. "Good morning, are you Mrs. McDowd?"

She was a plump little woman with a bright smile. "I most certainly am. What do you hope to sell me?"

He waited by the gate. "Not a thing. I'm Joe Ezell, a private investigator, and I'm looking for Bertha Lloyd. I believe she worked with Dr. McDowd, and the family has lost touch with her. Do you happen to know where she might be?"

"I sure do, Forest Lawn. How can her family not know she's dead?"

"Some families aren't as close as others. You have a beautiful garden. My mother was also fond of zinnias."

"Right cheerful flowers, aren't they?" she replied. "Although I love my pots of pansies in the spring. If you're not in a rush, why don't you come up on the porch and sit with me for a spell?"

"I'd be happy to, Mrs. McDowd." Joe flipped the latch on the gate and followed her to the wicker chairs on the porch. He waited for her to take the rocking chair, and then sat down beside her. He pulled his notebook and pen from his pocket.

"I have another couple of questions about Bertha Lloyd, do you mind?"

"Not at all, although I didn't know her well."

"Thank you. She signed Phillip Fitzgerald's birth certificate on November 11, 1911."

She removed her hat to fan herself and revealed a head of thick, white curls. "That was a long time ago."

"Thirty-six years to be exact," Joe replied. "Another of Dr. McDowd's patients had a set of twins that same night. Ida Sparks was the midwife."

"I know Ida quite well," Mrs. McDowd interjected. "My husband always spoke very highly of her."

"That's wonderful. The twins were separated at birth, and just discovered each other recently. I'm helping them learn the truth about their birth. Do any of Dr. McDowd's records still exist?"

"His file cabinets are out in the garage. I haven't gotten rid of them and should. Do you want to take a look at them?"

He was tempted to kiss her, but restrained himself. "I'm only interested in November of 1911, so it shouldn't take me long."

"Take as long as you like. No one else is in any hurry to read them." She led him down a path beside the house to a small narrow garage built when the Model T Ford was popular.

Joe pulled open the double doors and sunlight streamed in to reveal a row of pale green file cabinets placed along a side wall. Boxes labeled holiday decorations were stacked on top.

"I've been meaning to sort the decorations and give most away. I'm just not as enthusiastic as I once was about dressing up the house for Christmas. You don't need me standing here looking over your shoulder, so I'll go back out front and finish watering."

"Thank you, Mrs. McDowd."

"You're welcome, son. If you find anything pertinent to what you're seeking, feel free to take it with you. It will save me the trouble of throwing it out."

"I will." Joe waited for her to walk away before he bent down to read the faded labels on the file cabinet drawers. Patient records were organized in alphabetical order, with the Cs one cabinet over. He found Lillian Cooper's and took it out into the sunlight to read. She'd visited Dr. McDowd several times during her pregnancy, but the doctor's handwriting was small and difficult to read. The birth of male twins was noted for November 11, 1911, with the comment only one boy had survived the birth. Ida Sparks was listed as the midwife.

That was definitely untrue, as Fred's aunt Ida had to know. He searched for the Fitzgerald family next. Pearl Fitzgerald had visited the doctor in August for a sore throat, with no mention of a pregnancy, and yet she became the mother of a son on November 11, 1911. Bertha Lloyd's name as the midwife had been added later in blue ink.

Joe carried the two files out to the front yard to speak with Mrs. McDowd. "Did your husband handle adoptions?"

She set the watering can on the porch before she answered. "A time or two he might have, but it wasn't a regular part of his practice. Girls from around here who find themselves in a family way usually go to live with a relative out of state, so no one here would ever learn they had a baby. Those babies would have been adopted there rather than here."

"I understand. Thank you again for your help."

"You're welcome. Please tell Bertha's family I'm sorry for their loss."

"Sure will." He waved and got into his car. Fees collected weren't given in the patient records, but if Dr. McDowd had been paid for handing Phillip to the Fitzgeralds, there wouldn't be any record of it anyway.

* * *

On the way to his office, Joe stopped by Fred Cooper's

barbershop. Glaziers were already installing a new plate glass window, and he walked around them to enter. The shop wasn't open while repairs were underway, and Fred sat at his desk at the end of the room working on his books.

Joe carried the brick to him. "Does this look like the one that came flying through your window?"

The barber turned it over in his hands. "Exactly. See the streak of white paint? Something must have been painted on them, and they might match up."

"Probably not. It was a big pile of bricks," Joe countered.

"All right, I'll drop it, but Phillip doesn't have to know. While I'm tempted to throw this through his firm's front window, I'm a better man than that. Can you come up with a way to let him know I'm on to him?"

Joe pulled up a chair. "I could just walk in and lay it on his desk. He'd think it was the one that broke your window, and immediately deny anything to do with it. While I'm there, I could show him Percival McDowd's records." He spread them out on Fred's desk.

Fred scanned them quickly. "Childbirth isn't easy on a woman. Do you suppose my mother was so exhausted by labor that she believed McDowd when he told her only one twin had survived?"

"Did she ever mention you'd had a twin?"

"Never. I'll call my sisters and ask if she ever mention twins to them."

Joe walked away to watch the installation of the new window while Fred made the calls. It didn't take long before the barber joined him up front.

"They never heard I was a twin either. Would Phillip's parents speak to you?"

"Florence, his wife, didn't believe so. First, I want to see Phillip's face when I deliver the brick. I can easily imagine the smoke spewing from his ears."

Fred laughed with him. "So can I. Between us, I believe I'm the luckier man."

"So do I," Joe agreed.

* * *

After dinner that night, Joe took Mary Margaret to Aunt Lucy's Ice Cream Parlor. She listened to Joe's discoveries and nodded thoughtfully. "The doctor's wife didn't strike you as someone who could have been involved in selling black market babies?"

"Not at all. She's the straightforward type. It's more likely Phillip's father, who is an attorney, planned and arranged the adoption."

She savored a particularly delicious taste of chocolate ice cream before she spoke. "With the doctor's involvement, of course. What if the attorney didn't stop with finding a son for himself? What if he made it known he'd welcome an infant whose mother had died in childbirth, or whose mother was unwed? He could have had a lucrative adoption practice."

"Yes, he could have handled such adoptions, but Dr. McDowd apparently told Mrs. Cooper that one of her twins had died. That's not just wrong, it's evil."

"I agree, but what if she was in on it? Maybe she couldn't handle the thought of raising two babies, and the doctor promised to find a good home for one, perhaps the smaller child?"

"Phillip's wife mentioned he had a heart murmur." He paused to take a long sip of his milkshake. "I need to speak with Fred's aunt Ida again. What sort of incentive can I use to inspire her to talk?"

"Other than Aunt Lucy's ice cream? Maybe if she thought Phillip wanted to meet his mother, she'd tell you why it isn't a good idea."

He reached for her hand. "That's inspired. I'll try it."

"That's one of the things I love about you. You're always willing to try something new."

"Let's wait until we've left Aunt Lucy's to begin, shall we?"

She blew him a kiss.

Wednesday morning, Joe gave Phillip time to stop by the construction site and reach his office before he arrived at

Fitzgerald, Finegold, and Sloan. He carried the brick he'd picked up in a shoebox as well as Dr. McDowd's records tucked under his arm. The receptionist recognized him, and looking for Fred, shot a fearful glance behind him.

"I'm by myself today. Is Phillip in?"

"He is, but he won't want to see you."

"I'm sure he'd rather see me than the police." Joe went by her down the hall and found Phillip in his office at his drawing board. "Before you start yelling at the receptionist, I forced my way by her." He placed the shoebox on the drafting table. "Fred sent you something."

"I don't need any shoes," Phillip replied. "Get out of here."

"Better open the box," Joe urged, his manner friendly rather than threatening.

Phillip yanked it open, and then stared at Joe. "What's this supposed to mean?"

"It's the brick you threw through Fred's shop window, and it's a perfect match for the bricks piled at your construction site. We could probably fit them all back together and discover where this one used to be. The police asked for a name of someone who might have caused the vandalism, but Fred didn't give them yours. Frankly, I believe he's too embarrassed to report his brother would resort to such juvenile behavior."

The architect looked ready to choke. "What's he want?"

"Nothing for his silence, but if there's any further trouble, he'll report you. Now on a lighter note, I have Dr. McDowd's records for Fred's mother and yours."

He waited for Phillip to absorb the additional distressing news. "Mrs. Cooper had several prenatal visits with the doctor, and had twins on November 11, 1911. Sadly, the doctor told her only one of the little boys survived. That same evening, your mother apparently also gave birth to a boy, without the benefit of any prenatal visits. The name of a midwife, Bertha Lloyd, was added to the record later."

Joe opened the folders so Phillip could read them, but he kept a tight hold on them so the architect couldn't rip them to shreds when he was through. "It's interesting that Pearl Fitzgerald saw Dr. McDowd in August for a sore throat. There's no mention of a pregnancy, undoubtedly because she wasn't pregnant. I'll be happy to go with you to talk with your parents if you like. They really should have told you about the adoption, if we can call it that, long before this."

When Phillip continued to regard him with a malevolent stare, Joe took another tack. "Fred closely resembles his fraternal grandfather and uncle. Do you look like any of the Fitzgerald family?"

"No," Phillip reluctantly conceded.

"I'd really like to ask your parents about November 11, 1911, and how your family came to have a baby boy Dr. McDowd had earlier declared dead."

"My parents are my parents," Phillip spit out through clenched teeth.

"Of course they are, they raised you, but there's a woman living in Pasadena who gave birth to you. Wouldn't you like to meet her?"

"Not particularly, no."

Joe closed the folders and shoved them under his arm. "Keep the brick as a token from your twin. You know how to contact me when you become so curious about your true parentage you can no longer hold it in."

He walked out of Phillip's office, wished the befuddled receptionist a good day, and drove to his office to decide how to proceed. He owed Fred a report, but before he could arrange a meeting, the telephone rang. It was former LAPD detective Henry Hilburn.

"Det. Lynch found the Thorntons."

"Where are they?" Joe asked, hoping they hadn't turned up as dead bodies in some nameless ravine.

"They're back home in Denver. Vince's father died suddenly." He shuffled his notes. "Looks like they got the word of his death early on Thursday, September 4th, and he and his wife grabbed everything and hightailed it for Colorado. Vince got a speeding ticket in Albuquerque on

Saturday, September 6th, and that was the last day Cookie Crumble performed. So they're off the suspect list. Looks like they took Route 66 out of LA, followed it across Arizona to New Mexico and made a left turn to go north up Highway 25 to Denver."

Joe sat back in his chair. "Is there anything in your notes about what they did with their keys?"

"Nope, and I don't have a telephone number for them. Does it matter?"

"Possibly. If they were in such a great hurry, they might have left the door unlocked and forgotten to leave the keys. Whatever they did, they were too far away to harm Cookie. Thanks, Henry. I'll stop by to talk with you soon."

He ended the call, hung his bulletin board on the wall, and removed the Thorntons' card to make a note they were in Denver. He could understand how a sudden death would make notifying a landlord slide, but at least they were accounted for, and it solved a part of the puzzle. He'd still like to know where Vince Thornton and his wife had worked, if only to tie up loose ends.

He called Leon Helms with the news. "My source tells me the Thorntons returned to Colorado before Alice Reyes died."

Leon sighed unhappily. "That's not good for us, is it?"

"It removes them as possible suspects, but there are still plenty of others who could be involved in her death."

"What did they do with their keys?" he asked.

"My source didn't know, but we'll keep asking until we find them. The missing keys could have fallen into anyone's hands. You can be sure Gladys will use the keys to every advantage."

"I sure hope so," Leon replied. "Let me know if you learn anything more."

Joe promised, and placed a call to Gladys Swartz. He gave her the news about the Thorntons.

She listened as he described his source as a knowledgeable former LAPD detective. "So you trust his information to be accurate?" she asked.

"I do. Now we need to find the keys, and identify who used them."

"Wasn't the apartment where Cookie was found unlocked? If the murderer had had the keys, wouldn't he have locked the door so her body wouldn't have been found?"

"Yes, unless he wanted her to be discovered," Joe suggested.

"Interesting thought. Keep in touch, and let me know if you find anything more related to Stuart's case."

"I will." He pulled a 3x5 card from his top drawer to list reasons the murderer could have had for wanting Cookie's body to be found. Almost immediately it occurred to him the murderer must have had a believable alibi for the time of her death, and wanted to shift the blame to someone who didn't. It was clever, but impossibly evil in its intent.

There was still plenty of time left in the day for a trip to Pasadena to chat with Aunt Ida. He'd paid close attention as Fred had driven there last week and had written her address in his notebook. He rehearsed what he wanted to say as he drove the curving Arroyo Seco in the midday traffic.

Ida Sparks answered his knock at the door, appeared puzzled momentarily, and then remembered him. "You're Fred's friend," she murmured without enthusiasm.

"Yes, I am, and if you have a minute, I'd like to speak with you." He kept Dr. McDowd's records clasped in his hand.

She glanced over her shoulder to make certain Lillian wasn't calling for her, and then stepped out on the porch. "A minute is all I have. Make it quick."

"As you know, Fred has recently discovered he has a twin. His brother, Phillip Fitzgerald, hopes to meet their mother. He loves the couple who raised him, but he'd still like to see his mother, if only once. Could you arrange it?"

"Lordy," she whispered under her breath. "My sister isn't certain who Fred is, and she's too forgetful to have an enjoyable visit with Phillip or anyone else. She was a proud woman, and wouldn't want anyone to see her now that a stroke has taken away so much of who she was."

"I understand, but Phillip would drop by to say hello, and leave promptly. He wouldn't tire her."

"You don't take no for an answer, do you?"

"It's considered a fine trait for a detective," he responded with an easy smile. "What Fred and Phillip really want to know, is how they came to be separated soon after they were born." He opened Lillian's folder. "Dr. McDowd wrote that your sister had given birth to twins, but only one survived. You were there. What really happened?"

Ida looked away. "It was nearly forty years ago, and it's best left forgotten."

"It might be the easiest course, but Fred and Phillip deserve to know the truth."

Pressed to explain, her gaze turned scorching. Her voice dropped to a breathless whisper, "I'll tell you if you promise to go away and leave my sister in peace. Do you understand me? You come here again, and I won't open the door."

"Fair enough." There were chairs on the front porch, but she didn't even glance toward them, let alone invite him to sit.

"The boys were William's children, not Paul's. Paul married my sister when William left town rather than do the honorable thing and marry her. Paul simply couldn't bear to see Lillian disgraced with an out-of-wedlock child. Our parents, may they rest in peace, never knew the truth. They believed Paul was the better of the brothers, and that Lillian had made the wisest choice.

"When Lillian had twins, Paul refused to raise two of his brother's brats, and told Dr. McDowd to take one away. My sister was too exhausted by a difficult labor to fully understand what had transpired. As soon as she regained her strength, I gave her little Fred to cuddle. She adored him instantly, and didn't need the grief of learning what Paul had done with their other little boy. The child simply didn't exist in her heart and mind.

"Paul soon fell in love with the baby, and if he ever regretted giving away his twin, he never admitted it to me. He was a wonderful husband and father. Paul and my sister were happy together, welcomed two daughters, and neither ever mentioned William's name. Is that a story either Fred or his brother will enjoy hearing? Fred loved Paul and believes he was his father. Do you really wish to reveal Paul was actually an uncle, and that he discarded Fred's tiny infant brother like a worn-out toy?"

She entered the house, closed the heavy oak door, and locked it before Joe could do more than stare in astonishment. He went out to his car to think rather than sit on her porch to gather himself. He felt as though he'd been punched in the stomach, and learning the truth had been more disastrous than satisfying.

He took Mary Margaret to Clifton's Cafeteria for dinner. He needed a plate of their soothing macaroni and cheese and offered very little by way of conversation while they ate.

"Clearly something is desperately wrong," she observed. "Do you want to tell me what it is, or should I try and guess?"

"I'm sorry. When I take you home, I'll tell you how another of my investigations has rendered the worst of results. Maybe all families have secrets, and the most painful ones should probably remain undiscovered. It shouldn't matter what I found."

She possessed the patience to wait for the whole story and once they reached her cottage she made coffee and offered chocolate chip cookies she'd made over the weekend. She'd added pecans, and they were especially good.

Comfortably seated together on the sofa, Joe repeated what Ida Sparks had told him. "Driving home, I asked myself whether or not Fred needed to have his world turned upside down. He doesn't, of course, but there is a value in knowing the truth, isn't there?"

She nearly choked on a bite of cookie and needed a swallow of coffee before she could speak. "Enormous value I'd say, but in Fred's case, I understand how difficult it will be to tell. The man who raised him stepped in when his brother abandoned Lillian, but then he handed one of his wife's twins to strangers, which is hardhearted. Phillip doesn't appear to care, so you can leave him out of it, if that's any consolation."

"Phillip is so impressed with himself, he would never have been content being the son of a barber, no matter how fine a man Paul may have been. Whoever made the choice, Paul or Dr. McDowd, Phillip was the right boy to send to a wealthy home."

"Interesting way to look at it. Have another cookie."

"I mean it, Mary Margaret. Are you and your brothers and sisters all alike because you have the same parents and upbringing?"

"No, each of us is a distinct individual. As the eldest, I was able to see their separate personalities from the moment they were born."

He nodded and took a second cookie. "Had Paul had two boys to remind him of his brother, he might not have been the loving father he was. He already knew he was Lillian's second choice, and that had to hurt."

"You could be over-thinking this, Joe. What if you told Fred his parents felt they couldn't raise two boys, and that Dr. McDowd found Phillip a fine home? It's a bare-bones account of what happened, but it is the truth. Maybe the Fitzgeralds had tried for years to have a child. They could have been overjoyed to adopt a baby boy."

Her explanation offered a justification for how the twins had been separated, but in his opinion, what was easy wasn't always right.

CHAPTER 13

CC came by Joe's office Thursday morning and found him with his feet propped on his desk, his attention focused on his new painting. "Good morning, Mr. Ezell, are you relaxing between cases?"

Joe swung his feet off the desk onto the floor. "I'm in the middle of two, that's the problem. I'm just taking a minute for an inspiration to hit me, and then I'll get busy."

"Well, sir, I've always found inspiration comes more easily if I'm walking toward it."

Joe stood and stretched. "You're a very wise man, CC. I do need to get moving, and I'll go out for a walk."

"It's a good day for it," CC agreed.

Once outdoors, Joe drew in a deep breath and walked twice as far as he usually did. With his long stride, he could cover several blocks easily and then several more. He knew exactly what he was doing, wasting time rather than typing a final report for Fred Cooper. He was leaning toward Mary Margaret's sterile version of the facts, but not far enough to actually go with it.

He'd want to know the full story, and he thought Fred would too. Still, the unvarnished truth disturbed him, and would needlessly hurt Fred. When he'd become a private investigator, he'd anticipated having cases where he'd discover and report the facts, and be well-paid for doing so.

Clearly, he'd known nothing about the actual work any private investigator would do, and how little he'd earn doing it.

He ate lunch at a new café where they had freshly baked bread for their sandwiches. He'd come by again when his walk took him off his usual route. By the time he returned to the office, he'd gathered the inspiration he'd been seeking. He'd prepare two reports for Fred Cooper and let him decide which one he'd prefer to read. He called him, and said he'd come by after Fred finished work.

Fred was busy sweeping the floor as Joe entered his shop. "Give me a minute," he called to the detective. "I sweep up a dozen times a day, but the last time has to be the most thorough."

Joe sat down in the waiting area and scanned his two reports. Perhaps it was cowardly to ask Fred to make the choice, when he was already certain the man would prefer the more detailed version.

After Fred put his broom and dustpan away, he washed his hands, hung up his white jacket, and joined Joe. "Let's go down to The Pepper Mill for coffee. It's been a long day, and I could use one of their brownies."

"Brownies?" Joe's mood improved instantly. "I never refuse a brownie." He waited until they were seated in the nearby café and had been served before he summarized his work.

"I talked with your aunt Ida yesterday, and she spoke at length on the promise I'd never again darken her door. Which would you prefer, a brief version that explains how you and Phillip were separated, or a longer report that includes what might be some disturbing news about your family? I brought both with me."

"I'll bet I know what my aunt told you," Fred offered. "I've always suspected there was a good chance I was my uncle William's son rather than my father's. If that's what she admitted, then it's not totally unexpected. It also implies something my mother would rather I didn't know, but I'd never fault the dear woman."

Greatly relieved, Joe eyed the delicious looking brownie, but he dared not take a bite yet. "Yes, my report details what she told me, and it's clear the man who raised you is the real hero of the story." He'd taken Mary Margaret's advice and softened how Paul had chosen to raise only one of the twins.

Rather than respond immediately, Fred took a bite of his brownie. "I never even suspected I might have a twin. Aren't twins supposed to have a connection other brothers and sisters don't share?"

"I've heard it, but perhaps you were parted too soon for it to develop."

"From what I've seen of Phillip, I'm glad it's true." He laughed with the thought of his arrogant twin. "What are you going to tell him?"

"Phillip? Nothing at all. He's made it clear he's not interested in having more than one family."

"I feel sorry for him."

"So, do I," Joe agreed, and he ate what proved to be the most delectable brownie he'd ever eaten.

Friday morning, Joe studied his bulletin board and rearranged the cards into different groupings. The other strippers at Sherry's were jealous of the attention Cookie Crumble received, and they could have killed her. They could also offer each other alibis, but Detective Lynch hadn't considered them serious suspects. Joe thought it a mistake to overlook the four women who knew Cookie best, and liked her the least.

He answered his telephone on the third ring. "Discreet Investigations."

"Mr. Ezell, this is Noel Sloan, one of Phillip Fitzgerald's partners. We met last week. Do you have time to see me this morning?"

"I'll make the time." Joe had nothing on his calendar so it wasn't difficult, and they agreed to meet in an hour. He turned his bulletin board to the wall, watered the philodendron, made a fresh pot of coffee, and considered himself ready.

Noel arrived a few minutes early. He took a chair in front of Joe's desk and removed his notes from his shirt pocket. "I'm glad you came by last week, because I'd been thinking of hiring a detective. I'm worried about Phillip."

"In what way?" Joe asked. He had a new folder ready for his notes.

"He's difficult to contact when he's in San Francisco. We leave messages at his hotel, and he responds, but I've come to believe he might be taking on outside work when he's there."

"Is that something your partnership doesn't allow?"

"It most certainly is. We work on projects together, or separately, but it's all for the firm. If Phillip plans to leave us, and take his clients with him, Jacob Finegold and I need to know it now."

"Have you asked him about his plans?"

"Not directly, because it would put him on his guard. Would you consider going up to San Francisco the next time Phillip does, and see what you can discover about how he spends his time?"

"I'd have to increase my fees for out-of-town work, and travel and hotel costs would also add to my expenses," Joe advised.

"Jacob and I have the money set aside to fund your investigation. Phillip must not even suspect we're doing so, however."

Joe nodded. "I understand. He'd accuse you of spying on him and leave the firm whether or not he'd planned on it."

"Exactly. Is it a job you'd care to do?"

In no position to turn down work, he offered a quick reassurance. "Yes, I can follow him and report on his activities without him suspecting he's being watched. Does he have another trip planned?"

"Not for a couple of weeks, but I'll let you know in plenty of time to make your own plans. Would you like me to leave a check today?"

He'd like it, but if Noel changed his mind and wanted a refund, the money might already be spent. "It's not necessary. Let's wait until we have a definite date to make plans." He rose as Noel stood and shook his hand.

Once alone, Joe turned back to his bulletin board. After the party at Casper Green's, he'd added Lawrence Mooney's name, but he considered the wealthy man too cold and calculating to strangle a woman. Lawrence had nothing in the way of charm as well, so Cookie might have met him at Casper Green's, but she wouldn't have liked him. The board was becoming cluttered, and no longer considering Lawrence a viable suspect, he removed his card, and tossed it in the wastebasket.

Joe had shied away from focusing on Mickey Cohen and his cohorts because they were such a dangerous crowd. Still, if Cookie had had such poor taste in men, they'd definitely be in that category. Mae had told him that about Cookie, and so had the strippers, but where was their evidence? Who were the men she'd chosen to date when she shouldn't have? It was time to make another trip to Sherry's to see the ladies and ask.

He arrived at the restaurant at six o'clock, checked for any sign of Corky Coyne, didn't see him, and made his way to the stripper's dressing room. Ginger Snap saw him first, and welcomed him with a pretty smile. "I hope I'm not intruding," he said.

"Of course you are!" she responded. "Come on in anyway."

Joe glanced over his shoulder, and the hallway remained clear. Carmela Cordova, and Patty, the Southern Belle, greeted him just as warmly. If they were carrying a heavy burden of guilt, they hid it well.

"Where's Lily?" he asked.

The girls exchanged puzzled glances. "Sometimes she's late, so we don't worry about her."

"Then I won't either." Joe opened his notebook. "If Cookie had poor taste in men, can you give me some names? They'll never know I got them from you."

Carmela rested a hip on the long counter. "Some were friends of Mickey Cohen, and I don't want to know their names. Others were men who saw her act and promised they could get her movie roles, but they didn't actually have any strings to pull. She'd drop them quick when she realized their promises were nothing more than hot air."

"She did like college boys," Ginger Snap offered. "I don't remember her ever dating Stuart Helms though. There must be some reason the police arrested him."

"Not really," he responded. "Did Cookie ever mention Lawrence Mooney?"

"Who's he?" Carmela asked.

"A man she might have met at Casper Green's."

"You've lost me," Ginger Snap added. "Who's Casper Green?"

Lily had taken Cookie to his parties, but apparently the other girls didn't know him. "He's a movie director."

"Really?" Patty asked. She was donning the ruffled slips for her costume. "Then Cookie would have stuck to him like a feather to honey."

Joe made a quick note. If Cookie were dating both Tom and his father, or using Tom to get to his father, she could have been caught in the crossfire between them. "Thank you, ladies. When Lily arrives, please tell her I'm sorry I missed her."

"Sure we will," Ginger promised, without a lick of sincerity.

Mary Margaret patted the place beside her on the sofa. "You were so worried about how Fred Cooper would take your report, and his reaction seems really mild."

Joe sat down beside her and pulled her into his arms. "Mild is a good word. How was your day?"

"We have a couple of difficult new patients, which makes tending them a chore, but we'll teach them how to behave soon enough."

"I bet you will." She managed him easily enough, and he kissed her soundly. When he'd caught his breath, he told her about Noel Sloan's concerns about Phillip Fitzgerald. "It means I'd have to go up to San Francisco for a few days, but if Phillip has an extra project, he'd go right to it, not wait several days to drop by."

"I want to go too," she replied. "Could we call it a honeymoon preview?"

He laughed at the idea. "We could, but I wouldn't get any work done with you there, and then I wouldn't be paid. It's still a lovely idea."

"I have others," she teased, and he enjoyed them all.

Joe looked forward to the relaxing hours of his Saturday morning golf games. Gilbert was unusually chipper, and while Joe and Hal exchanged amused glances, neither asked the young man why. They were playing the eighth hole before Gilbert paused after sinking his putt.

"A nice girl moved into my apartment building, and we went to dinner last night. We talked about going to the movies tonight, but do you think she'll get tired of me if we go out two nights in a row?"

Hal rested his putter on his shoulder. "If she does, then she isn't the right girl for you."

Gilbert looked to Joe for advice, and the detective couldn't help but smile. "Did you both have fun last night?"

A bright blush filled Gilbert's cheeks. "Yes, but I don't want to pounce on her. Well, not actually pounce, but you get what I mean."

"I do," Joe responded. "Why not take the newspaper section with movie times by her apartment this afternoon. Ask if there's anything she'd like to see."

"That's right," Hal agreed. "If she's not interested in spending more time with you, she'll say there's nothing she cares to see and maybe suggest you two go to the movies another time."

"I understand, let her use the movies as an excuse rather than force her to say she'd rather not see me ever again."

"You need a more optimistic view," Joe chided. "I'll bet

she's looking forward to seeing you tonight. She might even pick a movie she has no interest in just to go out with you."

Gilbert laughed in spite of himself. "I sure hope so." He moved back so Hal could make his putt, and kept smiling the rest of the morning.

Saturday afternoon, Joe had lunch at the counter downstairs and returned to his desk hoping something easy would come bounding his way. When the telephone rang, he answered promptly, "Discrete Investigations."

"Joe?" her voice was whisper soft.

Knowing something had to be very wrong, he sat up straight. "Yes, who is this?"

"Lily. I can't come to your office. Will you come to my place?"

He grabbed a pencil, wrote down the address in Hollywood and reached her within half an hour. The apartment building was the standard before war big box, but several residents had colorful flowerboxes that brightened the exterior considerably. Lily lived on the second floor, and he took the stairs rather than the elevator.

When he knocked at her door, she peeked out to be certain it was someone she wanted to see. Finding Joe, she released the chain, opened the door, and led the way through the narrow entryway into the neatly kept living room. Fresh flowers lent the sunny room a sweet perfume. He gasped when she turned to face him. Her right eye was black and swollen shut, and a vivid purple handprint marred the fair skin of her throat.

"Who did that to you?" he asked.

She gestured for him to take an overstuffed chair, and she sat on the sofa and leaned back. Her black satin robe was too tightly belted to allow for more than a glimpse of a slender ankle.

Her voice was hoarse, "The friend who meets me at Casper's parties called me yesterday to say the director had a role for me in an upcoming film, but he needed me to audition that afternoon. I've never considered myself much of an actress, but Casper's films aren't nominated for Oscars anyway, so we'd be even."

Anxious to hear the whole story, Joe leaned forward, and remained quiet rather than interrupt with questions she'd not had time to answer. Her hair curled around her cheeks, and without the dramatic make-up she wore at Sherry's, she looked years younger. Clearly she was a finer actress than she thought if she could turn herself into the sophisticated Lily Montell at will.

"I should have asked if you'd like something to drink."

"No, thank you," he assured her. "May I bring you something?"

She handed him a glass with melting ice cubes in the bottom. "Water would be good."

The kitchen was off the living room, and he added more ice cubes, and filled the glass with water from the sink. Just to satisfy his curiosity, he opened the refrigerator, and was grateful it contained only the makings for meals and condiments. He hurried back to her.

"How did the audition go?" he asked.

"In the beginning, quite well. Casper sent a taxi to bring me to his home, and I thought it wouldn't take long and had the man wait. I read the part of a guest at a wedding who makes small talk with the young man seated beside her before the ceremony begins. When the minister asks if anyone has a reason why the couple shouldn't marry, the young man next to me was to leap to his feet and insist he and the bride were already wed.

"A fight breaks out between the man and the groom. The bride sorts out her feelings, and leaves on her honeymoon with the man she'd previously wed. My character comforts the jilted groom, but I had no more lines.

"Casper complimented me and gave me the part." She closed her eyes and breathed deeply. "It was a comedy, and Casper's manner was so friendly, I didn't expect him to suddenly turn amorous. When he pulled me into his arms, I laughed and pushed him away, but he tightened his hold on me. I told him to let me go as forcefully as I could, but instead he slid his hands around my throat and frightened me so badly I kicked him hard in the shins.

"He punched me as he let me go and told me if I ever spoke a word to anyone about what had happened between us that afternoon, I could forget the movie role. I no longer wanted it, and took the taxi home."

"Last night, the ladies at Sherry's didn't know where you were."

"When I got home, I called the manager and told him I was ill and needed a few days off. Perhaps he told them later."

Joe thought of the crime photographer, but he wasn't ready to call Detective Lynch. "What do you think the chances are that Casper Green tried the same tactics with Cookie Crumble?"

"The thought terrified me, and that's why I fought him so hard."

"Would you object to having a photographer come and take photographs of your bruises?"

She took a sip of water, but it didn't ease her raspy voice. "Not at all. Casper grabbed me, and hit me with his left hand. Not many men are left-handed. Cookie's bruises might prove she'd also been hit by a left-handed man."

"It would be important evidence if they do." He used her telephone to call Pete Foster and ask him if he had time to take photos that would be vital in a murder case. Greatly intrigued, Pete said he'd close the shop and be right over.

"I'm so sorry this happened to you," Joe told her. "It makes me wonder how many other young actresses were afraid to complain when Casper Green took advantage of them."

"If they valued their careers, they probably went along with his advances," she responded. "I'd not thought of Cookie as being particularly principled, and the price may have been her life."

"Could your friend have known what Casper really wanted?"

She looked away. "I'd like to believe he didn't, but I shed a lot of tears over it last night. Maybe nothing he's told me is true."

Rather than volunteer to check on him for her, Joe remained silent until Pete arrived.

The photographer set down his equipment bag, took one look at Lily, and winced. "Shouldn't you be in a hospital?"

"Is my face really that bad?" she asked. "I'm avoiding mirrors."

"I'm sorry," Pete responded. "I don't want to make you feel any worse than you already do. The light is good where you're seated. Let's take a couple to show your neck and face, and then a few close-ups on your neck. That bruise will fade first, and the point is to document your injuries, isn't it?"

"It is," Joe answered.

Lily sat still for the photos, and then loosened the belt on her robe. She sloughed it off her shoulders to reveal deep purple bruises in her upper arms. "Get these too, please."

Pete took several more photos. "Did you make a police report?"

"We will soon," Joe assured him.

"Wait a minute," Lily raised a hand. "I want this to be about what happened to Cookie rather than what happened to me."

"It will be, but we need to do this right. May I use your telephone again to call Stuart's attorney? She'll know how we should proceed."

"Sure, go ahead," Lily responded.

Joe made a quick call to Gladys Swartz and described Lily's injuries. "We've taken photos, and her bruises may match those Cookie suffered. What should we do next?"

"Give me the address, and I'll be there within the hour."

He provided directions and turned to Lily. "Gladys will be over soon."

She glanced around her living room. "I didn't plan on entertaining company."

"Everything looks fine," Pete assured her. "I'll wait to see if the attorney wants more photos."

"Good plan," Joe agreed. "If you feel like taking a nap, Lily, go ahead, and I'll wake you when Mrs. Swartz arrives."

"Give me a hand up, please."

Joe offered a light hold on her fingertips and eased her to her feet. "Can you make it on your own?"

"Sure, there's nothing wrong with my feet."

Pete waited until Lily had closed her bedroom door before he whispered, "Is she a stripper?"

"She is, and a very fine one, but because of it some people will dismiss her testimony out of hand. We can't allow that to happen."

When Gladys arrived, she urged Joe not to wake Lily as yet. "We want to offer the DA a suspect so compelling the charges against Stuart Helms will be dropped." She took a place on the sofa, and opened her briefcase. She removed a pad of paper and a pen. "Tell me how your investigation has gone thus far."

Joe pulled his notebook from his pocket. He'd reviewed his notes so often he knew them by heart. "Cookie spent a lot of time with Casper Green's son, Tom, who often came to Sherry's to see her act. Lily had been invited to Casper Green's parties, and he asked her to bring Cookie. He might have seen her at Sherry's, or heard about her from his son. Either way, Cookie wanted to be a movie star, and she would have been thrilled at an introduction to a director. He could have asked her to come to his home to read for a part, just as he did with Lily."

Gladys nodded thoughtfully. "Tom might have objected, or maybe he and his father routinely shared pretty girls." Pete had been introduced as a photographer, and when he gasped, she directed her next remark to him.

"From the morning Cookie Crumble was found dead, this hasn't been a pretty story. I want you to stay a while longer in case more photos are needed, but you can't say a word to anyone about this discussion. Is that clear? You can't entertain your girlfriend with even a mention of Cookie Crumble, or brag to your friends about meeting a stripper."

"Yes, ma'am. I understand."

Gladys waited a moment to make certain she'd been clear. "You saw the crime scene, Joe. What bruises did you see on Cookie?"

"There was a clear handprint on her right arm, but the way she was folded in half, I couldn't see more. Lily is alive, and it's far easier to examine the vivid bruises on her."

"Would you call her now, please?"

Joe knocked lightly on her door, and she covered a wide yawn as she joined them. She handed Gladys one of her publicity photos. "This is how I look as Lily Montell. My real name is Bernice Ross."

"Very elegant costume and pose, Bernice," the attorney responded. She studied the young woman's injuries, and asked about the photos taken. "You need to make a police report, but you're much too weak to visit the station. We'll call and request an officer come here to take your statement."

Lily drew in a deep breath. "Go ahead, I've nothing to lose."

Gladys leaned close. "No, you've a great deal to lose. You're a lovely young woman, and can't perform your act in your present battered condition. If you suffer any permanent damage, your career could be jeopardized. Don't pretend to be strong if you feel like crying."

"I'm as miserable as I look," Lily responded, "and couldn't pretend to be otherwise."

"Did the taxi driver notice your injuries as you left Casper Green's?" Joe asked.

"I kept my head down, and I don't believe so. He wasn't the friendly, talkative sort, and I was only a fare to him, nothing more."

"Do you remember the taxi company? Was it a Yellow Cab?"

"I'm sorry, no. I was thinking about being in a movie

when he picked me up, and too hurt to care on the way home."

"Small problem," Joe assured her. "I know Casper's address, and I'll find which taxi company took a fare there yesterday, with a return trip to this address. If there's any question, we want to have proof you were there."

"Casper will say it's all lies, won't he?" Lily asked. "He could accuse me of attempting to extort money from him."

"Let's not borrow trouble," Gladys urged.

Joe understood Lily's concern. She was a stripper after all, and had been a frequent visitor to parties at the Green home. "I've had my suspicions about Brett Wayne. He lives in apartment one in my building, right across from apartment three where Cookie's body was found. He's written film scripts for Casper Green, and he could have known apartment three was empty, stowed the body there for Casper, and believed the murder would be blamed on the missing couple, the Thorntons."

"Brett comes to Sherry's and to Casper Green's," Lily added. "He's rather bashful, and doesn't bother anyone at either place. Could he know if Casper killed Cookie?"

"Why don't I have a chat with him and see?" Joe replied. "You should go ahead and make a police report. I made a note of Lily's number, and I'll check in with you here in an hour or so."

"Be careful," Gladys warned. "If Brett appears dangerous, call the police right away."

"I will," Joe promised.

Pete Foster left with him. "Abby lives in your building. Do you think she's safe?"

Joe paused with him on the front walk. "She and Brett never showed a particle of interest in each other, so I wouldn't worry. Remember you're not to breathe a whisper of what you heard or saw today, especially not to Abby, who lives so close to the crime scene."

"My lips are sealed. I'll get the photos developed this afternoon."

"Thanks, Pete." As he drove home, Joe considered ways

to approach Brett Wayne. The screenwriter knew Lilly Montell, and should be sympathetic to her story. It was a way to begin, and then all he'd have to do was watch and listen to Brett's response.

Brett came to his door, and greeted Joe warmly. Joe didn't expect to be invited in, and immediately launched into his spiel. "You know Lily Montell from Sherry's?"

"Sure, she has that great 1920's siren act."

"That's her. Casper Green asked her to come to his home to read for a part in an upcoming movie, but what he really wanted was sex. When she refused, he beat her up. Do you think the same thing could have happened to Cookie Crumble?"

Brett spent most of his time indoors, but what faint tan he had instantly paled to a ghostly white. He shook his head, and sagged against the doorframe. "Have you asked anyone else about Casper?"

"Not yet," Joe lied. "You know him, and I wanted your opinion first."

The writer made a quick glance toward the patio, to reassure himself they were alone. "Come in, this is too upsetting to discuss out here." He stepped aside to let Joe enter his apartment first.

There were stacks of movie scripts on the sofa and chairs just as Brett had once described. Joe waited for him to clear a place to sit, and didn't see the lamp coming before it connected with the back of his head. His knees hit the carpet first, and he was out cold before his cheek smacked the floor.

CHAPTER 14

Joe awoke in the trunk of a car, which was bad enough, and to make matters worse, his wrists were so tightly bound his fingers were growing numb. He cursed as he hadn't since he'd left the Coast Guard, and he blamed himself for turning his back on Brett Wayne when he believed him to be complicit in Cookie's murder.

They were traveling on a road with more bumps and potholes than smooth pavement and bursts of pain shot through his skull with an excruciating rhythm. He felt sick to his stomach, which might have been from the cramped quarters, or he had suffered a concussion. He opted for the latter.

Mary Margaret wouldn't worry when he failed to pick her up after work. She'd simply assume a job had filled his afternoon, and that she'd hear from him later.

He'd told Gladys and Lily he'd be in touch soon, and they'd known where he was bound when he'd left them. They would have expected to hear from him in an hour or two, and when they didn't, Gladys would surely have called his office to check on him. When no one answered, she'd probably called the police and sent them to Brett Wayne's apartment. It was unlikely the police would follow up and look for him when he'd only been missing a couple of hours though.

He had no idea how long he'd been unconscious, and stuck in a dark car trunk, he couldn't tell whether it was still daytime, or if night had fallen. Maybe not enough time had passed for Gladys to grow concerned about him. She could still be plotting strategy with Lily and only occasionally glance at her watch. With his hands behind his back, his watch was of no use even if there had been some light filtering into the trunk to see it.

There should be a tire iron close enough to reach if he wiggled a bit, but added to the bouncing road, his head ached too badly to try. Instead, he concentrated on the knots tying his wrists. The Coast Guard had taught him more knots than a Boy Scout knew, but Brett had used what felt like clothesline around his hands, and the knot was too small to untie with clumsy numb fingers. He tried anyway, and jerked as best he could to create enough slack to pull his hands free.

He awoke with a start when the car stopped, and realized he'd passed out again. He could hear voices, two men were talking, probably Brett and Casper. This wasn't a movie where an extra could play dead, and then jump to his feet at the end of the scene. He hoped they realized it before he came to any further harm. Grasping surprise as a weapon, when they unlocked the trunk, he played dead, but he'd had a fast glimpse at the night sky.

"You said you just knocked him out. Did you kill him?"

Brett reached into the trunk to check the pulse in Joe's throat. "No, his heart is still beating. Let's just leave him here. We're too far out of town for him to get home on his own, and there's no one around to rescue him. Help me get him out of the trunk."

Joe went limp and the two men struggled to pull him out and place him on the ground. From what he heard, they intended to abandon him. It wasn't much of a plan, and he waited without so much as a twitch for them to realize they needed to untie his hands.

"We could back the car over him."

"No! Let's just leave him be. If he dies of exposure, no

one can say it's murder, but if there are tire tracks running across his chest, they will come looking for us."

"We should untie his hands."

"You have a knife?"

"No, can't you just untie the knots you made, Brett?"

"They're too tight to loosen. Look in the glove box. There might be a pocket knife in there."

Brett's cohort opened the passenger door, and rustled around in the old maps, and half-empty cigarette packs. "Found one, but the blades don't look too sharp."

"I'm not trying to slit his throat." Brett had to saw the blade back and forth on the clothesline, and he was sweating when he at last cut through. He closed the knife, and threw the cut cord into the open trunk. "All right, let's get out of here."

Before Brett could slam the trunk shut, Joe made a flying grab for his leg, twisted it hard to trip him, and the writer fell with a bone-jarring thud, the breath knocked out of him. Joe went after his accomplice next and found Tom rather than Casper staring at him bug-eyed. Not wasting a second, he punched the kid on the chin with a force that dropped him in the dirt. Joe grabbed the pieces of clothesline Brett had tossed into the trunk and bound their hands behind their backs with the speed of an award winning rodeo calf roper. He picked up the dull knife.

Feeling dizzy, he stood back and leaned against Brett's Ford sedan. "Which of you killed Cookie?" he asked. "The law will go easier on the first one to tell the truth."

Tom was badly shaken, and his voice became a muffled whine, "Cookie was a lot of fun, I would never have hurt her."

"Really?" Joe asked. "Guess that leaves you, Brett, but I didn't think you had it in you."

Brett looked up from the dirt where he lay. He coughed and sputtered, "I'm no murderer."

Joe looked around. They were so far out in the desert, there were no lights twinkling in the distance. "Pardon me if I don't believe you, but I do appreciate your refusal to run over me a few times before you left me out here all by my lonesome." He stuck to the back of the car to keep from swaying and give away what poor shape he was actually in. His head ached so badly he was sure his skull had to be cracked.

"What did you hit me with, Brett? A baseball bat?" he asked.

"No, it was just a wrought-iron lamp."

"Is that all?" Joe looked up at the sky. Here, away from the light of town, the stars shown with a fiery brilliance. It was a spectacular sight, but this was no time to name constellations. He drew in a deep breath. "Do you really expect me to believe neither of you had anything to do with Cookie's death, and that you drove me out here simply for a bit of fun?"

Neither replied. Tom sniffed as though struggling to hold back tears, and Brett lay right where he'd fallen. "This could be a Laurel and Hardy comedy," Joe observed, "and there doesn't appear to be a brain between you two, which is fortunate for me, of course. Now we're going back into LA, and you're going to tell Detective Lynch how this miserable ride came about. I'll warn you now, he usually has plans for Saturday night, and he won't be pleased to be called into the station."

Joe waited for one of them to plead with him not to go to the police, or to offer something of value to silence him, but neither did. "Tom, I'm going to untie you so you can hoist Brett off the ground and stuff him into the backseat. I should make you ride in the trunk, but I'm in a generous mood." When Brett was tucked into place, Joe continued. "You're going to drive, Tom, while I keep my eye on both of you.

"By the way, Brett, several people knew I intended to talk to you, so you'd never have gotten away with this pathetic stunt. By now, the police have already been to your place looking for me, so don't think you can avoid the grief that's coming. You'll richly deserve every bit of it. Get into the driver's seat, Tom, and let's go."

Joe had considered it a good plan to get back into town without causing himself any additional pain, but Tom skidded into a curve on the uneven road, lost control, and sent the Ford flying into the air. Coming down hard, it rolled over twice in a clattering, gravel spewing screech, and landed with a loud thud on its roof. Already hurt, Joe choked on the flying dust and again lost consciousness.

The first pale light of dawn shone in the eastern sky when Joe awoke. He was lying half out of the badly damaged car in a bloody pool of broken glass. His jacket had protected his arms, but blood dripped into his eyes from a gash above his left eyebrow. He yanked his handkerchief from his hip pocket and applied pressure. It seemed to help, and he risked moving his legs to crawl away from the wreck.

He could see Brett from where he sat, but the writer's legs were twisted at an odd angle. "Brett! Can you hear me?" All he heard was the desert's eerie silence.

"Tom! Are you all right?" Again there was no answer, and he feared the kid had thought them both dead and run all the way home.

"This is a fine mess," he murmured, again reminded of Laurel and Hardy. He'd stemmed the blood dripping from his head, but his handkerchief had been soaked in the process. He dropped it into the sandy soil and pulled off his tie. It had been one of his favorites, but he needed a bandage more. He tied it tightly around his head the way he'd once used a strip of cloth when playing cowboys and Indians.

He sat still, but ached all over. At least it was October rather than August when the desert temperature would be over one hundred degrees. "That's indeed a blessing."

The radiator could be drained for water, but when he edged around the car, he found the front end badly damaged. Whatever water the radiator had once contained had dripped into the desert floor.

He lay back down to think. The natural landscape was perfect for Western movies, and that's how Brett and Tom could have known about this back road. He wouldn't hope that the cast and crew of such an epic were about to appear on the horizon.

"Where's the cavalry when you need them?"

A lizard appeared atop a nearby rock. It studied him with a quick glance before continuing his daily run. Joe wondered if he'd get hungry enough to eat a lizard, but in his present state, he wouldn't be fast enough to catch one.

By now, Mary Margaret would know something was wrong. Gladys could have called her. The police might be looking for Brett's car, but not out here in the desert. He continued his crawl around the Ford and found Brett looking horribly forlorn, but alive.

"Good morning," Joe greeted him. "I'd pull you out of the wreckage, but I'm too woozy to stand. I can free your hands though." He reached into the partially flattened car to untie the cord, and his knot was a lot easier to loosen than Brett's had been.

"Thanks. It hurts too badly to do more than snap my fingers," Brett murmured. "I'll stay put until the ambulance arrives."

"What an optimistic view," Joe chided. He pulled the cord through his hands. "Do you think Tom will call for one when he reaches civilization?"

"Why wouldn't he?"

Joe slumped down facing him. "Facing a murder charge might be a bit intimidating."

"Neither of us killed Cookie," Brett insisted, his voice tired as gravel.

"You intended to strand me out here in the desert with only lizards for company, and that's attempted murder. A donkey might stray by that I could ride into town once I convinced him to follow the road."

"We would have come back to get you in a day or two. Casper just wanted to frighten you off, not kill you."

"That's encouraging. While we're waiting out here with nothing else to do, why don't you tell me who did kill Cookie?"

Brett sighed sadly. "I'll deny it if you repeat a word of this to the police."

"There are no officers in sight." Joe looked down the road and hoped Tom hadn't been too badly hurt to reach a main highway and summon help.

"When the Thornton's left in the middle of the night, it gave me an idea for a noir mystery. I went to Casper's to pitch it. Maybe a prison escapee, who busted out to prove his innocence, or a woman hiding from a jealous lover could stay there. There had to be a threat of imminent discovery that would bring absolute disaster. Casper liked that angle, and urged me to devise a plot that would appeal to Humphrey Bogart and Lauren McCall.

"We were working in the house, and Tom and Cookie were in the pool. When it got quiet, Casper looked out the window, and murmured Tom was making good use of the pool house. He soon excused himself. I don't know how long he was gone, but when he came back, he told me there had been a horrible accident, and Cookie was dead.

"I thought she'd drowned, and wanted to call the police, but Casper said we couldn't let anyone know she had died there. He seized upon the idea of using the vacant apartment in my building as a good place to hide her body."

"And you obviously went along with it," Joe murmured.

"Not for a long while I didn't, but Casper swore he wouldn't buy another of my scripts, and no one else in Hollywood would either, unless I helped him. What choice did I have?"

"So he threatened to end your career?"

"It was no idle threat, Joe, he meant it. Tom was beside himself and ranting about how he'd invited pretty girls home for his father. He'd never thought Casper would play so rough he'd kill Cookie though. Casper yelled at him to shut up. It was awful."

Joe's opinion of Tom went up a several notches. "What happened to Cookie's purse and clothing, any evidence that she'd been there?"

"I don't know, but Casper must have gotten rid of them by now. We just wrapped her in a blanket, put her in my car trunk, and Tom came with me. Our building is so quiet in the evenings, no one saw us bring her inside apartment three. We left her in the refrigerator so her body wouldn't decompose before she was found."

"How thoughtful of you." Joe had to swallow hard to tamp down a surging wave of nausea. "When you strolled up to join us on the morning we found Cookie, you appeared to be merely a curious neighbor. You may have missed your calling, Brett. You might be a better actor than screenwriter."

"I don't feel well," Brett moaned.

"Neither do I, so let's relax and conserve our energy." He hoped help was on the way, but then had the awful thought Casper might come for them. The director could seize the chance to be rid of a witness to Cookie's death as well as a troublesome private eye who knew too much.

Alarmed, he crawled to the open trunk and rooted around for the tire iron. He couldn't mount much of a defense against an able bodied man holding a gun, but that was no excuse not to try.

He stationed himself at the front of the partially crushed Ford to have a clear view of the road. There would be a flowing dust trail heralding anyone's approach, and he wouldn't be caught off-guard as he had been at Brett's. Concerned about the writer, he moved down the side of the car to where Brett lay, but he was asleep or unconscious. With his arms tied behind his back, he'd had no way to brace or catch himself when his car had gone airborne and rolled. He hadn't blamed Joe for his injuries, but he might later.

If there were a later. The morning temperature had dropped several degrees, and ominous gray clouds churned in the northern sky and cast deep shadows across the desert floor. The air had gown remarkably still, and Joe feared a flash flood might be brewing. People had drowned in the desert, and he didn't want to join their sad ranks. The car had come to rest in a shallow dip that would quickly fill with rushing rainwater in a storm.

"Brett?" He didn't want to shake him, and instead squeezed his hand. "Brett?"

"What?" the writer whispered in a soft moan.

"It may rain, and we should move to higher ground."

"Wake me when the first raindrops hit. My legs may be broken, and I won't move unless I absolutely have to."

"That's undoubtedly wise, but flash floods hit with a powerful force, not a beginning trickle that will leave us time to relocate at our leisure."

"Sure, I know, but give me a few more minutes to rest."

The cloud-filled sky had darkened to an even more threatening hue, and Joe doubted they had any time to waste. Then again, if Brett had internal injuries, moving him could prove deadly. Choosing which way to let him die wasn't a choice he cared to make.

"Why didn't you bury Cookie's body out here?"

"It would have taken too long, and Casper was eager to remove any sign of her murder from his house."

"That's awfully cold." Joe grabbed hold of the side of the Ford and hauled himself to his feet. Other than the low place where they'd landed, the surrounding desert was a monotonous flat landscape. "I don't see any higher ground, but we have to get out of this ditch."

"Easy for you to say." Brett made the effort to drag himself out of the car using his elbows for leverage, but cried out in pain. "I can't do it. It hurts too badly, and drowning might not be such a bad way to go."

Joe withheld his opinion on that dreary subject.

When the ground had been scraped clean for the road, boulders had been pushed to the sides. If he wished to build a dam to keep the wreck dry, the materials for a high stonewall were handy, but he lacked the strength to pick up a rock larger than a baseball.

"Do you hear that?" Brett asked. "Is there a small plane in sight?"

Joe scanned the sky but saw only fearsome clouds. "Do you hear one?"

"Thought so. Can you gather enough rocks to spell out help?"

It worked in movies, and Joe was on his feet, but he hadn't regained enough strength for such an ambitious project. "I'll shoot for a giant arrow," he suggested instead.

He lined up the rocks he could carry to form the arrowhead pointing to the wreck, but then had to sit down to rest. A high-pitched whine, while faint, could be a small plane, and he looked up. Far to the south, a mere speck moved against the clouds, but at that distance, the pilot wouldn't be able to see the wreck, or his makeshift arrow.

"Is that a plane?" Brett asked.

"It is, but it's too far away to see us."

"If he's searching for us, he'll fly in big circles and come closer soon."

"Stop dreaming," Joe countered. "Tom knows where we are, and any help he sends will come by the road. There are people who know I'm missing, but they wouldn't hire a plane to look for me way out here. That's probably a flight instructor and student pilot getting in a few hours of practice."

"Still, they might see the arrow." Brett rested with his head on his outstretched arm. He jerked up suddenly. "I felt a raindrop! Come on, get me out of here."

Another huge raindrop splattered on the sandy soil near Joe's foot. He scrambled to his feet rather than risk being swept away in a flash flood. He bent over to grab Brett's arms in a firm grasp. "Scream all you like, but I need to drag you at least ten feet."

"Just do it!"

Joe hauled the writer away from the ditch as fast as he could travel hunched over and moving backwards. A chilly wind swirled around them, masking Brett's frantic cries until Joe had to stop to rest. He could no longer ignore Brett's sobs.

"That should be far enough," he told him. "Now I need to find something to use for splints on your legs."

"Don't you dare touch my legs," Brett growled. "I want to lay here and die in peace."

They heard the small airplane circling nearer. Joe took off his jacket and waved it in a frantic arc, but the pilot flew on without acknowledging him.

Raindrops splashed against the ground all around them, and Joe feared he might have to move Brett again. "I wish you'd had an umbrella in your car."

"A flare gun to shoot emergency flares a pilot could see would be even better," Brett posed. "Remind me to get them when I buy my next car."

"You don't see serious jail time in your future?" Joe asked.

"I didn't kill anyone, and Casper forced me to help him."

"Good luck with that defense." They were both getting wet, and the scrub brush was so sparse Joe couldn't raise even a humble shelter. He walked back to the ditch, and found it already running with several inches of water. "We moved you just in time."

Brett responded with a sarcastic grunt.

Joe let him be. Water rose around the wreck, threatening to become the horrendous torrent he'd feared. He sat down where he had a good view of the car and road, but the dark, miserable day hid anyone who might be approaching. He was too tired and sore to be hungry, but if help didn't appear tomorrow, he'd have to hike down the road and hope he met a geologist collecting rocks, or a lizard fancier out on an excursion who could give him a ride into town.

"How long did you drive on this back road, Brett?"

"Fifteen, maybe twenty minutes. We just wanted to go far enough to make it difficult for you to get back into town on your own."

"It's a shame you didn't realize your own health would depend on it."

"Someone will come, won't they, Joe?"

"Hold that hope. You couldn't have driven very fast on this wretched road, so you probably covered less than ten miles in twenty minutes. Tom should have been able to walk that far by now, unless he was hurt and had to stop often to rest."

"What if he were bitten by a rattlesnake?" Brett asked fretfully.

"It didn't occur to you that might happen to me if you abandoned me out here?"

P.J. Conn

"No, I guess it should have."

Joe stood up, and checked his watch to see how long he could remain on his feet without growing dizzy. It wasn't long enough to go more than twenty yards, let alone ten miles. Maybe he'd feel better tomorrow, but without food, the odds weren't good. He looked up, and opened his mouth to catch the fat raindrops on his tongue.

CHAPTER 15

The sky cleared as quickly as it had clouded over. Joe's clothes were a soggy mess, and Brett was too miserable to complain about damp clothing. Water had tumbled stones around, over, under, and through the wreck to leave whatever wasn't buried in mud heavily camouflaged. Unless a pilot saw Joe waving, he wouldn't fly close enough to see the arrow pointing toward the wreckage.

Brett lifted his head. "Do you hear a siren?"

Joe focused on the road. The rain had left it too wet for flying dust to signal a car in the distance, but the siren's high-pitched whine was unmistakable. Casper wouldn't be approaching in an ambulance, which meant rescue must be only a few minutes away.

"Yeah, I hear it, but why would anyone need a siren when there's no traffic out here on the desert?" He pushed himself to his feet, shaded his eyes with his hand, and recognized a deputy sheriff's black and white car on the horizon. An ambulance followed in close pursuit.

"What's our story?" Brett asked.

"How about the truth? You and Tom kidnapped me, intending to leave me stuck out here to die. I foiled your plan, and Tom flipped the car driving us back to civilization. You and I were too badly hurt in the accident to walk out. That covers the pertinent details of our present situation."

"That's awfully harsh. No one wanted you dead."

"Easy for you to say now."

The deputy sheriff parked ten yards away, climbed out, and came toward them. He was one of the tallest men Joe had ever seen and lean as a whip. "Afternoon," Joe called.

"Are you Joe Ezell?" the deputy called. His deep voice rolled on the crisp air.

"I am, and this is Brett Wayne. We're afraid his legs are broken. We're grateful you came looking for us. How did you know we were here?"

The deputy removed his hat, wiped his forehead on his sleeve and plunked the hat back on. "Tom Green flagged down a truck and reported an accident. He said you'd been out scouting movie locations. Is that how you see it?"

"Yes!" Brett called. "That's what happened."

"There are a few pertinent details," Joe added. "But they can wait until we're at the hospital to relate." When the deputy slanted his head and peered at him like he was nuts, Joe had the horrible thought the lawman, and ambulance crew as well, could all be from central casting. Maybe this wasn't a rescue after all.

"May I see your credentials?" Joe asked.

"Credentials? Are you kidding? You think I drive around in a sheriff's car with a star pinned on my chest for the fun of it? You must have hit your head awfully hard."

"Yeah, several times, but I still want to see your credentials."

The ambulance driver and his assistant had already carried a stretcher to where Brett lay. They looked as though they knew what they were doing, but actors would as well. Joe waited, and the deputy finally fished his wallet out of his hip pocket and flipped it open to his identification with the sheriff's star printed on the background. He stepped closer to Joe.

"There, you see this? I'm Robert Jessup, and I've been on the force fourteen years."

"Impressive," Joe responded. It had been a brutal day, and he couldn't stay on his feet much longer. "I'm going to go sit in the ambulance." He started in that direction, but wove slightly angling to the right.

The deputy caught his arm. "Lean on me, and I'll get you there. I see people all the time who want their friends treated first, when often they're the most badly hurt."

Joe stumbled along beside him and thanked him when he reached the back of the ambulance and could sit down. There were two narrow cots inside, and he definitely deserved one. "How is Tom?"

"When I last saw Mr. Green, he was at the hospital having a cast put on a broken arm. He was all bruised and scratched up, so nobody doubted he'd been in an accident. You ought to drive a jeep or truck when you come scouting locations, rather than a sedan meant for city streets."

"Excellent advice." Joe was now embarrassed he'd doubted the deputy's identity. Had Casper Green wanted them dead, he would have come himself or sent a goon like Corky Coyne. His head hurt so badly, it was no wonder he wasn't thinking clearly. Everything was muddled around the edges.

The medical technicians carried Brett to the ambulance, one entered first to pull the stretcher up inside, and they carefully shifted Brett to the cot. He had temporary splints on both legs, and he looked as white as the ambulance sheets.

One of the technicians turned his attention to Joe. "You don't look good. Are you in pain?"

"Only my head, but I'm awfully thirsty if you have some water."

"We do." He poured a cup from a Thermos and handed it to Joe.

He had to hold the cup with both hands, but got more to his mouth than in his lap. "Thank you. Now if I could just lay down."

The young man continued his exam as though Joe hadn't spoken. He placed a wet cloth over the tie headband to loosen it before pulling it free. "That's a big lump on the back of your head, and the gash above your brow will require stitches. It would be better if you sat up until we reached the hospital."

"Where are we?" Joe asked. "I'm all turned around, or I'm sure I'd know."

"We're near Lancaster. Did you start out from Palmdale?"

"I wasn't driving, and I really don't know." Joe recognized the names of the towns. They were northwest of Los Angeles, in the Antelope Valley in the western Mojave Desert. He had never been to either place.

"We didn't see any antelope," Joe continued. "Are there any out here?"

"Back when the first settlers arrived, there sure were. Supposed to have been deer and elk too, but most were gone by 1900. One still wanders by every once in awhile though."

"That's good." Lizard Valley was a better description now, but it lacked the necessary Western flavor to draw new residents.

Mary Margaret rested her hands on her hips, her expression fierce. "Is it impossible for you to stay out of trouble? Maybe I should consider marrying a man who shoots himself out of a cannon for a living."

"He'd be with the circus and travel so often you'd probably forget what he looked like between visits home."

"That might not be such a bad thing."

He loved her red curls, but he seldom saw her spitfire side. It was an awfully cute combination. Of course, she did have a point, since he got beat up rather often. "Did Detective Lynch come with you?"

"No, Lancaster is out of his jurisdiction, as you must know. Did you think he'd come along because he's so fond of you?"

"I could have grown on him. May we go home and make a date to argue tomorrow or the next day?"

She took hold of his chin and stared into his eyes. "Head injuries are serious, Joe. I'd leave you here a day or two, but then you'd have to take a bus to get home, and all that bouncing around wouldn't be good for you."

His head still hurt so badly he didn't need to be reminded, but she was a nurse, after all, and prone to giving medical advice. "Whatever you say, dear."

She kissed his cheek. "That's better. I love you."

"I love you, too." He had to cover a wide yawn. "Is it still Sunday?"

"Late Sunday, but there will be less traffic on the road if we leave now rather than wait until tomorrow morning."

He moved to ease himself off the bed, and she stopped him. "Wait, I'll call for an orderly to bring a wheelchair."

"I don't need a wheelchair."

"Do you want to ride home on the bus?"

He shook his head and instantly regretted it. "No, ma'am, I don't. So if you insist, I'll sit tight."

"I insist."

"Wait, what's happened to Brett Wayne?"

"He's in surgery. Do you want to wait until he comes out?"

"Not really." With two broken legs, Brett wasn't likely to ride for the border, so Joe felt justified in leaving him there. "And Tom Green?"

"He'd left by the time I arrived. Maybe his dad came to get him."

Joe thought Tom would have called a fellow Kappa Sigma brother rather than his murdering father. "I appreciate the fact he told the authorities Brett and I had been hurt. We'd still be sitting out in the desert otherwise."

"I'm not even tempted to throw him a party," she murmured and left to summon an orderly with a wheelchair.

Mary Margaret had found Joe's car keys under the floor mat and had driven his Chevy to Lancaster. Joe rode in the backseat on the way home. He tried to stay awake to keep her company, but drifted to sleep rather often. He was wide-awake when they reached his apartment building and wished he had a place on the first floor. Number three was available, but he'd marry Mary Margaret and move into her cottage too soon to merit a move now.

He liked having her arm around his waist, and didn't protest as they climbed the stairs to apartment six. "Will you make me breakfast now?" he asked. "I haven't eaten in more than a day."

"Let me check on what you have on hand before I make any promises."

"That isn't encouraging." He sat down in the easy chair in the living room rather than head to bed. He heard her rummaging through the refrigerator, and slamming cabinet doors.

She leaned out of the kitchen doorway. "There isn't anything here to prepare other than toast and coffee."

"That's fine, just make coffee and lots of toast."

She came in and leaned down to kiss him. "You need a good woman to take care of you."

"I'm lucky I found one." He kissed her back. He would have pulled her down across his lap, but the mere thought hurt. "There's jelly, isn't there?"

"Yes, both grape and raspberry. I'll make a variety of toast using them."

"Thanks."

She cut each slice of toast diagonally making two triangles. He usually ate the toast whole, but he thought it was wonderful all the same. He knew people argued about silly things like how a piece of toast or sandwich ought to be cut, but it was a waste of precious time in his view.

"Now that you've rested and had something to eat, tell me how you ended up in a car wreck in the desert. That's a bit much even for you." She'd made a couple of pieces of toast for herself, and covered them with raspberry jam.

Joe whittled the tale down to the facts and related them briefly. "I need to talk with Detective Lynch tomorrow."

"Let's hope he has enough evidence to arrest Casper

Green. However, if Casper killed Cookie, he'll go to prison, and it will undoubtedly be the end of your movie career."

He couldn't tell if she were teasing. "The whole point of pretending to be an actor, which seems redundant, was to solve her murder."

"I know, and I can't wait to see *Arizona Sunrise*. You'll have that screen credit at least. You look so serious, Joe. What are you thinking?"

"How nice it is to be sitting here with you," he responded. "Will you spend the night?"

"I'm tempted to stay and keep an eye on you. Do you want more toast?"

He almost shook his head before he remembered how badly it would hurt. "I'm fine. I'll take the couch, and give you the bed."

"No, absolutely not. You're the invalid and will take the bed." She stood and carried their empty plates into the kitchen. "It's late, and you need to get some sleep."

He was as tired as he had ever been. "Will you be here in the morning to make sure I wake up?"

"Yes, and I'm taking your car to work. You need to stay here and rest for several days before you go to the office."

Joe touched the bandage above his left brow. "I'll bet I don't look too good, and I wouldn't want to scare away new clients."

"There's also that to consider. Good-night, love." She kissed him, eased him out of his chair, and made certain he didn't walk into the wall on his way into the bedroom.

Mary Margaret went to the market early to stock Joe's refrigerator with orange juice, cold cuts, cheese, bacon, eggs, bread, milk, a box of corn flakes, and ginger ale. She put three cans of chicken noodle soup in the cupboard along with a box of Ritz crackers.

She made him a big breakfast, and then gathered up her things. "That should hold you until I come by after work."

Joe was still in his robe and drew her close for a warm,

fuzzy hug. "I'll be fine. I need to call Lynch, Gladys Swartz, and Leon Helms. Maybe I'll read some Sherlock Holmes stories in between, and take a nap. That should fill the day."

"If you have any trouble at all, if you become dizzy, or feel faint, call me at the hospital."

"Compared to how I felt yesterday stranded out in the desert, I'm doing real well. Go lavish your attention on your patients today."

She looked at him askance. "I mean it, Joe."

"I promise to behave." He kissed her good-bye, decided it was too early to make any calls, and pulled the Complete Works of Sherlock Holmes from the bookcase. He sat down to read, began to yawn, and would have fallen asleep, had someone not knocked on his door. He struggled to his feet, and pulled his door open only two inches to peer out.

"Leon, I'd invite you in, but I'm not dressed. I do have good news to report. Brett Wayne was at Casper Green's when Cookie died, and said Casper killed her. Gladys will confirm the details, but the charges against Stuart should be dropped soon."

"Really? When no one could find you Saturday, I feared the worse. Stuart has been to the Green's home, but he never said anything about Tom's father. Why would he kill Cookie?"

Joe rested against the door. "Apparently she slept with Tom, but didn't care to sleep with Casper. It will take a while for the whole story to shake out, but it's clear Stuart wasn't involved. Now I had a rough couple of days, and need to rest."

Leon backed away. "Sorry to have bothered you. I just wanted to make certain you were all right. Oh, yes, there's one other thing. I haven't worn these pants in a while, and I found the key to apartment three in the pocket." He pulled it out to show Joe. "The key just came off the ring, and that solves one mystery at least."

"It does. Thank you for checking on me." Joe closed the door as Leon started down the stairs. No need to call him now. It was after nine, and he poured himself a glass of ginger ale before searching through his small notebook for Detective Lynch's telephone number. He sat down, and had just reached for the phone when it rang.

Startled, he let it ring twice, and barely caught himself before answering with Discreet Investigations. "Hello."

"This is Jacob Lynch. I need some answers about your lost weekend. I tried your office first. I'll be at your home in ten minutes. Stay put."

"Yes, sir." Joe looked down at his robe. It was comfortably worn red plaid flannel, and not something he cared to wear while verbally sparing with Detective Lynch. He took several fortifying sips of ginger ale before searching his closet for something comfortable to wear. He pulled on khaki pants, and a dress shirt, and with his slippers considered himself well enough dressed to meet with Lynch.

The detective burst into Joe's apartment the instant the door opened. His suit was a subtle gray plaid. His shirt nearly glowed it was so white, and his vivid maroon silk tie was held in place by a gold clip engraved with his initials. Joe was even more convinced his wife dressed him.

Lynch dismissed the minimally furnished apartment with a quick glance. "Saturday afternoon, Gladys Swartz called me and swore something dreadful must have happened to you. I thought you were probably in some dimly lit bar at the beach."

"Well, there is a lot of sand in the Antelope Valley," Joe replied. "I need to sit down, help yourself to the sofa." He returned to the comforting warmth of his chair, and reached for his glass. "I'm serving ginger ale today. Would you care for some?"

"No." Lynch unbuttoned his jacket and sat down. His leather-covered notebook looked new, and he shuffled through a few pages to find a new one. "Tell me how you managed to disappear, and then reappear so quickly."

"Did Mrs. Swartz tell you I'd come home?"

"She did, which I appreciate, but we don't consider

anyone missing after only a few hours. She did point us to Brett Wayne, who also conveniently disappeared. He's in a hospital in Lancaster with two broken legs. Are you taking credit for that?"

"No, certainly not." Joe drew in a deep breath, began with Lily Montell being assaulted by Casper Green, and told the story with more detail than he'd given Mary Margaret. "I think Brett and Tom meant to kill me, or they at least hoped I'd die of exposure before I found a way out of the desert. Even if Brett wasn't a witness to Cookie's murder, he was in Casper's house, heard him confess, and then hid the body for him."

"None of which you can prove," Lynch responded with his usual aloof distain.

"Proof is your department," Joe countered. "The bruises on Lily Montell's arms should match those on Cookie Crumble's, and tie her murder to Casper Green. Have you picked him up? He might be so frightened to learn I've gotten out of the desert alive that he'll be eager to talk."

"I spoke with Mr. Green on Saturday, when looking for you was a good excuse. He was horrified to learn you were missing."

"I introduced myself to him as an actor looking for work, not as a private investigator. Cookie's brother and I had minor parts in *Arizona Sunrise*, his latest Western. Why would he give a fig about me?"

Lynch flipped back a page in his notebook. "He told me you were a good friend of Brett Wayne, and that he strongly suspected Brett had killed Cookie, and you had helped him hide her body."

Joe thought of an appropriately inventive string of scalding obscenities but simply savored them in his mind. "Casper's son, Tom, had taken Cookie to his home in Beverly Hills the day she died. He knows his dad killed her, and he's the one who helped Brett hide her body."

"I spoke with Brett Wayne on the telephone," Lynch offered. "He's a writer, remember, and earns his living telling tales. When you two were stranded in the desert, didn't it occur to you that he might not be telling the truth?"

"No, he was in too much pain to lie. Have you questioned Tom? Both he and Brett are guilty of kidnapping me, and I've got the lump on the back of my head to prove it. We all could have died in the accident, and our bodies wouldn't have been found for weeks."

"Tom," Lynch replied, "backs his father's story. It seems he brought Cookie home to swim on more than one occasion. The day she died, Brett offered to give her a ride home. Tom swears she was alive and well when he and his father last saw her."

"That makes no sense," Joe responded. "If Tom had nothing to do with the murder, why would be help Brett kidnap me?"

"He said he thought it was a practical joke."

Joe couldn't comb his hair without hurting himself, and it stuck up like black feathers. There was a square bandage above his left brow, and the whole side of his face was bruised. He was too weak to leave his apartment, and Tom's comment was the last straw.

"Do I look as though I were involved in a practical joke? With two broken legs, Brett Wayne doesn't either."

Lynch spoke slowly to make his point. "The three of you were in a car wreck, Mr. Ezell. Your injuries could have stemmed from that."

"Let's see," Joe recounted. "Casper Green roughed up Lily Montell when she refused to sleep with him. That could well have been his pattern. She was luckier than Cookie Crumble and got away. She telephoned me, and I called Gladys Swartz because she's representing Stuart Helms, who has no idea what happened to Cookie. I told Mrs. Swartz I intended to speak with Brett, and would get right back to her. That's when I 'disappeared'.

"Brett and Tom can't possibly be friends, so why would he call the kid to help him play a practical joke on me? I was out cold when they put me in the trunk of Brett's car. That doesn't sound like a practical joke either. Tom hasn't impressed me as being too dim to notice something so obvious as an unconscious man. He helped Brett because his father told him he had to."

Lynch nodded. "Maybe. Mrs. Swartz should have a field day with that account when Stuart Helms comes to trial. It might even create sufficient reasonable doubt for a not guilty verdict." He stood and turned toward the door. "Stick with cases involving philandering husbands, where you won't overstep your talents."

Joe was too angry to tell him to get out before he had gone. He gave himself a few minutes to calm down before calling Gladys Swartz. She was equally upset by Lynch's failure to believe Joe's account of how Cookie had died.

"Right after you left us on Saturday, Bernice, or Lily Montell, reported Casper Green's assault. An officer came to her place to take the report, but he wouldn't have been from homicide where Lynch works. Casper should have been picked up for questioning by now. I'll make a quick call and see what's happening there."

"Thanks, Gladys. There have to be other girls who were too worried about their film careers to report Casper, and I'll bet he's pressured a great many to sleep with him."

Joe hung up and when he thought of how often MGM turned out a film, and how many Casper Green had directed, he knew he had his work cut out for him. However, all he had to do was find one young woman who'd tell the truth about Casper Green and Detective Lynch would have to listen.

CHAPTER 16

By the time Mary Margaret came by that evening with the groceries to prepare spaghetti for dinner, Joe was nearly beside himself. He related his conversation with Detective Lynch. "I didn't believe it was possible to dislike him more than I already did, but he's reached a whole new level on the abomination scale. Gladys called to let me know the police questioned and released Casper Green without charging him. I doubt they will investigate Lilly Montell's report of an assault any further."

"That's distressing. Do you feel well enough to put the pot of water on the stove?" Not knowing what Joe might own, she'd brought her own cooking gear and utensils.

He wasn't ready to let go of Detective Lynch's endless shortcomings. "Sure I do, and Lynch should land in very hot water when the truth is readily known." He filled the pot with water, and griped the handles tightly to give it a practice lift before he turned to the stove. Refusing to appear weak in front of his beloved, he drew in a deep breath, and carried the pot the three steps to the stove.

"Thank you. I like cooking with you, but I don't want to tire you," she said.

"I've rested all day. You can trust me with the car tomorrow."

"Let's see how you feel in the morning."

Joe spun her around and kissed her so soundly she had to hang onto him. "My goodness, but that was convincing," she claimed through a sparkling giggle.

He laughed. "It was meant to be."

Joe drove Mary Margaret to work the next morning with the assurance he'd sit quietly in his office all day. As soon as he'd dropped her off, he began the nearly two hour drive to Lancaster. He drove north through the Simi Valley and then angled west to pass through the Angeles National Forest and the San Gabriel Mountains. When he arrived, he was disappointed not to find Brett Wayne handcuffed to his bed.

"Didn't expect you to come for a visit," Brett murmured. He reached for his glass of water and took a long drink. Both legs were in casts with traction pinning him to the bed like an overturned turtle. "The service here leaves a great deal to be desired, but it's far better than what we encountered in the desert."

Joe pulled up a chair. He'd smoothed his hair down with water, and his bruises were fading. He'd put a fresh band-aid over the stitches above his left brow and didn't think he looked too bad. "I had a good reason for coming. Have the Lancaster police questioned you?"

"No, and I haven't seen any of the sheriff's deputies since the desert. You complained so loudly about being kidnapped, haven't you reported it?"

Joe had expected to be questioned before he checked out of the hospital, but no one had come to interview him. His head was beginning to ache just thinking about it. He had reported the crime to Detective Lynch, however.

"That's not why I'm here. Casper Green is accusing you of murdering Cookie Crumble." He provided the director's account as Lynch had put it.

"What?" Shocked, Brett's glass slipped from his hand and shattered as it hit the pale green linoleum tile. "He's not going to get away with it."

"You did hide her body."

"Only because he forced me to," Brett swore.

"I have the telephone number of one of the extras on *Arizona Sunrise*. She might know of other young women who've had trouble with Casper. Maybe it's well-known among the actresses who star in his films. Cookie was a stripper, and maybe none of the girls knew she was involved with Casper. If I point it out, they might come forward to testify."

"They wouldn't risk their careers," Brett argued. "Hollywood is flooded with beautiful girls, and a few actually have some talent. The stories about the casting room couch are true."

Joe sat back in his chair. That he'd reported the kidnapping to Lynch would be enough to figure into Cookie's murder. He had been kidnapped in Los Angeles, after all. He'd just ended up in the Antelope Valley. Tiring faster than he'd hoped after the long drive, he stood slowly.

"I need to get back to my office." He handed Brett one of his cards. "Call me if you think of anything else that will reveal how Casper Green typically abuses women."

"Look up who starred in his films, that would be a good place to begin. Victoria Ray starred in *Arizona Sunrise*. She has a firm foothold in Hollywood, and might talk with you if you ask her nicely. You could give her my name."

"Thanks, I will."

"Why are you trusting me rather than Casper?"

"The bruises on Cookie's arm matched those on Lily's. That's evidence enough for me."

"I'm sick over Cookie's death. I hope you realize that."

"Sure, we're all sick over it. Before I go, do you have the Thorntons' keys?"

"No, they left in such a hurry, they apparently forgot to leave them. I saw they hadn't locked the door behind them, and I went in to look around. The empty apartment prompted so many story ideas I hurried back to my place to work on them. I just closed the door when I left, but couldn't lock it without the key."

"It didn't occur to you to tell Leon that the Thorntons had moved out?"

"No, I thought they would have told him." He covered a wide yawn. "Did you ever see Cookie's act?"

"No. Sorry, I missed it."

"I must have seen her a dozen times and each one was different. She would have been a great actress if she'd had the chance. Everything about this awful mess is so unfair. Westerns appeal to people because the good guys always triumph. Unfortunately, real life doesn't work that way."

"Depends on where you're standing," Joe replied. He stopped for a hamburger and large soda before leaving Lancaster. As he left town, he realized he'd not asked Brett about Corky Coyne, but he wasn't going back. It was a shame Corky hadn't been with Cookie on her last day alive. Everything would have ended differently, and Casper might have turned up floating face down in the pool.

Joe managed the return trip to Los Angeles without incident. Fortified with a large soda from the fountain in the drug store downstairs, he spent the remainder of the day in his office, dozing with his feet propped on his desk. If CC came by, he didn't wake him.

When he picked up Mary Margaret after work, he asked about her day so he'd not have to lie to her about his own. She deserved the truth, of course, but not after the fact when it would only worry her. They ate leftover spaghetti at his place, played a few games of Cribbage, and he took her home in plenty of time for them both to get a good night's rest.

Wednesday morning, Joe could barely get out of bed, ample proof he'd overdone it the day before. Moving slowly, he showered, dressed, ate some toast with strawberry jelly and got to the office without collapsing.

He'd kept Pamela Smyth's number when she'd told him about the wrap party at Casper Green's and waited until after 10:00 o'clock to call her. "Good morning, this is Joe Ezell, and I'm still working on Cookie Crumble's murder. I wonder if you've heard anything about the way Casper Green treats starlets."

"Other than badly, no," she responded. "But he's no worse than many of the other directors. I'll not mention any names, but one loves to put his hands all over girls, and then swears he's only tickling them when they complain."

Joe took notes as fast as he could write them. "I'm sorry to hear that, but right now, I'm only interested in Casper. Did he ever invite you to his house to read for a part?"

"No, I've just gone to his office on the MGM lot. Maybe he isn't all that found of redheads, although I'm included in the invitations to his parties. What did you think of the one you snuck into?"

"It was a great party," he replied. "Casper's son Tom was there. Do you know him?"

"Do I ever." She began to laugh. "He's cute, and knows how to treat a lady, not that I'd include myself in that refined category, you understand."

"You shouldn't think so little of yourself," he scolded softly. "Do you have Victoria Ray's telephone number? She wasn't on the set the days we shot the saloon fight, but she's done several Westerns with Casper. I'd like to ask her a few questions."

"Sure, I've got her number here somewhere. Give me a minute to find it."

"Take all the time you need." Joe rested the telephone receiver against his cheek. When she came back, he wrote down the number and thanked her.

"Maybe we'll work on another film together," she replied.

"You can never tell," Joe responded, but as far as he was concerned, his film career was over.

He placed a call to Victoria, but no one answered. Perhaps she was at MGM shooting a picture.

His next call came from Neal Sloan. "Phillip is going up to San Francisco tomorrow. I'll make the reservation for your train ticket and hotel. I'll cover all your fees and expenses. I've traveled on the Coast Starlight, and it's a gorgeous trip along the Pacific Ocean through Santa Barbara and on up to San Francisco. Your only chore will be to keep Phillip from seeing you. He stays at the Mark Hopkins, but it's a large hotel, and you can avoid him there. Our new building is also on California Street, so you can use cable cars there and back to the hotel. If Phillip is spending his time elsewhere, it doesn't matter if he goes to museums, or the movies. All I want to know is whether or not he has an additional project. It should only take you Friday and Saturday to discover if it's true, and you can come home on Sunday. What do you say?"

It took the whole day to reach San Francisco, and Joe looked forward to viewing the coast and snoozing the whole way. With his hat pulled low and the collar of his overcoat turned up, Phillip wouldn't recognize him unless he walked up and shook the architect's hand.

"I can clear my schedule," Joe offered agreeably. They went over his out-of-town rate, and he asked for fifty dollars in cash to cover initial expenses.

"I'll messenger the cash to your office, and details of our project in San Francisco. Your ticket will be at Union Station. I hate to think of what you might discover, but under no circumstance is Phillip to suspect you're working for Finegold and me."

"If we should cross paths, I'll convince him I'm searching for a little old lady's lost grandson. I can bore him to tears in a few minutes, and he'll forget me as soon as I'm out of sight."

"Good. I'll expect your report next week."

"Give me Monday to type up my notes, and I'll talk to you on Tuesday." Joe could use a few days out of town, and he'd earn enough to take Mary Margaret to San Francisco for their honeymoon, if she wanted to go there, of course. No bride should be stuck on a honeymoon somewhere she didn't wish to go.

Mary Margaret didn't view the trip with Joe's enthusiasm. "Can't you postpone the job for a week or two when you'll be feeling better?"

"No, I have to go when Phillip Fitzgerald is traveling.

This will be such an easy job, sweetheart. San Francisco is a civilized city, and you needn't worry I'll hang around the docks after dark."

"Promise?"

"I promise." He meant it too. "I called Leon Helms so he'll know I'm out of town. I also let Gladys Swartz know I'll be away, and will get back on Stuart's case next Monday."

"I always think of it as Cookie Crumble's case," she responded. "Maybe a couple of days away will be a good distraction for you."

"It should be, and I've leads to follow up on next week." He pulled her close. "I'm going to miss you."

She relaxed into his arms. "Show me how much when you come home."

"I'll look forward to it." He thought a sample might be nice, and covered her face with teasing kisses.

Thursday morning, the Coast Starlight pulled out of Union Station early. Joe found a window seat where he could appreciate the incredible seaside view once they had left Los Angeles proper. He expected Phillip Fitzgerald to find a place in the lounge car where he could sketch, or read, or whatever else the man might wish to do. He'd follow him once they reached San Francisco, but there was no need to trail him on the train.

A pretty young woman in a fur coat sat down beside him. "Please, pretend we're traveling together."

She had puffy pink lips as though she spent hours each day whistling. "Why would I do that?" Joe asked.

"There's a man following me, and I'm avoiding his company," she whispered.

"So you're risking mine?" While his bruises had begun to fade, he still had a Band-Aid over the stitches above his brow, and thought any sensible woman would take one look at him and find another seat.

Her eyes widened slightly as she studied him more closely. "You try anything funny, and I'll call the conductor."

Joe turned to observe the other passengers in their car. There were several men, a family with small children, and two other women traveling alone. "Why not sit with one of the women?"

"I wouldn't wish the creep on anyone else."

"Which man is he?"

"He was in the last car. Maybe he got the hint when I came forward a car."

He handed her his card. "This sounds like a job to me, and I don't come cheap."

"You're a detective?" She handed back the card, called him a most uncomplimentary name, and moved across the aisle to sit beside a young man who welcomed her with a broad smile.

Joe leaned back and closed his eyes. He bet when they reached San Francisco she'd claim to be a little short, and beg to borrow money to cover a taxicab, and hotel. The poor chap would naively come to her rescue. She might then need train fare to Seattle. It would go on and on until she'd taken the sucker for all he was worth. The man had to learn for himself though, so Joe kept his thoughts to himself.

He'd once been easily impressed by a pretty woman. Patty had seemed so damn sincere that most young men would have fallen for her scheme. They'd gone out a few times before she asked for help paying her bills. It hadn't been much, and he'd been glad to pitch in. The next month she claimed she'd used most of her paycheck to cover her mother's medical expenses, and needed help with her rent. Alarm bells went off in his mind with a loud clang. He'd offered to help her go over her income and expenses to discover a way to save for future emergencies.

She'd responded to his sensible offer with such furious anger he'd walked out on her and never looked back. After December 7, 1941, war had been declared, and Los Angeles had been flooded with soldiers and sailors on their way to the Pacific. He bet Patty had had dozens sending her part of their pay every month, and he pitied any man she might have married.

When Mary Margaret had hired him to discover whether or not her boyfriend was faithful, she'd been so cute he had liked her immediately. She was also as level-headed as he was, and when he found her sweetheart had more girls than had toured with the USO, she dropped the man without a blink. While it wasn't usually part of his services, he'd offered amusing comfort, and asked her out before she left his office. It had been the beginning of a beautiful friendship. He grinned and concentrated on the spectacular scenery for the remainder of the trip.

When the Coast Starlight train arrived in San Francisco that evening, Phillip Fitzgerald hailed a taxicab to ride to the Mark Hopkins Hotel. Joe carried his small valise and hopped on a cable car to the Nob Hill hotel. He strode through the three-arched entryway and up to the impressive mahogany registration desk. They had his reservation, and as he signed in, he looked up.

"I have a meeting with Phillip Fitzgerald scheduled for the morning. Has he already checked in?"

"Yes, he has, Mr. Ezell, about fifteen minutes ago."

"Great, thank you." He didn't need a bellhop to carry his bag and made his way up to his fifth floor room on his own. The elegantly furnished room had twin-sized beds, and the tall windows provided a stunning view of the bay. The hotel had suites costing five times what his room did, but he doubted any offered a better view.

He unpacked what little he had brought, a couple of fresh shirts, underwear, socks, and a second pair of pants. He'd also included a copy of Mickey Spillane's detective novel, *I, the Jury.* He ordered a steak dinner from room service, kicked off his shoes and sat down on the bed. With his back propped on pillows against the headboard he had a comfortable pose to read. Immediately caught up private detective Mike Hammer's quest to punish the man who'd killed his best friend, the waiter from room service had to knock twice to get his attention.

* * *

Friday morning, Joe awoke at 7:00 a.m. His goal was to leave the hotel and find a place to observe the Fitzgerald, Finegold and Sloan building before Phillip arrived. There was a café conveniently located across the street from the project. He entered, took a table by the front window, and ordered a breakfast of bacon and eggs. He'd bought a copy if the *San Francisco Chronicle* and opened it to form a screen while he waited for Phillip to appear.

He had just finished the last bite of his hash-browns when Phillip Fitzgerald arrived in a taxicab. The architect entered the gate in the chain link fence surrounding the lot, and was met by a burly man who appeared to be the construction foreman. An illustrated sign out front advertised the coming structure as the future home of professional offices and exclusive shops. With handsome modern lines and the planned landscaping, it would be an appealing addition to the city. Men were installing windows on the six-story building.

"More coffee, hon?" his waitress asked.

"Yes, thank you." Joe kept his attention on the two men as they walked along the front of the new building. The foreman waved his arms in sweeping gestures, and Phillip nodded as though he were pleased with the progress being made.

Joe paid his bill and left the café. He strolled down the street and stopped often to observe the construction site. He was surprised when Phillip soon came back through the gate, and walked in the opposite direction of their hotel. Joe followed him from across the street, and Phillip didn't once glance over his shoulder, so clearly he wasn't worried about being followed.

Three blocks from his professional project, he turned into a magnificent stone church that looked as though it could have survived the 1906 earthquake that destroyed much of San Francisco. Joe took out his notebook to note the time, and jotted down the address of St. Edmund's Episcopal church. Phillip hadn't impressed him as a man who would lose himself in prayer, and when he didn't soon reappear,

Joe risked mounting the steps, and pulled open one of the tall front doors.

He found a beautiful sanctuary with vibrant stained glass windows and a colorful altarpiece of Saint Edmund that could have come from Europe. The pews were empty, and it was eerily quiet, but the sound of hammering could be heard in the distance. He went back outside and circled the church. A stonewall enclosed the courtyard but he was tall enough to peek over.

A small construction crew was working on a one story wooden building that looked as though it were intended for Sunday school classrooms. Phillip had removed his jacket and shirt to work beside a man framing a door.

Joe walked back to the sidewalk. If Phillip were volunteering his time to design and build a Sunday school, why wouldn't he have told his partners? Was it so unlike him to do a good deed that no one would have believed him?

A woman parked her Chevrolet at the curb and opened the trunk to remove two flower-filled buckets. "Could you help me take these inside?" she called to him.

"Certainly."

"I like having the altar flowers here well before Sunday morning."

"The chrysanthemums are especially colorful this year," Joe exclaimed. She'd brought yellow, bronze, and orange with springs of green lemon leaf foliage. "How long have you arranged the bouquets for the church?"

She was a slim, gray-haired woman who walked with a spritely step. "Let me think, it's been either eight years or nine. I enjoy it, and not everyone wants to accept the responsibility."

"I know exactly what you mean," he sympathized. He pulled open a heavy front door for her.

"Thank you." She strode up the center aisle ahead of him. "I don't believe I've seen you here before. Are you working on the new Sunday school building?"

"I'm visiting from Los Angeles, so I doubt I'll have the

time. Tell me about it." He followed her up on the chancel and placed his bucket beside hers.

"The old building was dark and drafty, not a welcoming place for children. We were lucky Phillip Fitzgerald had a project being built nearby. Are you familiar with his work?"

"I've heard his name."

"He's the best of the young California architects, and when one of the vestry approached him about donating plans, he said he would. Whenever he's in town, he comes by to join in the construction. He's certainly not a talker, but he's been so generous with his time and talent, I don't criticize his lack of charm. Now I can take everything from here. Will you be attending church on Sunday?"

"If I'm in town," Joe responded, and he left before she's thought to ask his name.

Phillip had looked as though he planned to remain there for the day, and Joe saw no reason to stay close and watch for him to leave.

San Francisco was such a colorful city, and now he had a couple of hours to ride the cable cars and explore. It was a great opportunity to find a nice hotel he could afford for a honeymoon, and line up places to take Mary Margaret. Inspired, he whistled as he walked away thinking he'd begin with Fisherman's Wharf for lunch. He'd missed the sea since leaving the Coast Guard, and the San Francisco Bay was a wonderful place to visit.

Three hours later, Joe swung by Saint Edmund's again and nearly ran into Phillip as he was leaving. He ducked into a small grocery store, bought a pack of gum, and watched the architect walk by. Trailing Phillip to the hotel was easy, and he waited in the lobby ready to follow Phillip should he again leave. The desk had a variety of brochures on places to visit and tours, and he read them all while he waited.

San Francisco had so many fine restaurants, he was surprised when Phillip left the elevator and crossed the lobby for the hotel's dining room. He'd changed his clothes, and his dark hair still looked wet from the shower. Joe waited fifteen minutes before he entered the dining room. Phillip was seated alone, and didn't appear to be waiting for anyone to join him.

"May I help you, sir?" the maître d' asked.

"Thanks, just checking for a friend, and I don't see him."

He left and took the elevator to the Top of the Mark on the nineteenth floor, a bar and restaurant with a spectacular 360 degree view of the city. Drinks tasted better there, he was sure. He savored a scotch and soda and could have sat there all night enjoying the city lights in the distance, but he did have a job to continue tomorrow. When his stomach began to rumble, rather than stay to eat, he returned to his room to order another steak from room service.

He sat at the desk to expand on his notes while they were fresh in his mind. Other than volunteering at Saint Edmund's, Phillip hadn't surprised him, and he wondered if tomorrow would be a repeat of today. If so, Neal Sloan and his partner had nothing to worry about where Phillip Fitzgerald was concerned.

He'd bought a postcard for Mary Margaret on Fisherman's Wharf. It wouldn't arrive before he returned home, but she'd love it anyway. He took care to write how much he missed her. After he ate dinner, he read more of *I, the Jury*, and called it a night.

Saturday morning, Joe stopped at the desk to buy a stamp for the postcard. He licked it, slapped it on the card and handed it to the desk clerk to mail. As he turned away, he came face to face with Phillip Fitzgerald. His heart dropped to his shoes, but he smiled as though he were happy to see him.

"Good morning," Joe greeted him.

Phillip frowned, which appeared to be his favorite expression. "What are you doing here?"

"It's a very fine hotel," Joe replied, deliberately misinterpreting his question.

"No, what are you doing in San Francisco?" He took a step away from the desk, and Joe followed him.

"I'm here on a job. A sweet little old lady from Pasadena lost track of her grandson, and I came to find him. I got a lead from a friend at his last address and spoke with him yesterday. He was thrilled to hear from his grandmother. People have moved around so much since the end of the war, it's no wonder family members have difficulty staying in touch. Now why are you in San Francisco?"

"We have a building under construction not far from here. Have you had breakfast?"

"No, I haven't. Can you recommend someplace good?"

"Let's eat here." Phillip gestured toward the dining room where he'd had dinner the previous evening.

"Fine." Joe had never had anyone he'd been trailing invite him to share a meal, but he was game for it.

Once seated, Phillip spent a few minutes viewing the menu before slapping it down on the table. "You must think me an arrogant ass."

Joe couldn't help but laugh. "I don't become involved in my clients' lives, and I've made no assumptions whatsoever."

Phillip looked away. "I doubt it. My parents, and they are my parents, are elderly, and they needn't be forced to explain how I became their son. As for Fred, I wish him well, but I'm content with my life as it is."

"Merely content?" Joe asked. "You're successful and have a nice family. Shouldn't you be happy with your life?"

"Let's not quibble over terms," Phillip responded. "I'll not argue that I've been luckier than most men, but I've also worked hard to be a success. It's enough. Let's leave it at that." He focused on the bandage on Joe's forehead. "What happened to you, were you in a fight?"

Joe touched the fresh Band-Aid he'd applied that morning. "I was kidnapped and abandoned in the desert, but it only set me back a couple of days."

"You're kidding." The architect looked decidedly skeptical.

"It's the truth." Joe raised his hand. "I'm working on the Cookie Crumble murder, and got too close to the man who killed her."

"And now you're tracing missing grandsons?"

It was a good story, and Joe stuck with it. "I like variety in my work. I'm not going back to LA until tomorrow, is there any place I ought to see while I'm here?"

"Take one of the tours the hotel offers. They'll show you the sights and give you the city's history."

Joe could have gotten that advice at the desk. Phillip Fitzgerald was one of the coldest individuals he'd ever met. He appeared to be devoted to his work, and his concern for his parents was touching, even if he hadn't displayed any pride in his own family.

"Thanks, I will. I'm getting married at Christmastime, and I'd like to bring my bride here for our honeymoon."

"Lots of people vacation here over the holidays. Better make your reservations now."

"I'll do that." He gave up on drawing Phillip into a meaningful conversation and enjoyed bacon and eggs with a side of pancakes while they sat in a somewhat companionable silence. Each charged his breakfast to his room.

As he rose from the table, Phillip paused. "I've never been considered friendly. Don't take it as anything personal."

"All right, I won't." Fred Cooper had already drawn that regrettable conclusion, and Joe wouldn't waste his breath attempting to convince Phillip having a twin brother was well-worth changing his long standing solitary habits.

Mary Margaret met Joe's train when it pulled into Union Station on Sunday night. Opened in 1939, it was an unusual mixture of Mission Revival architecture enlivened with Art Deco elements. With high vaulted ceilings, the building welcomed travelers to Los Angeles with a view to the past as well as the future.

"I love this place, and you," she exclaimed. "So many of

the movies filmed during the war had soldiers passing through here and kissing their girlfriends good-bye. It's a wonderfully romantic place, don't you think?"

"Only if I'm with you," he insisted, and he hugged her tight. With his many cuts and bruises, he did look like a war veteran, and he was elated she didn't mind at all.

CHAPTER 17

Monday morning Joe typed his notes for Neal Sloan, and while he'd only confirmed the work Phillip Fitzgerald had been expected to do, he felt he'd earned his pay.

He hung his bulletin board on the wall and sat back to study it. He really wanted to speak with Tom Green, even if the college student was unlikely to name his father as a murderer. He needed to touch base with Gladys Swartz as well.

Interrupted by the telephone, he answered without hoping for a new client. "Discreet Investigations."

"This is Archibald Kimble. Is Joe Ezell there?"

"Speaking." Joe had been too busy to remember he'd signed a six-month contract with the agent.

"I've got work lined up for you. When can you come by the office?"

"How's Friday?" Joe replied. He had too much on his plate to deal with Kimble any earlier, but another couple of days filming would be a welcome break. "Casper Green won't hire me again though."

"He's not the only director filming in this town. You told me you could ride a horse. Can you?"

"Sure, and I can stay in the saddle too."

"Roy Rogers is casting his next film for Republic

Pictures, *Under California Stars.* He's looking for men that fans haven't seen a dozen times in his Westerns."

Joe covered the telephone so the agent wouldn't hear him laugh. "We'll then, I qualify."

"Be here early Friday morning."

"Will do." Joe hadn't ridden a horse since he was a kid, but he thought it must be like riding a bicycle and once you'd learned how, you wouldn't forget.

He made a pot of coffee, enjoyed a cup, and then called Gladys. "I hope you have good news," he greeted her.

She sighed. "You're not going to believe this."

"That doesn't sound good."

"It isn't," she explained. "Casper Green claims Bernice, or Lily, attacked him, and he manhandled her to keep her from stabbing him with a pair of scissors. He claims she'd read for a part, but wasn't accomplished enough to hire. When he told her so, he says she went berserk. He sent her home in a cab and didn't report the assault because he didn't want to make trouble for her."

"Snake," Joe responded. He hadn't tracked down the taxi driver who had driven Lily to Casper's, but with Casper admitting she had been at his home, there was no need.

"Snakes have more character than he has. There are no witnesses to what happened at Casper's, so it's a wash, and the DA won't consider prosecuting either allegation."

"I want to talk with Tom Green. He's claiming Cookie was alive when she left his home with Brett Wayne, but I'll bet her body was already cold. I also want to talk with Victoria Ray, who's starred in several of Casper's films. If Casper has pressured her to sleep with him to be hired, she might say so under oath."

"She might not," Gladys mused. "You'll need to find as many actresses as you possibly can who've had a similar experience to give substance to Bernice's story."

"I'm on it," Joe promised.

He dialed Victoria, and this time found her at home. She listened as he explained why he needed to talk with her. "Can we meet somewhere?" he asked.

"Frenchie's is a bar not too far from where I live." She gave him the address. "I'll meet you there at 5 o'clock tonight. I'll wear sunglasses and a scarf, so don't expect to recognize me from my movies. Sit at a table in the back, and I'll come to you."

"Got it. I'll see you then."

With plenty of time on his hands, Joe drove over to USC, and parked across from the Kappa Sigma fraternity house on Twenty Eighth Street. He doubted he'd see Tom Green coming or going from class, and preferred a more direct approach. He went up to the front door and knocked.

A young man answered and looked surprised to find a stranger on the doorstep. "May I help you, sir?"

"Yes, I have a prize certificate for Tom Green. It's worth quite a bit of money and I need to place it in his hand."

"Tom Green?" he repeated. He pushed his glasses up his nose, and peered at Joe more closely.

"Yes, it's a common name, do you have two here?"

"No, only one, but he was in a car accident, and is recuperating at home."

"I'm so sorry to hear that. Please don't tell him I was here. We want the certificate to be a surprise when he receives it."

"All right, I guess I could do that."

"Thank you."

As Joe walked back to his car, he debated driving to Casper Green's home, but if the director were there, he wouldn't let him speak to Tom. Then again, Casper might not be home. He stopped at the closest gas station to use the pay telephone. He still had the information for the MGM lot in his notebook, and put a call through to the gate.

"Good morning. I'm calling from the *Los Angeles Times*. We want to interview Casper Green. Is he shooting a film there today?"

"Yes, he's on the lot. Do you want to leave a message?"

"No, thank you. I'll catch him later."

* * *

Joe drove into Beverly Hills, and made his way to Casper Green's home. He parked on the street as he had the night of the party and took the path around the garage to the patio. Just as he'd thought he might be, Tom was asleep in a chaise beside the pool. He was dressed in shorts and a knit shirt, his left arm in a sling.

After quietly pulling up a patio chair, Joe tapped Tom's leg. When Tom sat up with a startled gasp, he was quick to reassure him. "I came to thank you for alerting the Sheriff's Dept. to the accident in the desert."

Tom looked ready to run, but he couldn't escape the determined detective. "I wouldn't have left you out there for the buzzards."

"Your generosity of spirit is most inspiring. You knew you weren't involved in a practical joke when you and Brett Wayne shoved me in his car trunk and drove me out to the desert. Did you really expect the police to believe that tale?"

"They did believe it!"

"Oh, really? Are you sure they aren't letting you think so while the DA gathers evidence against you?"

Tom had a glass of water on the small table beside him. He reached for it, and took a long drink. "They didn't arrest me."

"That doesn't mean they won't," Joe cautioned. "How far will you go to protect your father? Will it merely extend to perjury in court, or are you willing to spend the rest of your life in prison for him?"

Tom leaned forward. "I don't have to listen to you. Get out of here."

Joe stood and swung his chair aside. "It's a lot to think about, isn't it? First your father told you to get rid of Cookie's body, and then to get rid of me. What's going to be next, son? Think you'll look good in stripes?"

He walked away before Tom could voice a frustrated moan, but he'd planted the necessary seeds to frighten him into wondering about his own loyalties and his father's.

* * *

Joe walked into Frenchie's at ten to the hour, ordered a beer and carried it to one of the two tables near the rear exit. He took Mary Margaret to the movies so often, he thought they must have seen Victoria in something, but when she slid into the seat across from him, she didn't look familiar. She had startling blue eyes and dark curly hair only partially tamed by her blue scarf.

"Tell me your name," she began. Her voice had a low, husky depth.

He handed her his card. "Joe Ezell. That's a smart move, make whomever you're meeting say his name first. Otherwise, you might spend the whole night talking with someone who claims to be the person you'd hoped to meet."

"Care to ask how I learned such a valuable trick?"

She was a beautiful girl with smooth, creamy skin and a lively, intelligent gaze. "Clearly it's a mistake you didn't make twice."

The bartender brought her a Shirley Temple, a ginger ale with grenadine syrup and a maraschino cherry. "No, I didn't." She pulled a small notebook from her purse. "Casper Green is a competent director, but he expects more than a performance on screen. He's not nearly as repulsive as some of the other directors in town, so I went along with his amorous demands, but only to get screen credits."

"Was he rough with you?"

"No, but I didn't put up any resistance. That sounds as though I lack any sort of moral standard, I'm afraid, but I considered sex with him the cost of getting work."

"I believe he killed Cookie Crumble, and he may have come close to killing a stripper from Sherry's. Do you know of any young women he might have forced to sleep with him?"

She tore a sheet from her notebook and gave it to him. She ran a red tipped nail down the first four names on the list. "I've heard each of them complain he made it clear what he wanted in exchange for a role in one of his films. None of them was eager to go along, but they might have, so you should talk with them.

"As for the fifth name, Marsha Kincaid, the first time Casper hired me, it was to replace her in *Showdown at Sundown*. He said she'd thrown away the chance to become a star and gone home to Tulsa. She was new in town, not many people knew her, but it struck me as odd she'd quit after landing such a good part."

Chilled by where his imagination took him, he drew in a deep breath. "You think it's possible she never left Hollywood?"

Victoria nodded. "If Casper has an old refrigerator in his garage, you ought to look inside."

He hadn't expected another murder to drop into his lap, but if he couldn't get Casper for killing Cookie, he'd see what he could do for Marsha.

When Neal Sloan arrived at the Discreet Investigations office Tuesday morning, Joe had his report ready. He read it aloud before handing it to Neal.

Neal leaned forward to take the typed pages. "Phillip is working at a church?"

"Yes, St. Edmund's Episcopal. It's just a few blocks from your firm's office building. I couldn't have taken photos without giving myself away, but you can call the church and ask about the new Sunday school building. They'll confirm Phillip is the architect. He's volunteering his time and talent. Does it violate the terms of your partnership?"

"No, not at all. If Phillip wants to build Sunday schools up and down the state, Finegold and I would have no reason to complain unless he ignored our contracted work to do so."

"Good, then you have no reason to worry about him any further. While I did my best to avoid Phillip, he saw me at the hotel Saturday morning and invited me to have breakfast with him. I gave him a believable story for the case I was supposedly on, and he didn't appear to be suspicious."

Neal sat back and rubbed a hand over his face. "The

Phillip I know would rather go without eating than invite someone he barely knew to join him for a meal. It sounds as though you met an entirely different man."

"He surprised me too, but he may have wanted a chance to justify his behavior toward his newfound brother," Joe replied. "Share my report with your partner, and then throw it away at home so Phillip doesn't come across it accidently at your office."

"I will. You've taken a lot off my mind." Neal had brought cash to settle up the Discreet Investigation's bill, and shook Joe's hand before parting. "I'm glad we met."

"Thank you."

As soon as Neal had left, Joe telephoned Marty Streech, the reporter with the *LA Examiner*. "Good morning, what do you know about an actress named Marsha Kincaid? She was chosen to star in *Showdown at Sundown*, one of Casper Green's Westerns, and then supposedly quit and returned home to Tulsa."

"I remember her. She had long blonde hair, and I mean long, like illustrations in *Alice in Wonderland* books. Casper Green showed her off as his new star, and then dropped her. Want me to ask our entertainment editor what he knows?"

"Yes, call me if you learn anything useful."

"Does it have anything to do with Cookie Crumble's murder?"

"It may, and I'll give you the story when it's sorted out." Joe hung up and took out a folder to create a new file.

That night, Mary Margaret made pork chops with stuffing, mashed potatoes, and green beans, one of Joe's favorite dinners. She ladled the gravy on his plate in a graceful swirl and sat down to join him. "You haven't said much about Cookie since you came home from San Francisco. Have you hit a dead end? No pun intended."

"I have an interesting lead, but let's wait until it proves to be helpful before I give you the details."

"If you insist." She scooped up a forkful of stuffing and

P.J. Conn

savored it before changing the subject. "We need to talk about the wedding."

He swallowed without making an audible gulp. "Yes?"

"My mother thinks it would be a good idea for you to meet the family before our wedding."

Her father had passed away two years ago, and he understood how important it was for her mother to like him. "I'd love to, but I can't swing a trip to Seattle as well as a wedding and honeymoon this year."

"We could get married in Seattle," she offered without meeting his eyes.

"Aren't most of your friends here in LA now?"

"Yes." She pushed aside her half-eaten dinner. "I hate to ask my mother to make two trips to LA rather than just one for the wedding."

He was also fast losing his appetite. "There are your sisters and brothers to consider as well."

"True. It would be a lot easier for my family if we married in Seattle."

She didn't look happy about it though. He reached across the table for her hand and squeezed her fingers. "I'll marry you in Timbuktu if that's what you want."

"Thank you, but that's a little extreme. Just think about it, and we'll talk about it later. It's only October, so there's plenty of time."

"You'll need a dress."

"My mother wants me to wear hers. It's sweet, but dreadfully old-fashioned. My sister, Rose, wore it when she married Roger, but she'd have much rather have had her own. She couldn't bear to hurt our mother's feelings though."

"Your other sister, Sharon, she's not married?"

"Not yet, but she's had the same boyfriend since grade school, and they'll probably marry one day. My two brothers are still in college."

"So there's the two of us who could go to Seattle, or your mother, two brothers, one single sister, and one sister and her husband, six of them who'd have to come to LA?"

"When you put it that way, it seems selfish to ask that of them."

"We could get married here first, and travel to Seattle and get married again."

"You'd do that?"

"Sure, why not? Of course, that would mean your mother wouldn't have a chance to meet me before I became her son-in-law."

"That's a complication, it's true." She picked up her fork. "My family might object, but if they didn't know about wedding number one, they couldn't complain about it, could they?"

The sparkle had returned to her gaze, and he grinned with her. "We could have an engagement party here, and the wedding there. Or after the wedding there, we could have a second reception here when we came home."

"I hadn't realized there were so many choices." She smiled at the thought.

"As long as I'm your first choice for husband, nothing else matters to me."

"You are an absolute peach, Joe Ezell. I don't tell you that often enough."

He laughed with her. "I'm not keeping count. I could use a little more stuffing if there's any left."

"You know I always make plenty."

Joe went into the kitchen to help himself. He liked the homey feeling of her cottage, and most especially the magic she created in the kitchen.

Wednesday, Joe hadn't heard from Marty Streech, and rather than wait, he placed a call to the *Tulsa Daily World*. He asked for the newspaper's society editor, and had a long wait for her to come on the line.

"Good morning, this is Eloise Parker. I hope you'll invite me to whatever wonderful party you're planning."

Her voice had an excited trill, and he hated to disappoint her as he introduced himself. "Rather than plan a party, I need information on Marsha Kincaid. I wondered if you'd written a story on her when she left for Hollywood."

"Why yes, I did. She was a very popular girl, and everyone wished her well."

"Have you spoken with her since she returned to Tulsa?"

"I hadn't heard she'd come home. Who told you she had?"

"Casper Green, the director who'd hired her for one of his films."

"He must have been mistaken, because I've not seen her, or heard a word about her either."

She sounded as though she knew everyone worth knowing, and in a town of more than 150,000, that was no small feat. "Perhaps I should speak with her parents. Do you recall their names?"

"Of course, they're Minnie and John Kincaid. He's in oil, as many men are here in Oklahoma. Now you have me wondering what's happened to Marsha. We'd expected to see her on the screen long before now."

Joe thought it was possible Marsha had been so humiliated by her brief involvement with Casper Green that she might have gone home and laid low. Or, she could have disappeared somewhere between Hollywood and Tulsa. Hadn't she been missed?

"Thank you for your time." Joe hung up and placed his next call to the telephone information operator in Tulsa. He asked for John Kincaid's number, got it, and placed a call. A woman answered, and he asked for John.

"Mr. Kincaid is at his office this morning. You should call that number."

"I'm sorry. I've mislaid it. Are you Mrs. Kincaid?"

"No, I'm Miss Ivy the housekeeper."

"Nice to speak with you, Miss Ivy. Could you give me John's office number, please?"

"It's no secret." She recited the number. "Make a note of it this time."

"I certainly will. I'm also a friend of Marsha's from Hollywood. Is she there by any chance?"

"Yes, she is, but she's not taking any calls."

Joe was greatly relieved to hear Marsha had arrived home. "Will you please give her my number and ask her to call me at her earliest convenience?"

"She's finished with Hollywood."

"I don't blame her, but I'd still love to talk with her about her experiences here."

He provided his number, but hung up without any real hope Marsha would ever return his call. He tried her father's office and told the secretary who answered that he was with the *Tulsa Daily World.* She put him through to John, and Joe hurriedly pulled together what he hoped would be a believable story.

"Good morning, this is Eloise Parker's assistant, and we're following up on a feature story Miss Parker did on your beautiful daughter, Marsha. Is she filming a movie in Hollywood, or perhaps appearing in a play there?"

"Good lord, have you no shame about poking your nose into everyone's private business?"

"I'm so sorry to have disturbed you, but we want to wish your daughter every success with her movie career."

"She's done with Hollywood. Now don't bother us ever again."

Joe hung up without making any effort to defend himself. It sounded as though Marsha Kincaid was alive, if perhaps traumatized by her California experience. He wished he'd had her name when he'd spoken with Tom Green yesterday. Perhaps he'd mention her the next time he dropped by to see the young man.

The telephone rang just as Joe was locking his office door ready to go home. Hoping it might be Marsha Kincaid, he hurried back inside to answer. "Joe Ezell."

"It's Lily Montell. I've missed nearly two weeks of work at Sherry's and came in this afternoon to brush up on my routine. When Corky Coyne got here half an hour ago, he asked me where I'd been, and I told him the truth. He became furiously angry with Casper Green, and left here swearing he'd sort him out for good. I don't actually care what happens to Casper, but could you go by his home and keep Corky from getting into too much trouble?"

There was no way Joe was going to put himself between Corky and Casper, but he'd go to cheer Corky on. "I'll leave right now."

CHAPTER 18

W ith the heavy late afternoon traffic, Joe couldn't make good time, but Corky wouldn't have either. He worried about what he might find, but not enough to stop and call the police with a request they intervene.

Near the corner where he'd turn for Casper Green's home, a stalled car backed up the right lane. The drivers behind him leaned on their horns, as though the cars ahead of them had stopped for no good reason. He could sail through town on most days, but without exception, whenever he was in a hurry, the going would be painfully slow. Blaring horns only worsened the situation. Finally able to seize a break in the left lane traffic, he drove around the car causing the problem, and made the turn.

He needed a confession from Casper and hoped he'd not arrived too late for the man to give one. A big Lincoln sedan that looked like it could have belonged to Mickey Cohen, or one of his close associates, was parked in the circular driveway. He parked behind it. Angry shouts came from behind the house, which he took as a good sign. He ran along the path around the garage to the patio, where he found Corky dangling Casper by the scruff of the neck. The toes of the frantic director's shoes barely brushed the flagstone. Casper was the one yelling, or rather begging, while Tom stood back out of the way rather than defend his father.

"What's going on here?" Joe shouted, intending to startle Corky, even if he could not stop the assault in progress.

"This piece of trash killed Cookie," Corky growled. "And he's not getting away with it." He swung the director toward the pool, forced him over the side into the deep end, and shoved him under the water. He counted to ten, and then yanked him up by his hair. Casper drew in a sputtering breath.

Tom hadn't moved. "Did he kill her?" Joe called to him, and the young man nodded.

"It was an accident!" Casper screamed, and Corky dunked him again.

"You might want to call the police," Joe suggested, but there was no urgency in his tone.

"It's too late," Tom answered. "Cookie's dead, and my dad deserves whatever Corky gives him."

Corky again hauled Casper to the surface. The director gasped and blustered and grabbed hold of Corky's arm to save himself. "I never meant to hurt her," he sobbed. The water streaming from his wet hair mixed with his tears.

Joe took a step forward. "I heard him, and Tom's a witness to what happened to Cookie. Brett Wayne will also testify against Casper. You needn't drown him."

"How do you know what I need?" Corky shouted back at him.

"Looks like it's up to us, kid," Joe pointed out. "Go call the police while I rein in Corky."

Tom again shook his head. "They aren't needed."

Although Joe was on Corky's side, he had his limits. When Corky dipped Casper into the pool for what could be the last time, Joe picked up a heavy patio chair and swung it at Corky's head. He barely distracted him.

Corky glanced over his shoulder. "This guy believes in accidents, and I'm giving him one. Stay out of it."

There was a circular life buoy with an attached rope hanging on the patio wall, and Joe went for it. He dropped a loop of rope over Corky's head, and before the bodyguard could free himself, Joe ran the rope around the closest of the wooden columns supporting the patio roof. He used it for traction and pulling hard, yanked Corky away from the edge of the pool.

Casper broke free, swam with a desperate stroke to the pool ladder, and heaved himself out. He leaned over, coughing, and shaking badly. "Enough," he moaned. "I'll confess. I'll tell the police everything."

Finally satisfied, Tom went inside to make the call. Corky ran toward Joe to slacken the rope around his neck, and ripped it off over his head. Joe wisely stayed on the opposite side of the column.

"I know you loved Cookie, and she wouldn't want you to go to the gas chamber for killing Casper. That wouldn't honor her memory." Joe was prepared to argue with the brute until the police arrived, but Corky's legs abruptly collapsed under him, and he sat down hard on the flagstone. He covered his face with his hands, and sobbed Cookie's name over and over in a mournful howl.

Joe felt sorry for him, but he couldn't even get his arms around the guy, let alone hug him. He kept his eye on Casper, and the half-drowned man continued to weep and tremble beside the pool. A nearby wrought-iron rack held folded towels. Joe tossed one to Corky, but he left Casper to deal with his own misery alone.

The city of Beverly Hills had its own police force, and Joe hadn't met any of the officers who responded to Tom's call. Completely undone, Casper insisted through copious tears that Cookie had loved rough sex play, and that her death had been a terrible accident.

Tom admitted only to hiding the body. Corky retreated behind his usual fierce bodyguard pose and admitted absolutely nothing. Joe stood back and let the scene play out without interfering. When an officer asked for his statement, he gave him his card and made it brief.

"Mr. Green has been making sexual demands on the young women who appear in his films. I've been investigating one such incident, and came by to speak to him. Mr. Coyne was here also discussing the issue. Casper's conscience finally got the better of him, and he confessed to killing Cookie Crumble. Her real name was Alice Reyes. I'd like her to be remembered that way."

"Fine, I'll make a note of it. You'll be asked to come to the station to give a formal statement."

"I'll look forward to it." As soon as they were permitted to leave, Joe urged Corky out to his car. The big Lincoln proved to be his. "Nice car."

"It runs." Unable to meet Joe's gaze, Corky looked back toward the house. "You won't tell anyone what really happened, will you?"

"As far as I'm concerned, Casper slipped and fell into the pool."

"Yeah, that too, but don't let anyone know I cried."

"Your secret is safe with me, Corky."

"It better be."

Joe tried not to laugh, but he was actually beginning to like the guy.

He called Gladys Swartz the minute he got home, and gave her a brief recount of the afternoon. "Casper's admitted to killing Cookie. How long will it take the DA to drop the charges against Stuart Helms?"

"I'll see he drops them tomorrow. We should go to our favorite place in China Town and celebrate the end of the case with Mary Margaret and Hal. Are you doing anything Saturday night?"

Joe laughed. "I am now. See you then."

While Casper might not be charged with Alice Reyes's murder until tomorrow, Joe couldn't wait to call her brother, Max. "I hate to describe this as good news," he began. "The director we worked for, Casper Green, has confessed to killing your sister, but he insists it was an accident. His son, Tom, and a writer who lives in my apartment building, hid her body here in an empty apartment to throw suspicion off Casper."

Max was silent a long moment as the news soaked in. "I

wish I'd known the truth when we met him. How can he call strangling Alice an accident? Won't the authorities see it as a bald-faced lie?"

"I'm sorry to say there are men who abuse women before having sex. Casper must be one of them, but there may have been more going on. Alice had dated his son, and when Casper liked her too, she must have objected."

"And he killed her?"

"Yes, but knowing he did it doesn't ease the hurt. I'm so sorry you lost your beautiful sister."

"Well, yeah, that pain will last an awful long time. Guess we won't be doing that war movie after all."

"MGM will probably assign it to another director, but I've lost interest in it. Say, can you ride a horse?"

"Sure, I can."

"I may be able to get you some work on a Roy Roger's Western."

"Roy Rogers? That would be great."

They talked a few minutes more, and Joe hung up thinking how much he'd like to see the kid again.

Joe's next call went to Marty Streech to let him know an arrest had been made in the Cookie Crumble case. The reporter came to see him Thursday morning.

"This story is bigger than a single murder," Marty exclaimed. "Starlets are coming forward to describe their own awful experiences with Casper Green, as well as other directors who've taken advantage of them. I have enough material for more than a week's worth of columns."

"I'd hoped you'd do a lot with the subject," Joe mused aloud. "Too many girls come to Hollywood with their eyes so full of stars they can't see the dangers at every turn."

"Like the Black Dahlia," Marty added. "I often think of Elizabeth Short, but there aren't any new leads on her case."

When Marty got ready to leave, Joe had a suggestion. "I've found a great barber across the street from the El Capitan theatre. His name is Fred Cooper, and he'll give you the best haircut you've ever had for a reasonable price."

Marty brushed his hair off his forehead. "Thanks, I guess I could use a trim."

Joe smiled as though that was all the slovenly reporter needed, but it was a start.

Saturday night, Joe and Mary Margaret met Hal Marten and Gladys Swartz in one of China Town's finest restaurants. Leon Helms had been so grateful for all Joe had done for Stuart, he'd given him a generous bonus when he'd paid his bill. Joe now had the money for a honeymoon, and quite a few nice dinners as well.

Mary Margaret wore an enticingly seductive new perfume. This didn't seem like the time to comment on it however, when she might insist all he smelled was the luscious aroma of barbecued ribs.

"We've two things to celebrate." Mary Margaret raised her glass. "Joe not only solved the Cookie Crumble case, but he'll play a role in Roy Roger's next film, *Under California Stars!*"

"I wouldn't go so far as to describe it as a role," Joe objected with a good-natured humor. "The casting director was looking for lanky types, that's all. I'll probably only be kicking up a lot of dust riding out of town on horseback. I doubt you'll be able to recognize which cowboy is me."

"Of course, we will," Gladys interjected. "We should all go together when the film is released."

"Sure," Hal added. "I like Roy Roger's Westerns."

Their waiter began bringing their dinner choices, and the conversation settled into soft murmurs as they passed around the platters. Every dish was better than the last, and they appreciated them all.

Mary Margaret finished a delectable egg roll, and spoke softly, "I'm not looking for free legal advice, Gladys, but I do have a question."

"I'm in a celebratory mood," the attorney responded. "Ask whatever you'd like."

"Let's say a couple decides to marry here in LA, and then later wants to marry again in Seattle. Is there any law against it?"

"Not if you're marrying the same person. There are couples who renew their vows every year on their anniversary. You have such a lovely engagement ring. Are you thinking of marrying twice?"

"Our friends are all here," Joe explained. "Mary Margaret's family lives in Seattle."

Gladys nodded thoughtfully. "I see the problem. Would your family object to attending your second wedding rather than your first?"

Mary Margaret looked at Joe. "Not if they didn't know about the first wedding."

"Secrets," Hal breathed out. "There's a much better argument for telling the truth."

Lou King's sister, Jade, entered the restaurant with a tall, good-looking date. Rather than pause at their table, she simply waved. Dressed in a red *cheongsam* with her long, black hair falling free, she stopped the conversation at every table she passed.

"Who is that?" Mary Margaret whispered, her eyes wide.

"Jade King," Joe replied. "Her brother, Lou, is a bail bondsman who's been very helpful."

She looked at him askance. "A likely story."

Hal quickly stood up for his friend. "No, it's true. I'd not have met Gladys had Lou not given me her name when I needed an attorney. Jade is his receptionist."

"If that's the receptionist, I'd sure like to see Lou," Mary Margaret murmured.

Gladys giggled. "Didn't you just ask me about getting married twice?"

"That's true, but we're not married yet," Mary Margaret countered.

Joe brought her hand to his lips. "We can be at the courthouse Monday morning when the wedding license office opens." He knew she was teasing him, but he'd never let her go.

She batted her eyelashes. "Let's discuss it later, sweetheart."

When she wore such an exotic perfume, he doubted they'd remember to talk before dawn. While they were in China Town, however, he wondered if there might be a good place to buy silk tassels.

Turn the page for an
excerpt from

MURDER
ON
STILETTOS

A Joe Ezell Mystery

Book Four

P.J. Conn

Bloody footprints surrounded the body with dancing steps. Joe Ezell had come across a more gruesome murder scene only once, and he'd done his best to forget it. He bent down to get a closer look, and the sickening stench of freshly spilled blood immediately straightened his spine.

There was no sign of a fight, so apparently the deceased hadn't seen the first blow coming, and had had no chance to mount a defense. Blood splattered the wall in a sweeping arc, spoiling the pristine décor. The once beautiful apartment had been a serene mix of black and white, making the bright red splash doubly jarring.

Not wanting to smear whatever incriminating fingerprints might have been left behind, Joe knocked on a neighbor's door. "I'm Joe Ezell, a private detective. There's been a murder, and I need you to call the police."

The slim brunette who had answered the door swayed slightly and grabbed the doorknob to steady herself. Dressed in a tightly belted pink satin robe and feathered mules, she appeared to be getting a late start on the day. She gasped and glanced down the hallway to the door Joe had left standing ajar. She raised her hand to her throat. Her nails were painted a bright red.

"I've never called the police. What should I say?"

"Give them your name and address and tell them there

has been a murder in apartment eight. They'll take it from there."

"All right, I can handle that." She closed her door, and then yanked it open. "I'm sorry, but I'm not dressed and can't invite you to come in."

"I'd prefer to wait out here in the hallway. Please hurry and make the call. Then it would be a good idea to get dressed."

"Oh yes, right away." She closed her door and this time left it shut.

Twenty minutes later, Detective Lieutenant Jacob Lynch stepped out of the elevator. Handsomely dressed in a well-tailored suit, as always, he took one look at Joe, and swore under his breath.

"Have you recently moved into this building, Mr. Ezell? This is quite a step up for you."

Lynch knew where Joe lived because there had been a murder in his building, but Joe considered the comparison between his home and these high-priced apartments rude in the extreme. He'd never liked Lynch anyway.

"No, I haven't moved. I was in the neighborhood working on a case."

"Really? You've shown a rare talent for showing up at murder scenes."

Joe nodded. "Yeah, I'm lucky that way."

When he'd been hired, he'd expected the usual follow and photograph work, and he wondered how he could have been so badly mistaken.

MURDER ON STILETTOS

available in print and ebook

THE

DETECTIVE JOE EZELL MYSTERY

SERIES

A native Californian, P.J. Conn attended the University of Arizona and California State University at Los Angeles where she earned a BA in Art History and an MA in Education. Her Historical Romance and Futuristic novels, written under Phoebe Conn, have won many awards.

Phoebe is the proud mother of two grown sons and two adorable grandchildren, who love to have her read to them.

.

www.ingramcontent.com/pod-product-compliance
Lightning Source LLC
Chambersburg PA
CBHW020804250626
47155CB00003B/1197